adriane on the edge

TITLES BY PAUL MANDELBAUM

Adriane on the Edge

Garrett in Wedlock: A Novel-in-Stories

TITLES EDITED BY PAUL MANDELBAUM

First Words: Early Writings from
22 Favorite Contemporary Authors

12 Short Stories and Their Making:
An Anthology with Interviews

adriane on the edge

Paul Mandelbaum

BERKLEY BOOKS, NEW YORK

THE BERKLEY PUBLISHING GROUP
Published by the Penguin Group
Penguin Group (USA) Inc.
375 Hudson Street, New York, New York 10014, USA
Penguin Group (Canada), 90 Eglinton Avenue East, Suite 700, Toronto, Ontario M4P 2Y3, Canada
(a division of Pearson Penguin Canada Inc.)
Penguin Books Ltd., 80 Strand, London WC2R 0RL, England
Penguin Group Ireland, 25 St. Stephen's Green, Dublin 2, Ireland (a division of Penguin Books Ltd.)
Penguin Group (Australia), 250 Camberwell Road, Camberwell, Victoria 3124, Australia
(a division of Pearson Australia Group Pty. Ltd.)
Penguin Books India Pvt. Ltd., 11 Community Centre, Panchsheel Park, New Delhi—110 017, India
Penguin Group (NZ), Cnr. Airborne and Rosedale Roads, Albany, Auckland 1310, New Zealand
(a division of Pearson New Zealand Ltd.)
Penguin Books (South Africa) (Pty.) Ltd., 24 Sturdee Avenue, Rosebank, Johannesburg 2196,
South Africa

Penguin Books Ltd., Registered Offices: 80 Strand, London WC2R 0RL, England

This book is an original publication of The Berkley Publishing Group.

Grateful acknowledgment is made to *Colorado Review*, which first published "Adriane and the Fibroid Tumor," and to *Glimmer Train*, in which "Animal Shelter" first appeared.

Cover design by Rita Frangie.
Text design by Stacy Irwin.

First edition: December 2005

Library of Congress Cataloging-in-Publication Data

Mandelbaum, Paul, 1959–
Adriane on the edge / Paul Mandelbaum.—1st ed.
p. cm.
ISBN 0-425-20803-6
1. Single women—Fiction. 2. Conduct of life—Fiction. 3. Monk, Thelonious—Influence—Fiction. I. Title.

PS3618.O8455A65 2005
813'.6—dc22

2005048257

PRINTED IN THE UNITED STATES OF AMERICA

10 9 8 7 6 5 4 3 2 1

To Mica,

The Goddaughter

acknowledgments

Heartfelt thanks to Betsy Amster, my guardian agent, and Allison McCabe, my champion editor; to Tom Lutz, Nancy Schwalb, Elena Song, and Laurie Winer, my tireless over-seers; to Carolyn Birbiglia for spreading the word; to sharp-eyed Jenny Brown; to Bernie Horn, savvy political operator; to Stephen Lohrmann and Alan Sea for meeting so many of my funereal needs; to Robin Bartlett, Terence Cannon, Ramsey Flynn, Margot Frankel, Betsy Keller, Maryjane Krasnoff, Maria Möller, Rachel Resnick, and the Song family for their valuable input, aid, and goodwill.

adriane on the edge

This is the time the swooning soul hangs . . .
between the new day and the old. . . .

—Dorothy Parker, "The Little Hours"

1. adriane and the personal ad

fall 1996

"Why *not* write a personal ad?" urged her friend Joan.

Adriane considered the subject dropped already. "Because I hate sales."

She smeared some triple-crème Saint Andre on a cracker and passed it along, then topped off their Manhattans from the iced carafe. On TV, the Ravens were fumbling away her five hundred dollars. Rookie underdogs, this hapless home team. She'd glimpsed opportunity in the point spread; just her own wishful thinking, it now seemed.

"But you've got a great product. Guys should be lining up around the block," said Joan, holding the new issue, November '96, of *Baltimore* magazine. "These other ads don't sound so great."

"Let me see." Adriane began scanning a column of "Women Seeking Men."

There were so many! Some ads in bold, others in large type. How desperate, depending on font size to attract a mate. Her eye settled in the middle of a column, and she read a few–typical romantic psychobabble about *secure self-image* or *looking to share my enthusiasm* or *seeks friendship first, possibly leading to more.* She was just starting to feel she could compete with such lame efforts when she came across the following:

> Brit brunette, 25, better looking than you, tattoo on bum, likes a nice bonfire, civil disobedience & illegal carburetors, ISO real man to bone me like you own me.

"Listen to this!" Adriane yelped. She read the ad aloud.

"Holy cow," said Joan, reaching for her nicotine gum.

"What's up with this chick?"

"Maybe she's a hooker," offered Joan. "They sometimes slip in."

"This is not the prose of a prostitute. It's too–" She paused to consider what exactly surprised her so. "It's too *abandoned*."

"A little self-demeaning at the end?" Joan wondered.

"It *pretends* to be." Adriane peered closely at the page. "But she only says *like* you own me. Nobody's going to own this girl."

"Her prose *is* kind of wild," acknowledged Joan.

"It's totally abandoned." Adriane felt a slight rush just saying the word. Despite her one or two flirtations with outré behavior, Adriane had never been completely abandoned–except by other people.

"You can write a better ad than that," said Joan. "We'll both do it."

"I wouldn't even know where to begin," Adriane realized.

"We need to create your *profile*, Adriane Gelki." Joan reached for a pen. "Let's start with assets. You're attractive, you're smart, you're funny, you're barely twenty-eight, and you watch sports. Plus you're a gracious hostess," she added. "Call out anything that comes to mind."

"I don't think so," said Adriane.

"Modest," Joan added to the list. "Well, then how about your turn-ons?"

Adriane snorted loudly, then made herself another cracker. "Cheese," she said. "I like cheese."

On TV, the final seconds of the game clock ticked away, and just for emphasis, her underdogs fumbled one last time. A $500 mistake. Though her winnings from the day's other games would more or less cover it, she still felt upset with herself. Football handicapping remained one of the few areas of her life where she expected not to lose.

Monday morning, at her desk in the Mayor's Office of Neighborhood Enhancement, Adriane resumed work on her latest project, organizing Baltimore's first Painted Screen Door Slam. A few local artisans on the east side of town still practiced the old handicraft of adorning wire screen doors with alpine vistas, seascapes, and the occasional portrait of Jesus or Elvis. Adriane had proposed a friendly competition to bolster public interest in the art the way slams were popularizing poetry. Actually, she'd been half-kidding, but her boss seemed so happy with the idea, she felt moved to follow through. She couldn't decide whether to coordinate a walking tour or to ask the contestants to bring their doors and window screens to a central location.

"What do you think?" she asked her boss when he stepped out from his office.

"Walking tour," he said as he propped a worsted wool haunch on the edge of her desk. "You'll get more screens that way."

"Yes, but fewer viewers maybe."

"Without screens, the viewers won't have anything to look at."

"Without viewers," argued Adriane, "the screens won't be seen."

As banter, theirs fell short of, say, Katharine Hepburn and Spencer Tracy, but it helped pass the day.

"I brought pictures," he said.

"Pictures?"

"Of the baby."

"Oh, I want to see," said Adriane anxiously, if not eagerly. Garrett Hughes, after all, had once been the object of her fumbling attempts at seduction. He'd been going through such a hard time–Adriane could still picture his bruised face and leg cast from that nasty fall he'd taken, poor man–and she had reached out to him as a kind of healing gesture, even though he was married. The whole episode was awkward and shameful, and it ended almost before it had begun–and yet, getting over him had taken several years.

She looked now at snapshots of his eighteen-month-old daughter–laughing, licking a cupcake, being held in one secure pair of arms after another. And then: a picture in which she fed blissfully at her mother's bared breast–like Adriane needed to see that! Just a little bit indecent–not the nudity so much as the flaunting of mother-love. The sight raised in her a disturbingly simultaneous revulsion and longing.

"Isn't she a little old to still be breast-feeding?"

"My wife says it's well within the normal range."

Adriane handed back the photos, whipped out a blank piece of paper, and wrote at the top of it: *cheese.*

To which she added, in a flurry of self-assessment:

settles debts promptly
smart-ass
Vince Lombardi

"What's that you've got?" he asked.

"My profile," she declared. "Traits, turn-ons. I'm composing a personal ad."

"Good for you!" said Garrett, a bit too gung-ho for her liking. He peered upside down at the list, which she quickly covered with her hand.

"Buoyant," he said, smiling with encouragement.

She looked at him, repressed a distant urge to add his name as a turn-on.

"It's a good word to describe you," he added. "It suggests resilience and humor."

This may have been guilt talking. She wondered if he ever worried about her, and if worry was anything like love. It seemed kind of in the love family.

"Doesn't *buoyant,*" she asked, feeling the sudden need to embarrass him, "sound like I'm promoting my big bouncy breasts?"

Garrett reddened, right on cue. "Maybe." He removed his haunch from her desk and slunk into his office, closing the door behind him.

She wrote it down, *buoyant*, and tried to visualize her ideal man, her target audience: He'd have a pleasant face but not too fancy. An average build so he wouldn't begrudge Adriane her own love handles. A certain height seemed desirable and maybe a world-weary look around the eyes, a sense of resolve emanating from the jaw line. (This was all starting to resemble her boss, wasn't it?) Moving inward now: a lithe, nonacademic intelligence, an appreciation of human frailty without too great a taste for it. A conscience would be nice, some sort of moral equilibrium. Everyone always asked for a sense of humor, but that was meaningless unless you specified which style of humor. She seemed particularly drawn to men who needed a good cheering up.

Men like Garrett. And her father. Yes, her father, but preferably without the manic streak, the alcoholism, and the suicide.

"As ads go," said Joan, "this sounds a little off-putting." The two of them were sitting at the edge of the fountain in Hopkins Plaza eating pita pockets. "What are the chances the Dalai Lama has a kid brother who shoots craps?"

"It's just a rough draft," mumbled Adriane, her mouth full. "Oh, who am I kidding? The Dalai Lama's kid brother is probably writing to that 'bone me like you own me' girl right now." She couldn't get the phrase out of her mind; it was beginning to taunt her, to mock her fragile sexuality.

"Would you forget about her?" said Joan, wiping a crumb from Adriane's lapel.

"I can't. It's like she's shattered the mold. A regular ad, it just pales."

"Thanks a lot."

"Not yours, Joanie. Yours is good," she said, squinting at her friend's sheet of legal paper: *Cutie cable exec seeks merger with business-savvy professional. Must have secure self-image.* "But this other girl is writing in an entirely new language, reinventing the discourse of personals. She's the *über*-date, Joanie. Don't you want to see what she's like? You know, maybe arrange a meeting?"

"Not really." Joan swallowed the last bite of her pita pocket.

"We'll ask her for writing tips. Buy her a drink and size her up. Get to know the enemy."

"She's our enemy?"

"Oh, you know," said Adriane. "The competition."

Joan sighed. "We're getting sidetracked here."

The following Saturday afternoon, they were sipping whisky sours in a trendy outdoor café by the harbor, awaiting the arrival of one Shelley Addison, who, according to her e-mail, could be recognized by her long brown hair and a pair of blue jeans that fit her like skin.

"I have to admit, I do wonder what she'll be like," said Joan, fishing the maraschino cherry out of her glass.

She's going to be everything I'm not, it suddenly occurred to Adriane. She summoned their waiter and said, "I'm ready for my two-for-one freebie."

The waiter looked to Joan, who said, "I'm still nursing my first round."

Adriane felt a flutter of self-consciousness. She didn't mind having inherited her father's taste for gambling, but would prefer to avoid becoming an alcoholic. As forms of abandon went, alcohol was tainted.

At that moment, a strange motorcycle rumbled toward them. Strange, because it hauled a sidecar, and not a typical sidecar, either, but one enclosing a wheelchair. After parking–in a regular spot, not a handicapped one–the petite rider removed her helmet, loosing a flow of lustrous brown hair. She clambered into the adjacent wheelchair and then pulled a lever, converting the back door of the sidecar into a ramp. With apparent ease, she now rolled toward Adriane and Joan.

In a crisp British accent, the newcomer asked, "Are you the tarts interested in writing personals?"

Too stunned to speak, Adriane merely nodded.

"Yes we are," said Joan; she cleared a space at the table and introduced herself and Adriane.

Shelley Addison pulled forward, then beckoned their server and ordered a gin and tonic. "Sapphire, please, if you have it. And could we have things a little toastier?" she asked, nodding toward the space heater, which the waiter immediately set out to adjust.

From a storage pouch on the side of her wheelchair, she produced a pack of cigarettes and offered them all around. Adriane shook her head, had difficulty accepting this person as the girl from the ad.

"No, thanks," said Joan, who reached for her nicotine gum. "I'm trying to quit."

"Bully for you." Shelley lit up and expelled a set of smoke rings toward the center of the table.

"That's the trouble with nicotine gum," said Joan, ever the good sport. "You can't blow bubbles."

Shelley Addison laughed, a throaty chuckle steeped in condescension.

"We're very impressed with your ad," Joan continued. "It leaps off the page!"

"Thanks," said Shelley, sending an extra smoke ring Joan's way, as though it were a gift.

"Do you get many responses?" Joan asked. "You must."

"It's quite time consuming sorting through them all. I should hire a secretary."

She withdrew from her chair's side pouch a sheaf of letters, many of them with photographs attached, and passed them around. Men of virtually all ages, races, and backgrounds seemed represented. A forty-nine-year-old radiologist wrote on office letterhead a poignant essay claiming to be just the man she was looking for. Via e-mail, a Gen-X Web-page designer was proposing marriage without having met, or indeed ever having spoken to her. There were more than a few replies from prisoners.

"Your ad," stammered Adriane, her first words since the woman's arrival. "Isn't it a magnet for creeps? I mean, what if one of them decides to attack you?" She could not stop staring at Shelley's wheelchair.

"There are always a few unviables to screen out, I suppose," Shelley admitted between puffs.

"But isn't your ad offering advance consent?" Adriane pressed. She hated sounding so reactionary, but all her assumptions about Shelley Addison's wildness, self-possession, and abandon had been deflated by that damn *wheelchair*. Adriane felt duped, as though she'd answered the ad herself, which in a way she had.

"More like advance inclination," Shelley responded curtly.

"Adriane's frustrated," interjected Joan, "because she's having trouble positioning herself in the marketplace."

The waiter arrived with Shelley's gin and tonic and three whisky sours.

"Gracious," he said. "I messed up. Oh well. No extra charge."

He set all of the glasses on the table. Suddenly Adriane felt surrounded by drinks.

"Joanie," she begged, "help me with these."

"Let me ask you something, Adriane," began Shelley, lighting up another cigarette. "When you meet some bloke, are you inclined to like him or be wary of him?"

"You mean right when I meet him? I don't even know him; how am I supposed to like him?" She reached for a cocktail.

"You see, guys sense that," said Shelley. "They resemble horses that way."

"But," Adriane argued meekly, "I'm like that about women, too."

Joan turned the question back on Shelley. "What about you?"

"I like guys," declared the newcomer. This sounded like an old election slogan. "I start from there, and if there's a reason not to like one, I deal with that when it arises. By then I've usually met some other guy I like even more." She took a long pull from her gin and tonic. "Sweet Christ I adore booze, don't you?"

Adriane could stand it no longer and blurted, "What do those *blokes* think, who answer your ad, and then see, you know, your wheelchair?"

Joan cringed, but Shelley remained unfazed. "A lot of them don't really seem to notice it," she said.

"How can they not notice it?" said Adriane, too far gone now to turn back. It rattled her that Shelley Addison made no outward acknowledgment of her own disability; it seemed like . . . cheating.

"Surely they *notice* it," said Shelley, "but they don't make a big squawk about it. At some point we discuss the matter, but not for very long, and none of them would ever bring it up so bluntly as you have."

Adriane cast her eyes downward. "But we're on a fact-finding mission."

Shelley stubbed out her butt and explained that five years ago she'd been diagnosed with multiple sclerosis, and that she went through periods of needing her wheelchair interspersed with long stretches when she did not. Draining her gin and tonic, she proceeded to light up another cigarette.

"Should you be drinking and smoking?" Adriane wondered aloud.

"Listen," snapped Shelley, "if you want me to tell you how to get laid, I suggest you stop sounding like my mum this very instant."

"*Please* forgive Adriane," said Joan. "She's had . . . a bad experience."

Shelley Addison arched an eyebrow. "What sort of bad experience?"

Adriane shook her head. "No, nothing." She wondered which bad experience Joan meant.

"She had an affair with her married boss," Joan whispered.

"That's ancient history," said Adriane, who then felt obliged to point out, "It wasn't fully consummated." *What a waste*, she thought, *to have gone through all that and not even* . . . She took a deep breath and tried to keep her composure. Her failed seduction–coming just weeks after her mother's death–had heralded a spiritual crisis for Adriane and a setback to her humanity. She'd pursued this affair with more tenacity and mourned it with more grief than it probably deserved. Even now, four years later, the two events–seduction and death–seemed magnetized by a strong Oedipal current that flowed as well through her father's earlier death and her long-standing resentment of her mother. Adriane had, she knew, a few issues.

Shelley cocked her head. "Well," she coaxed, "have you moved on? Sexually at least?"

During the ensuing silence, Adriane slouched deeper into her chair. She'd had two sexual partners since the Garrett debacle: A few months ago, she'd slept with an Italian pianist in town to play Rachmaninoff's third with the Baltimore Symphony Orchestra. He'd been, alas, a professional rival of Adriane's mother–a man so senior, his scrotum hung low as a set of concert tails. Before that came another one-night stand–technically the deflowering of her virginity–with an Oriole Park pretzel vender. Neither experience seemed to count as moving on.

"We didn't ask you here to tell us how to get laid," she mumbled.

"Oh, excuse me. You want to become better copywriters, is that it? All right, have it your way. As long as I'm being treated. I'm famished."

The original invitation had been for drinks, but Adriane was grateful for the chance to sop up her whisky sours and buy back some of the table's goodwill with food.

After they ordered dinner, she made an attempt to be sociable. "So, what do you do for work?"

"I teach preschool," Shelley replied.

Adriane dragged her lips across her teeth, trying to smile.

"I *love* young children," Joan gushed.

Shelley concurred. "They're completely uninhibited."

One hour later, Adriane found herself strong-armed into visiting Screwdrivers, a blue-collar, South Baltimore rock club, which echoed tonight with the din of a band called Blood Brain Barrier.

"They used to be metal, then they became a techno band at raves, now they're metal-nostalgia," Shelley'd said on the way over.

"They're allowed to switch like that?" wondered Adriane.

The air was hazy with cigarette smoke, the fumes of cheap alcohol, and free-floating lust. Eager to leave already, Adriane chided herself for being such a stick in the mud. This was one of those no-win situations she had such a talent for finding.

Shelley was dancing already with a burly flannel-shirted stranger named James, who moments earlier had bought their table a round of beers. Dancing, sort of: Her arms were wrapped around his neck and her legs around his waist, and he was carting her back and forth across the dance floor, heedless of tempo–part slow dance, part traction. Joan passed Adriane some Kleenex, and both women stuffed their ears with it.

"You didn't have to tell her my . . . stuff!" Adriane groused, eyeing the half-empty beer in the cup holder of Shelley's wheelchair.

"Sorry!" Joan shouted. "But you were being so rude! I felt I had to explain you!"

They continued to watch Shelley's dance partner cradling her buttocks, the tattooed "bum" referenced in her ad. This tattoo, Adriane had learned over dinner, portrayed a cheetah, the world's fastest land animal. Apparently the image spanned Shelley's entire ass and appeared to run when she clenched and unclenched her cheeks, a trick more easily effected in times of remission–which was more information than even Adriane needed.

"Oh my God he's, like, in her jeans!" shouted Joan.

Adriane heard her friend correctly but pictured James inside Shelley's *genes*, and wondered if there was a guy-gene Shelley possessed. A marker that guys, like horses, were drawn to. That predisposed a person to make such inane pronouncements as "I like guys." Could Adriane ever adopt such a blithe policy herself? As she watched the sweating couples on the dance floor, she wondered if some women–say, the Madonna and Emily Dickinson and Sister Wendy, that art historian with the gigantic overbite, and maybe Adriane herself–were genetically inoculated against the pleasures of abandon.

The band segued from a tumultuous ballad about a girls' tennis team wrongfully busted for solicitation to an ear-splitting cautionary tale about a teenager stalking his aunt. Adriane's mother used to call this stuff *devil music*. Not in a born-again way, but as a classical pianist and a snob.

Adriane longed to have inherited even *half* of her mother's talent instead of the sliver she got. But better to remain a mediocre musician, if it meant avoiding her mother's primness, Valium addiction, and of course, suicide. This suicide came as less of a surprise than her father's, but their upshot amounted to the same: Adriane felt indicted. Her parents had both essentially disowned her. Whatever charms she might flaunt in a personal ad had not been enough to entice either of them to hang around. She pictured her parents bailing, sequentially and without parachutes, from a rickety airplane that she alone was left to pilot. Usually she brooded over such existential matters in the quiet Sunday hours before kickoff. But the cacophony of Blood Brain Barrier was driving her inward, the tissue paper in her ears amplifying her own thoughts. What were the odds, she wondered, of being the offspring of two suicides? And what about her own odds from here onward? Was there some actuarial formula to compute the likelihood that her genes would spare her? At least her thoughts about suicide, her own suicide, had so far remained abstract, and Adriane took some measure of comfort in this. Wasn't that the common wisdom? That your thoughts had to get specific, practical, logistical, before you were an imminent danger to yourself?

Feeling parched all of a sudden, she finished off her beer, then took the bottle from the drink holder in Shelley's armrest, where it was just going warm and flat, and chugged that one down, too. Shelley, who had transported them all on her cycle contraption, did not seem ready to leave any time soon.

"Smart-ass, SWF, 28," mused Adriane, taking another crack at her hypothetical ad, *"ISO reader, music lover, for palling around, possibly leading to suicide. . . ."*

"Come on," Joan yelled, motioning toward the dance floor. "We might as well work out."

Adriane followed and watched her friend flex arm and leg in time to the band. Discarding her tissue, Adriane let the shrieking sounds pierce her head, which she shook from side to side as though trying to expel a nagging drop of water. She began flinging her limbs, just to feel the blood rush to the edges of her fingers and toes, then wriggled like a snake shedding its skin. For the next twenty minutes, she tried to lose herself in the music, except that all her movements, wild as she might will them, remained corseted in self-consciousness.

No one approached either of them to dance, which was for the best, considering the hillbilly vibe of the place, but still. . . . She surveyed the men around her. Were they like horses after all? Why were they prepared to overlook Shelley's damage–obvious and exterior–but not Adriane's? Could they actually sense her trauma–all that leftover Oedipal electricity and grief over her parents, over her boss? Also that possible suicide gene of hers? As though she projected these things somehow–through her gaze or her scent or the rigid, martial style of her dancing.

Joan suddenly grabbed her sleeve and shouted, "Am I fat?"

"No!" Adriane shouted back. Then added, to be polite, "Am I?"

"Of course not!"

It seemed, without either of them needing to say so, time to leave.

Shelley still clung to tall, muscular James as though perched in a swaying tree bough. Adriane reached to tap her on the shoulder and shouted, "We wanna head out. Should we call a cab?"

"No, that's all right. I'll take you," said Shelley. Her lipstick was smeared up to her nose. "Time to say good night, James."

"But I thought, you know," he shouted over the band, confusion creasing his low brow, "we'd be, um, together."

"Not tonight." She gave him a peck on the cheek. "Perhaps some other time, love. You can have my number."

James looked toward the clock at the back of the room. "Just a few more dances then," he said. His interests seemed decidedly short term. On the other hand, it occurred to Adriane, maybe Shelley Addison operated on a not-so-distant time horizon herself.

"I can't," she said. "Be a gentleman and escort me to my chair, will you?"

But James apparently didn't care to be remembered as a gentleman, because he let go of her jean-clad cheetah and unwrapped her legs from around his waist so swiftly that Shelley jerked toward the ground, as though a gallows trapdoor had opened beneath her. Her hands unclasped from around his neck and, completely detached from him now, she began to stumble, pitching first one way then the other, her lustrous hair swaying wildly behind her.

Adriane lunged forward, caught Shelley under the arms, and despite the strain on her own back, held on tight. All this out of more than simple human kindness. As though Adriane somehow *needed* the other woman not to fall.

"Asshole!" Joan called after James, already halfway to the bar.

Her fingers damp from Shelley's warm armpits, Adriane guided her into the wheelchair, easing her down with great care.

Shelley chuckled, a bit more thickly this time, then looked up and squinted. "That certainly was a first," she sneered, as though daring Adriane to suggest otherwise.

They drove, rumbling through a light mist, Adriane ensconced in the wheelchair with Joan heavy on her lap–she was just a little bit fat, that Joanie, to tell the truth. Fortunately, her Federal Hill town house was not far from the club.

"Will we see you again?" she shouted, clambering off Adriane and removing the helmet that Shelley had lent her.

"Stranger things have happened," said Shelley Addison.

Joan passed the helmet to Adriane, who offered it to the driver.

"No, I insist," said Shelley and smiled, more softly than at any other time in the evening. "There's no sense both of us ending up in chairs." This acknowledgment–however sardonic–of her condition seemed intended as a sort of olive branch, a glimmer of fellowship. Adriane put on the helmet, and Shelley revved her engine.

They sped through the quiet Federal Hill streets. Adriane had never ridden in a sidecar before, or on a motorcycle at all, and the exposure to the elements, the wind and moisture, while a little uncomfortable, felt invigorating.

They approached a stoplight and were about to pull alongside a beat-up pickup truck with mud flaps featuring a buxom silhouette, when Shelley leaned over and shouted against the side of Adriane's helmet, "Let's lead this wanker on a merry chase, shall we? Retribution must be swift and proportionate."

Shelley soon motioned for the driver, a young bearded man wearing a Makita power tools hat, to roll down his window.

"What's your name, love?" she called out.

"Um–Carl."

"Care for a date, Carl?" she shouted gaily.

"A date?" he said, looking at Adriane's wheelchair. "With both of you?" The young man bore a clannish resemblance to James and might even have been on his way home from Screwdrivers. The idea of leading him on a wild goose chase through the streets of Baltimore as a way of making up for the evening's earlier humiliation contained a certain poetic justice, as well as a therapeutic symmetry. Had James dropped Adriane on the dance floor, she would likely nurse that wound for months. Yet Shelley had devised a way to act out her frustrations in one outrageous, adolescent gesture. It seemed almost healthy.

"Don't be scared," said Shelley, "by a few spasms."

Adriane smiled. Twitched obligingly.

"How much?" Carl asked.

"The girl's got quite a nice body." She chuckled with condescension and nodded toward Adriane, who was beginning to suspect maybe Shelley's guy gene was not so blithe after all. Then, a darker thought, and closer to home: She briefly considered the joke might be on her. That maybe Shelley's retribution, swift and proportionate, was directed not so much at James for dropping her but at Adriane for catching her.

"Well, go on, love, show the nice man your tits."

Feeling suddenly vulnerable in her helmet and wheelchair, she wondered how easily Shelley might disengage this sidecar contraption and race off without her, stranding her in the middle of South Baltimore with–with Carl. Adriane searched the other woman's face for a clue. Shelley's stare, soft yet urgent, suggested only that she was offering Adriane an opportunity. Abandon was within reach. The chance to behave heedless of consequence or loss. Without the guarantee of safety, or any guarantee at all.

The motorcycle and truck growled next to each other like two hungry stomachs. Adriane shrugged off her coat and reached for the hem of her shirt; watched the young man as he adjusted his cap as a pretext for dabbing the sweat on his forehead. He seemed almost relieved when it became clear Adriane wasn't likely to go through with it, her hands fiddling with the fabric. . . .

"Um–I," said the man, groggily as though waking. "I'd better not." He tipped his hat and drove across the intersection as the light became green again.

Adriane blushed with shame, and watched the pickup truck's taillights mock her.

"Sweet Christ," said Shelley. "Live a little, why don't you?"

She gunned the motorcycle, which issued a long ripping fart of exhaust as they streaked around the corner and then the next and the next corner with such acceleration that Adriane was thrust deep into the wheelchair. They raced toward the Inner Harbor, which twinkled bleakly with holiday lights. The holidays were on their way. And beyond that, a mere couple years on the horizon, the new millennium, which in Adriane's current frame of mind loomed like the most imposing of deadlines. The thought of venturing across Y2K's threshold only to face herself on the other side made her groan with despair.

They blew past Harborplace, past lofty condos, past the U.S.S. *Constellation*, its venerable masts festooned with decorations–until a stoplight made them pause, like an invisible hand holding them in place.

While they idled at the intersection of Fayette and Calvert, Adriane noticed a trio of hot-panted streetwalkers on the far corner. Their long legs shimmered in the orange glow from the street lamps, and they ambled back and forth across the sidewalk with the graceful lope of giraffes.

A brown Chevy slid to a stop in the lane on Adriane's right. She turned toward its driver, a haggard smoker with stained fingertips. He regarded her with hooded, world-weary eyes, a more tired, forlorn version of the man she had pictured for her personal ad. His mouth, especially, sagged from the weight of some ineffable burden, and he was in such obvious need of cheer, Adriane didn't think twice before removing her helmet and shaking forth her hair the way she'd seen Shelley do earlier. She felt a buoying wave of release and, despite the constricting wheelchair, a quiver of sexual power, which to prolong: She yanked high her shirt and bra, launching the heft of her flesh out into the world, her very personal flesh. So *her* and yet so thrillingly *not* her. Just a glimpse of this other her, the blink of a camera, before re-covering herself; she wanted to turn the man on, not embarrass him.

"How much, sweetheart?" he asked in a voice tinged with melancholy.

"Fifty," she heard herself say, some sort of declaration, however paltry, of self-worth. She wondered if she should have asked for more.

Meanwhile the man was climbing out of his brown Chevy and now flashed a police badge between his stained fingertips. The cool metal of handcuffs clicked onto Adriane's wrist. He attached the other half to Shelley's and took the key from her ignition. The motorcycle coughed into silence.

"Take 'em away, Officer!" called the streetwalkers. "She a ho!"

Shelley tapped out a cigarette with her free hand. "That was an admirable gesture," she said. "But you should know, money talk is not part of this particular game."

Adriane looked up at the cop and made an effort to explain. "We're not real hookers, Officer."

He was already busy radioing for a tow truck and a wheelchair-accessible van. Adriane looked at her watch, felt surprised by the hour's lateness.

"Hey, G-man," said Shelley, "how about a light?"

It seemed noteworthy that even when she was being arrested, Shelley got men to do her bidding.

As though passing a torch, she handed her lit cigarette to Adriane, who stared at it a moment before taking a long drag. She exhaled, and through the veil of smoke, she considered her immediate prospects: She had managed to get herself busted for exposure and solicitation; she and Shelley Addison would soon be taken in a patrol wagon to a police station, where they'd be photoed and fingerprinted; and she would now have a criminal record permanent as her own DNA. Adriane dangled her feet over the edge of the wheelchair–swinging them back and forth with determination–and thought to herself, *Things are finally starting to look up.*

2. animal shelter

fall 1996

Every once in a while, whenever she felt the loss of him most keenly, Adriane visited her father's grave, where she would arrange before his headstone a smoldering cigarette and a chilled Manhattan, straight up. On this brisk Friday afternoon, wearing his lucky shirt, she studied a printout of the Vegas line and made her preliminary picks for Sunday's NFL games, while nibbling the maraschino cherry from his drink, which he'd always let her do when she'd been a girl.

"Patriots plus four over Colts?" she said out loud, as though consulting him. "Nimble defensive line," she mused.

He'd always liked to gamble, had in fact come to own the cemetery plots–nestled between the Spevacks, Lottie and Julius, on the left, and the Gubermans, Lena and Leonard, on the right–by winning them in a poker game. It was the only way he could stomach the thought of funeral arrangements, she knew, and he'd seen no problem that Shalom Gardens was an Orthodox cemetery. He'd been Jewish himself, after all, though not much.

His name and dates occupied the left side of a doublewide headstone. And bordering this two-person plot, a granite railing around its perimeter that called to mind a full-sized bed. The right side of the plot and headstone remained empty, her father, it turned out, having failed to think through a few matters. Logic was never his strong suit, but he knew how to burn a candle at both ends. Adriane had lost him when she was fourteen.

On the back of her writing arm, above the elbow where the delicate fabric of the lucky shirt had become threadbare, Adriane felt something strange and a little spooky, like a puff of warm breath. Her stomach pressed against her heart–that exhilaration she would sometimes feel in her father's speeding car when he'd crest a hill–and she whipped around to see a medium-small dog, with a thick brown coat and a pointy nose.

He continued to sniff Adriane, gave her a thorough going over–starting again with her shirt, then her hair, now the soles of her shoes–before deciding to lie down next to the Manhattan on her father's grave. A couple of warty little growths clung to his eyelids, but overall he was a handsome animal. She couldn't tell if he was wearing a collar buried within that thick coat of his, and when she reached to check, he rolled over, inviting her to scratch his belly. He felt even softer than he looked–a small, warm cloud. Whenever she scratched near his armpit, his hind leg would wave spastically in a way that seemed to indicate pleasure. After her fingers eventually grew tired, she returned to handicapping. He watched her for a while, then closed his eyes and fell into a nap.

On the horizon, she now saw Daniel Minick, the cemetery manager, striding downhill toward her.

He carried a large black binder that matched his peacoat.

"Good afternoon, Ms. Gelki," he said, sunlight glaring behind him.

Adriane squinted up at him, nodded hello.

Minick seemed a little older than Adriane, maybe thirtyish. And though he looked quite dashing–like a slightly smaller George Clooney, but with a yarmulke–Adriane couldn't help associating him with death.

"Haven't we discussed smoking and drinking on the grounds, Ms. Gelki?" he asked, folding his arms across the binder, like a schoolgirl.

"I'm not," she insisted. "These are the things my father liked."

Minick smiled wearily. "You're not cold in that *schmatte*?"

"I don't know what you mean by *schmatte*, but if you're talking about this imported cotton Oxford shirt, I'm fine," she insisted, though she was feeling a chill.

Minick sighed, surveying the cemetery around them. "So. Have you decided anything about the adjoining plot?"

Four years earlier he had prevented Adriane's mother from being buried at Shalom Gardens after inferring from the maiden name on her transit permit that she was likely gentile. It remained a very sore subject, which he seemed compelled to bring up whenever he and Adriane crossed paths, as though he felt guilty and needed her forgiveness.

She usually told him she had no idea, which was true. "Maybe I'll convert and use it myself," she decided to say now. "Like you suggested. Would that be incestuous?" she asked Minick. "A daughter sharing a plot with her father?"

He began to blush. "You could have the markers redone singly. And we'd remove this border," he said, pointing to the granite perimeter that made the plot look like a bed. Talking about logistics seemed to calm him momentarily, but when Adriane didn't respond, the silence quickly became awkward again and he continued to blush and look down at his shoes. "You're going to have to put out that cigarette," he said at last. "Those are the rules. The rules are the rules."

Could there possibly be a more circular argument? Adriane glowered at the large black binder–*Robert's Rules of Death*, no doubt–and stubbed out her cigarette. She wondered if he would insist she pour out the cocktail.

"That's not your dog, is it?" he asked.

"Yes," she lied. "He is."

"No, he's not. I saw him here yesterday. Go on," he told the dog. "Scram!"

The dog slowly opened his eyes, yawned widely before padding off.

"He wasn't hurting anything."

"Loved ones are buried here!" shouted Minick. And then, softer: "It's almost sundown."

He walked away, waved his arms wildly at the dog, who'd paused to dig at the base of a large gray headstone. Daniel Minick whipped out a cell phone and trooped over the hill. Trying her best to forget about him, Adriane returned to her handicapping.

"Miami Dolphins plus nine?" she asked her father's grave. Then she lit another cigarette, the fancy European brand he would smoke on Sunday mornings when he would sit on the edge of the bathtub reading the sports pages and let Adriane shave his beautiful face with a creamy lather that smelled of meadow grass. Chilled Manhattan at his side. Adriane would hold her breath as she drew the bone-handled razor across his dimpled chin. So very carefully. After he phoned in his bets, the two of them would retire to the den and watch NFL football, while Adriane's mother practiced the piano or vacuumed or performed some other loud task. Her father continued to sip Manhattans and smoke, sheltering Adriane under his free arm, the comforting cotton of his lucky shirt soft against her cheek.

She sprinkled a few drops of the cocktail over his grass, slugged down the rest, and wiped the glass. Then she stashed her things in the Maryland Public Television tote bag she'd received for succumbing–whether from altruism or shame, she couldn't tell–to MPT's recent pledge drive. And now as she set out across the cemetery, she saw in the distance a white truck with a city emblem on its side, and a uniformed man leading a dog–it looked like the pointy-nosed dog–up a ramp into the back.

"Hey!" shouted Adriane. "Wait up!" She began running toward them, past rows of headstones chiseled with Hebrew letters and Stars of David, some inset with small oval portraits of Beloved Mothers and Beloved Fathers, always in pairs, Beloved Mothers and Beloved Fathers, like creatures aboard the ark. But the truck drove off before she even got close. Stopping to catch her breath, Adriane didn't know what she would have done if the driver had waited. Pretended the dog was hers again? And then what? Her building didn't allow dogs.

A vaporous dread seemed to follow her home, up the elevator, into her apartment. She stowed her MPT tote bag under the baby grand piano, grateful tonight was poker night, because she really didn't feel like being alone.

"No offense," she said, toward the piano, on top of which rested the silvery urn that contained her mother's ashes.

* * *

Usually poker night provided a pleasant diversion. Chips clicking happily into the pot, a sound from early childhood when her father would let Adriane sit on his lap and toss his bet in for him, the other men around the table smiling indulgently. . . .

But tonight's game had gone badly. For starters, Fiona, who worked downstairs from Adriane at City Hall in the mayor's public relations office, had invited a lesbian couple, which Adriane wasn't crazy about, the couple aspect really. There was an ethos to any poker game–an undercurrent of conjugal wistfulness in the case of Adriane's–and including a couple threw off the whole vibe. Plus they tended not to compete against each other, couples, giving them an unfair advantage.

But what really perturbed Adriane, what threw her off her game and now riveted her with insomnia, was that awful remark one of the newcomers made about the animal shelter. Adriane had told her story about the pointy-nosed dog and watching him be taken away. "What'll become of him?" she asked the group.

It was more a rhetorical question than anything, but for some reason, Monique, the more masculine of the couple, said this terrible, terrible thing: "I heard they put them in a sealed room," she said, "and then suck the air out."

Everyone at the table stopped betting and stared at Monique.

Her girlfriend gaped. "Why would you share that?"

Shelley, a newer addition to poker night and the first player to regain her aplomb, raised the pot and said, "How charming, the things one hears."

"Please tell us that's an urban legend," said Fiona and promptly folded her hand.

"*I* don't know," said Monique defensively. "Maybe it's cheaper that way."

Adriane herself was too distraught to say anything. She retrieved the pack of fancy cigarettes from her MPT bag, then opened the French window in her living room. She rarely smoked, but suddenly felt the need. She was picturing a room full of deflated dogs. Dogs flat as Salvador Dalí watches. The vacuum taking not only the new air they needed to breathe, but whatever air was inside them to begin with. Their very personal dog breath. She inhaled deeply and blew the smoke out her window.

Now, her insomnia already past its third hour, she tried to quell the little bursts of adrenaline that continued to wind her muscles tighter and tighter. She shrugged her shoulders, raising them as near her ears as possible, in the isometric search for relief. But she couldn't edge that stupid painting out of her mind–*The Persistence of Memory*–those dripping watches, that sinister mindscape. As a teenager, she'd thought it was cool; now she'd never be able to enjoy it again. Feeling foolish and defeated, she stumbled toward the kitchen to heat some milk.

She fished a few graham crackers out of their box and brought her glass of warm milk into the living-dining room, the scuff of her slippers whispering against carpet. The table still brimmed with cards and chips. After that dog remark, she'd badly misjudged a hand of Texas Hold 'Em, and things went downhill from there. The trick to winning in poker was to not dwell on a bad hand, which she was normally able to do, in cards if not life. But she'd kept thinking about those poor animals, and nothing seemed to go right.

She sat at the piano now and set her glass on the folded-down music rack–over a placemat, in a small concession to her mother. Moonlight reached through the French window and beamed against her mother's urn. Adriane dunked a cracker and watched her hand moving in the container's reflection. It had cost her a bundle: silver plated and pretty in that ornate style her mother liked–though, of course, her mom had not picked it out herself.

I'm soon to rejoin my beloved husband, she'd written in her suicide note. *You'll find the deed for the adjoining plot in my safe-deposit box. Everything's paid for and taken care of, your father assured me, so there should be no problems.*

But there had been problems, of biblical proportion, and Adriane could still hear Daniel Minick's sanctimonious tone from four years ago:

"The guy who used to run things here," he'd said, "sometimes got a little bendy with the rules. But this I cannot do for you. Even setting aside the cause of death, I cannot admit your gentile mother. If your father cared about being buried next to his wife," added Minick, "he shouldn't have chosen an Orthodox cemetery."

"He didn't exactly choose it," said Adriane.

Minick blinked, confused. "How did you come to own this deed?"

Her lower lip quivering, she told him about the poker game. Daniel Minick sighed and, as she recalled now, passed her a box of tissues.

She blew her nose. "What do you mean 'even setting aside the cause of death'?"

"It's against Jewish law to kill yourself," he told her, taking a seat behind the desk in his cramped office. "So there's debate over the proper burial of a suicide. Some cemeteries have a separate section. But we make every effort to construe the death as an accident. Take the person who jumps off a bridge, for instance, but then renounces her choice. Before hitting the water, I mean. Suicide?

Depends on your philosophy. How did your mother kill herself, if you don't mind my asking?"

Yes, she did mind his asking! She doubted her mother had renounced any choice–ever. For instance: her choice to punish Adriane for her father's death. By and large this punishment took the form of silence. Even the lone compliment Adriane could savor from those years–a reference to her alluring eyes–seemed tainted by innuendo and malice. The two women waged a cold war through a series of passive and not-so-passive aggressions; her mother even went so far as to filch the lucky shirt from under Adriane's pillow and launder it. Washed her father's exhaled smoke right down the drain. Surely her mother's suicide had been willful and unbending, because that was her mother's . . . *style*. Too demoralized to explain any of this to Daniel Minick, Adriane simply answered his question. "Pills."

He perked up. "You see? She might very well have come to regret her decision," he said, as though this were consolation. "Why don't you take Mother to one of the better gentile cemeteries in town?" he suggested, and he produced a printed list. "Or if you want, we can help transfer your father to a more liberal place, alongside your mother."

Adriane shook her head. She would not move her father, who'd been so pleased with himself: Securing death care in such a roundabout way had made it seem like a game. He liked the spot, had taken her there once on a picnic. They'd sat on Orioles seat cushions and eaten ham-and-cheese sandwiches.

Adriane wouldn't move him. So whatever else she did from that point forward, her mother would remain mad at her. For eternity. Which may have been fitting, may have even felt normal to Adriane; in any case, she wouldn't move him.

"Or if you convert," Minick was saying, "I mean officially, with a *teudat gerut*, the whole schmear, *you* can be buried next to your father. How's that?"

She still remembered, sitting here on the piano bench, the self-satisfaction in his voice. He was being so reasonable and helpful. *How's that?* Laughable that was. What a lucky thing Minick wasn't in charge when her father had committed his own suicide; shooting your face off, well, that left damn little window for renunciation. Though her father's death had never seemed like a choice to Adriane to begin with. Yes, it had come by his own hand–she acknowledged this eventually–but her father seemed merely to have given in, after exhausting struggle, to a force much larger than himself.

She watched now as her reflected hand lifted the glass of milk to her mouth. In the moonlit stillness of three A.M., a person could really hear herself swallow.

Her agitated funk continued into the weekend. She often thought about the dog with the pointy nose and whether his owners had rescued him. On Monday, from her office, she decided to call the pound. A twangy, coarse voice answered, and Adriane began describing the animal. "You nabbed him at Shalom Gardens. Someone must have snitched and got him kicked out of the cemetery. He wasn't even hurting anything."

"There's a lot of dogs here," said the twangy voice, barely rising above the welter of barking and howling. "You'll have to come down and see."

"I'm calling from City Hall."

"We're about twenty minutes away."

Adriane had meant, "My boss knows the mayor," but the guy hung up before she could float that thinly veiled threat. Feeling even more frustrated than before, she poked her head into her boss's office and said, "Hey, you guys have a nice yard. You should get a dog."

From his window a beam of sunshine bathed his face and shoulders in a very agreeable light, like in a Flemish painting. He glanced up from his computer and smiled at her. "You're trying to find a home for someone?"

"Sort of. He's at the pound. Maybe."

"Does he have hair or fur?"

"What's the difference? He's a great dog!" She thought of the animal's expressive face and genteel manner.

"Dogs with hair don't shed, I think. May-Annlouise is allergic."

"They have pills for that."

He smiled, as though she'd made a joke, when in truth her remark had tapped a small vein of resentment left over from their fling. Brief, awkward, and unconsummated. His wife had pretty much nipped it in the bud. In the four years since, Adriane believed she'd done a pretty good job getting over him, but there remained the occasional wistful moment.

"Listen, I'd love a dog," he said. "But she'd kill me if I brought home a shedder."

Adriane left it at that.

But on Wednesday, she was back in her boss's office talking about it again. "Maybe his owners came already," she said miserably. "They get a week, right?"

"Five days, I believe," said Garrett.

"Five business days?"

"I wouldn't think so."

Adriane felt her guts churn. She began ticking off days on her fingers. She returned to her desk and phoned the pound again. Heard the same hillbilly voice.

"Do the dogs get a week or five days? A week, right?"

"Five days," he said over the yelping and barking and howling.

"Five business days?"

"Five days."

"Okay, I called you Monday. And today's his fifth day. You've got to look for me. Put him on reserve or something. Because my boss knows the–"

"Just come before four-thirty," he said and hung up.

Adriane checked her watch; it was already three-fifteen. She threw on her coat and ran back into Garrett's office. "Can you come to the pound with me? Please?"

"I can't," he said. "I'm supposed to meet May-Annlouise at five."

"But this is a matter of life or death," said Adriane. "She'll understand."

"She might not, and honestly, I really can't," said Garrett. "Are you going to adopt him?"

"My building doesn't allow pets," she reminded him, and quickly left before he asked any other logic-bound questions she didn't know the answer to.

She ended up running most of the way home, stopping into her apartment just long enough to throw on a dry shirt and grab her tote bag and car keys. And now she was driving–the ancient Checker Marathon she'd inherited from her father–recklessly, still unsure what to do if she found her dog or why she'd begun thinking of him as "her" dog. As she crested a hill on Calvert Street, she felt her stomach rise against her heart, and within that weightless moment, a giddy flutter of something like nerve, or maybe even abandon. She continued to speed, and about forty-five minutes after having left the office, she pulled into a parking spot near the drab bunker of the city animal shelter.

Cinder-block walls baffled the relentless noise of dogs in distress, as though the building itself were whimpering. The disembodied sounds seemed ghostly to Adriane, and she quickened her pace.

"Help you?" asked the clerk, a wiry man with a large Adam's apple and a gauze bandage wrapped around the meat of his left hand.

"Yes, I'm looking for a special dog, but you wouldn't help me on the phone."

"People ain't serious on the phone."

"I'm serious on the phone." She felt dizzy from the smell of disinfectant. "Where are the five-day-old dogs?"

"Farthest down," he said. "We close in half an hour."

The main room reminded Adriane of two long rows of shotgun apartments. Bare bulbs hung from the ceiling and cast a dingy twilight. The dogs closest to her began yapping louder as she approached the gauntlet of cells on either side. A large spotted beast howled forlornly at the ceiling. Some sort of one-eared mottled thing pressed his flank against the wire mesh so heavily his flesh extruded through the holes, as though he were trying to strain himself to the other side. Adriane didn't know much about breeds, though even she could tell there were lots and lots of pit bulls. As she wandered deeper along death row, each passing cage of dogs responded to her in sequence, like football fans performing the Wave.

In the far corner of the last cage, Adriane saw him, the dog from the cemetery. He was curled in a ball, trying to nap through all the ruckus. She bent down to touch him through the chain link, and before he'd even woken up, all his cage-mates had flocked to the corner and begun vying for her attention. A lanky hound with a silvery coat and liquid brown eyes stepped over him in an effort to make an impression.

"I found him!" she shouted to the room in general. Her cemetery dog wore a plastic, institutional collar with the number 314 painted large enough to see from a dozen feet away. "I want three-fourteen!"

No humans seemed around to hear, but all the dogs in the last cage were barking in full frenzy, even hers now, their passion for life fully inflamed, tongues slithering through the wire mesh trying to taste her. Baying for their mothers and the memory of warm teats or their own long-lost litters, Adriane imagined. For everything large or small that had ever given them comfort. Faced with such naked yearning, she found herself dropping to her knees. She pressed her left cheek against the cage, fingers intertwined with wire, and let the dogs rasp their tongues across her skin, drink in the oil of her hair, slipping occasionally into her ear or eye.

Her knees began to ache against the concrete floor, but only after she'd been inadvertently scratched a few times did she stand up. She didn't want them all trampling one another in their excitement, especially not her 314, now that she'd found him.

Adriane returned to the front desk in search of that clerk with the swaddled hand, but he wasn't around. She poked her head into a small side office and sat down to wait for him. After a few minutes, she noticed a stock-car calendar that seemed turned to the wrong month; then she realized the whole thing was years old. Anxious of the time suddenly, she ran back to the hall of cages.

At the far end of the row, a different attendant, large and hulking, bent over a dog and affixed a length of rope to its collar.

She called out: "Hey, buddy, it's not even four-thirty yet, is it?"

He began to lead the creature out of the cage, and in the dim light, Adriane discerned the docile, puffed-out profile of 314.

"I said I wanted that dog! I'm taking that dog. Stop! Hold on a minute!"

The attendant's head bowed forward as he led 314 through a small back door. Adriane tried to follow, but it locked behind him. She flung herself against its metal.

"Come back!" she shouted. "Come back!"

All the dogs were barking now, a prison riot of sound, and the man from the front desk was running toward her, zipping up his pants with his good hand. "What's the matter?" he asked.

"I want three-fourteen!" she said, pounding on the locked door with both her open palms.

The front desk attendant withdrew a walkie-talkie from his pocket and said, "Corey, bring three-fourteen; this lady wants him."

They waited an endless minute before Corey shambled out with her dog–panting and wagging–and handed the rope to Adriane.

"Didn't you hear me?" she asked him.

Still without looking at her, Corey began to shuffle away.

"Hey!" She took a step after him, but a bandaged hand held back her shoulder.

"He's not trained to deal with the public, miss."

Her dog yawned and shook out his long thick coat. Then glanced up at her in quiet acknowledgment that she had done him a good turn. Crouching by his side, Adriane ruffled the top of his head and experienced a rare sense of destiny at having found him at the last possible moment. She felt meant to save him.

"Why didn't his owners come?" she wondered out loud. "He's a great dog. How could anyone dump such a dog?"

The attendant shrugged and spread his arms, a worldly gesture that said, dogwise, he'd seen it all.

The dog licked her hand, and she embraced him. There was a lot of give to him physically, from all that fluff.

"Is this hair or fur?" she asked, holding a clump that had fallen out. The whole distinction seemed specious to her.

"Fur." After leading them back to the front desk, the attendant handed Adriane a license application. When she asked what to write for breed, he guessed sheltie, a small herding dog. "He ain't pure, though. The pure breeds get snapped up by rescue societies."

"How freaking orthodox," muttered Adriane, taking the sting of such elitism personally. She was a mutt herself, after all. "Does he have a name?"

The attendant shrugged again. "Probably."

"Well, I don't know what to put here for name."

"You can mail it in when you decide."

As she and her sheltie began to leave, she glimpsed in the distance Corey the executioner lumbering back into the rear cage and attaching his rope to another dog. Adriane recognized the silvery-coated hound by its lanky profile. Even in the dim light, its scrawny legs seemed to be trembling.

Adriane wanted to call out, *Wait! I'll take that one, too!* But she knew it was impossible. She could barely imagine how to smuggle one medium-small dog in and out of her apartment building; a second, large dog was unthinkable.

And yet she continued to think about it, saw the silvery dog's soulful face long after she and 314 left the pound. . . . After she'd driven him home and hustled him into the elevator within her MPT tote bag. . . . After she'd improvised a first dinner for him out of leftover Chinese takeout and smuggled him out again for an evening walk, she remained haunted by the dog left behind.

When it was time for bed, 314 settled at the foot of her blanket and promptly went to sleep. Adriane, however, lay awake and continued to see the other dog, staring at her, eyes liquid with betrayal.

In her best phlegm voice, she called in sick the next day. Her boss sighed skeptically. She needed, in such occasional small ways, to have her way with him. Besides, his wife was much more high-maintenance than she was, she told herself, and even though she understood there was no logic to that thought, she still managed to squeeze justification from it.

"I'm all stuffed up," she said.

"Maybe you're allergic to that dog," noted Garrett, and Adriane had to laugh.

"I slept badly last night," she told him honestly. "I'll see you tomorrow."

"Don't forget to have your friend neutered," he added, just as she hung up.

After smuggling her "friend" outside for his morning walk, they hung out in the kitchen as she made a list of possible names. She did not want a traditional dog name.

"Aaron?" she asked, starting at the beginning. She paused to note any change in his expression. "Abner? Ace?" She went through a slew of *A*'s, and he responded to them all with the same earnest look, as though her next words were bound to contain the meaning of his life. "Arlo?"

When they got as far as "Barry," about ten minutes into the project, his lips curled a smidge further in a sort of enigmatic dog-smile. “Barry?” she asked again, seeking confirmation. It was hard to tell, but she put the list aside and made her choice: Barry.

They went to a pet store, where she bought a proper collar and leash, a large sack of food formulated for older dogs, and a dozen treats and playthings, including a rubber ball with raised pimples all over it to stimulate his gums, a rope bone that was supposed to floss his teeth, rawhide crudités, and a cloth mouse, though that was probably intended as a cat toy.

Just to be safe, he needed shots, so she took him to the Greater Baltimore Animal Hospital. The nurse on the phone had also suggested Adriane bring along a stool sample to test for worms, so after breakfast, she'd collected one inside an empty Chinese take-out carton. At the hospital, they told her Barry had already been neutered. They showed her how to clip his toenails and douche his ears with a diluted vinegar solution and how to cut out matted fur.

When they got home, she tried a test run of all these things. She set him in the bathtub and clipped and squirted; the water in his ears annoyed him, but he put up with everything, and seemed generally to enjoy her ministrations. He even let her lift his lips and clean his teeth with a special fingertip brush. She bathed him with an expensive dog shampoo that smelled faintly of wildflowers. When she was done, she rewarded him with a smoked pig's ear.

They were each very happy with the other.

That night, when it was time to sleep, Adriane positioned him higher in the bed, so she could wrap her arms around him. He resisted at first, wanted to sleep at her feet, but she kept dragging him toward her, and eventually, he let her rest a cheek on the soft fur above his shoulder. Breathing in the smells of clean dog and meadow flowers, she felt a greater sense of contentment than she'd felt in a long time.

They awoke around seven the next morning, her arms still wrapped around him, the lower one tingling as her blood returned to it. Barry yawned and stretched across the top of the covers. It occurred to Adriane that this was the first time in her twenty-eight-year-old life she had woken up next to another living creature. How pathetic! And yet she felt overcome by the pleasure of the moment–of reposing side by side with an affectionate companion. They continued to loll in bed awhile.

When eventually they shuffled into the kitchen for breakfast, however, she experienced a prick of shame, a whiff of disapproval from the piano's direction, from her mother's urn.

"Come on, Barry, let's go for a walk." She smuggled him outside in his tote bag. It was a beautiful, crisp morning, and they explored several blocks together. He pulled her along, giddy at all the new trees, front steps, and hydrants at his disposal, and he managed to cast traces of himself on most everything they passed.

Back at home, he watched as she readied herself for the office. At the sight of her briefcase, he pawed its flap in what seemed a vain attempt to crawl inside. Adriane felt an ache not unlike homesickness–it had been a while since she had felt anything similar, so tightly had she bound herself against the demands of tenderness. She dreaded good-byes, no matter how routine or brief.

After making sure he had food and water, she spread some newspaper on the kitchen floor just in case, and she settled him onto the couch in front of the television, turned very low, before tiptoeing out. During her entire walk to work, she felt a tug on her arm, as though she were grasping a phantom leash.

"How's the mutt?" Garrett asked when he stopped by her desk.

"Charming," said Adriane. "You should have snapped him up when you had the chance."

"He doesn't mind being in an apartment all day?"

"I do feel a little guilty," said Adriane, recalling her recent unease.

From work, she called her friends to cancel that night's poker game, telling the other players she wanted to give her dog longer to adjust. But really, she wanted more time alone with him.

When she returned home, she found Barry asleep on the couch exactly where she'd left him; the newspapers clean and dry. They took a longer walk this time, in the twilight, then spent another pleasant evening watching television, as she brushed his luxurious coat and filed his toenails with an emery board.

But when they awoke the following morning, Adriane with her arms around him again, guilt seemed to press against her as solidly as the weight of his body.

She fed him, then sat down to some cereal, the *Baltimore Sun*, and the *New York Times*, but sensed, just beyond the horizon of the newspaper, her mother's censure. Adriane found an old silk scarf and draped it over the urn.

She spent most of Saturday on the couch with Barry, handicapping her NFL picks for that week. Occasionally she would glance toward the scarf-covered urn and wonder if her guilt pangs were a sort of allergic reaction to happiness.

That evening before bedtime, she moved her mother's ashes from the piano to a low shelf on the bookcase, where they'd be less conspicuous, though this still seemed like a paltry half-measure. She put on her pajamas and climbed into bed, and after Barry hopped up, she urged him toward the pillow so she could wrap her arms around him. Her cheek against the back of his neck, she closed her eyes. Drifting into the marshy area between wakefulness and sleep, Adriane thought of her mother falling into that heavier slumber, pulled along by the weight of all those pills and the liquor from the hotel minibar. *Had* she renounced her choice in those final drowsy moments? Had she panicked at being unable to say her own name, unable to pick up a phone and signal her changed intentions? Later, much later in the night, Adriane dreamed she heard the squeak of the crematory oven's iron hinge, the closing clank of its door. Then, a still grimmer turn: the whoosh of burners lighting, a sound like the flap of a gigantic wing, drawing all air to the dark breast beneath.

She woke up sweating against her dog, her arm numb, her legs pinned by the force of her dream. She took several hours to get out of bed. After she and Barry made their way into the living room, Adriane approached her mother's urn and removed the scarf, saw her own beleaguered reflection in its silver face.

Too rattled to call her bookie, she decided to skip football betting for one week. Instead, she got dressed, opened her hall closet, and brought out the MPT tote bag. She was reaching for her mother's ashes, to set their container inside, when Barry took it upon himself to climb in first. So she fished out a second, older tote bag and put her mother's urn into that, along with a serrated knife and a serving spoon. Looking at both bags, she took a deep breath and exhaled.

"All right," she said. "Let's go." She said again, "All right," before hefting a bag in each hand and leaving her apartment.

She drove to the cemetery, then walked with both totes past the rows of graves, the chiseled Hebrew letters and Stars of David, the cameos of Beloved Mothers and Beloved Fathers, always in pairs. She wondered if God had picked which animals got to ride on the ark and which had to stay behind and have the very breath taken from them–or whether He made Noah decide. And if Noah, how did he ever choose? Did he simply pick a random pair of aardvarks and move on? Or did he go nuts, agonizing about his own motives? Altruism. Shame. Altruism. *Which is it, Noah?* Did people even parse motives back then, she wondered. Or were feelings self-evident, deeds the simple performance of those feelings or, better yet, the following of divine orders? Only messianic narcissists claimed to follow divine orders nowadays; everybody else had to rely more or less on himself, with occasionally a little input from the oddsmakers.

When she arrived before her father's grave, she set Barry's tote on its side so he could lie down. A few gentle flurries, the season's first, floated earthward. Her dog lay quiet and still, except for the slight rise and fall of his bag.

Discreetly, she brought forward the knife and pierced the empty plot, then slowly and with some effort, cut a medium-small circle in the ground. After prying inward from the edges, she lifted the toupee of grass, then began scooping dirt to one side. Barry oversaw this work from his bag. She opened now the knobbed lid of the urn, still hidden within its own tote, reached inside, and seized a palmful of ash. It felt surprisingly light and almost delicate in her hand. Adriane brought out her fist and slowly opened it. Peered closely at her selection. Then tucked the ashes into bed beside her father. Handful by handful, she did this, until the urn was empty, then smoothed the grass coverlet in place. A few snowflakes settled on top and soon melted.

Regarding the mound of displaced earth, Adriane figured she would have to dispose of it elsewhere. She scooped it into the empty urn and had just finished when she saw Daniel Minick, bundled in his peacoat and carrying his large binder, marching swiftly against the cold. He waved at Adriane and began heading in her direction, but she refused to wave back. Her heart pounding, she quickly gathered her belongings, hefted her two bags, and headed toward the car.

From the shelter of his tote, her dog quietly sniffed the air passing above, converting it to small puffs of steam. Adriane wondered how well he knew the smells of this place. And if they evoked in him the memory of his own narrow escape, and with it, all the guilt and terror of surviving.

Or maybe he just felt lucky.

3. adriane and the court-appointed psychiatrist

winter 1997

TRUE OR FALSE: I USUALLY FEEL THAT LIFE IS WORTHWHILE.

In fact, Adriane felt life was only *occasionally* worthwhile, but that wasn't the question before her, and even though the doctor said there were no right or wrong answers, clearly there was a right answer to this one. A normal person would respond: *True, I usually do, yes, I most certainly do feel that life is worthwhile usually*. Adriane wasn't going to let herself be pigeonholed as "antilife." She didn't need that on her record! Determined to put forward her most winning personality, she bore down on her number-two pencil and filled in the little circle: TRUE. She was gonna ace this fucker.

She sat at a small desk in a small room–probably a converted den–and she could hear Dr. B. P. Harris shambling around the office across the hallway. He didn't seem to have any other patients. When she'd made the appointment, his schedule was wide open.

TRUE OR FALSE: I HAVE NEVER BEEN IN TROUBLE WITH THE LAW.

Hmm, she wondered, how carefully did they cross-check these things? "Trouble with the law," after all, had landed her here in the first place. She'd found it merry enough at the time, three months ago, when she and her new friend Shelley managed to get themselves arrested for impersonating streetwalkers. What a lark! Still, when the judge offered to expunge her record on condition she see a shrink, Adriane consented, even though she hardly belonged here, and coming represented a small step backward in her recently hatched ambition to pursue a life of abandon.

But hell, she only had to come three times–unless the doctor ordered more–the first session to be consumed by taking this test. She filled in the little circle: TRUE, no troubles with the law, nothing you folks need worry your pretty little heads over.

TRUE OR FALSE: WHEN PEOPLE DO ME A WRONG, I FEEL I SHOULD PAY THEM BACK IF I CAN, JUST FOR THE PRINCIPLE OF THE THING.

Well, of course she felt that! Who didn't? Still: FALSE. Why did these Minnesota Multiphasic Personality Inventory people presume they were entitled to the truth, *her* truth.

"Abandoneers"–she coined the term right then and there–rejected that premise. Abandoneers revealed the truth–assuming there even existed such a mutually recognizable thing–when it suited them. Didn't one of those German philosophers have something to say about this? Or was she thinking of Ayn Rand? Anyway, back to the test:

Only 574 questions to go.

The following week, she returned to Dr. Harris's north Baltimore brownstone and pressed the doorbell below his mailbox, one of three gray rectangles lined up like headstones. She waited until he buzzed her in, then climbed the two long flights of stairs to the top floor. He came to the door, wearing the same tweed suit and loosely knotted bow tie from the last time, and Adriane found herself wondering how such a frail old man made it up and down all those stairs. Maybe he never left home.

He led her to the office and sat behind an oak desk, in an oak swivel chair–the kind that were very retro, owing perhaps to premillennium nostalgia, except she suspected his was original–and she sat across from him on a ratty orange sofa and tried not to stare at the shrubs of gray hair that sprouted from his nose and ears. She couldn't stop staring at those saucer-plate ears. How closely they matched her erstwhile fantasy of God: Gentle Listener, she'd called Him and liked to imagine herself lying along the rim of this large, disembodied ear, the length of her cushioned by a pillow of silver hairs, and she would whisper her innermost thoughts as the ear hurtled through the cosmos. She'd concocted this fantasy–part of an urgent spiritual quest–shortly after her father's death, but gave it up a few years ago during a crisis of faith. Deep down, she'd always known her "prayers" were a kind of playacting. Which was not to say God didn't exist, but even if He did, He probably didn't have time for individual sessions.

Dr. Harris clutched her test scores in his liver-spotted hand. "Ms. Gelki, the Minnesota Multiphasic Personality Inventory contains diagnostic scales to indicate when someone manipulates her answers to manufacture an impression."

"Un-huh," said Adriane, crossing her legs, then immediately uncrossing them, lest her body language give her away. Maybe, from a strategic point of view, she should have owned up to a couple foibles.

"Your answers, I'm afraid, have run afoul of these diagnostics. And so what could have been a valuable tool for us both–" Here he began to cough, a racking convulsion that shook his entire body, but he insisted on finishing his sentence: "–has–[*cough*]–been–[*cough*]–squandered."

"Oh, dear." She sunk deeper into the couch. A flea sprang from the armrest onto her jeans. "Could there be some mistake? Some mix-up at the lab?"

The doctor shook his head, then unwrapped a lozenge from the candy dish on his desk and put it in his mouth. He splayed his fingers across his narrow chest, closed his eyes, and tilted back in his chair as though about to take a nap.

He remained that way for several long minutes before Adriane, seeking to fill the silence, asked: "Do you want me to retake the test?"

"No," he said, opening his eyes. "Why did you seek to undermine your personality portrait, Ms. Gelki? Do you know?"

She brushed another flea from her thigh. "I guess I wanted a more flattering portrait."

"Granted, but why do you find the idea of an accurate portrait intolerable?"

This had trick question written all over it, and Adriane proceeded with caution. "Intolerable," she said, "is a strong word."

"So the prospect of wasting my time and flouting the court is merely a matter of whimsy to you?"

She *knew* it had been a trick question! "Not whimsy, I'd–"

He held up a palm to cut her off, then reached for a legal pad. "What's the date?"

"Today? It's the thirteenth," she said.

"Thursday, February Thirteenth, Nineteen and Nine Seven," he muttered as he wrote. "Let's begin. Are you employed?"

Adriane told him she worked at City Hall, in the Mayor's Office of Neighborhood Enhancement, creating community-building events.

"Such as?" he asked.

"Oh . . ." She mentioned the soft-shell-crab-eating fund-raiser for the Dundalk Fire Department. The annual St. Patrick's Day Parade along Charles Street. Last month's Painted Screen Door Slam, which might have worked out okay if it were held inside, but the Convention Center space she'd reserved fell through due to a miscommunication, and the hastily arranged walking tour wasn't as popular as she'd hoped. Also, most people had switched out their screens for storm doors, it being the dead of winter. Adriane lowered her head. "Nothing all that important, I guess."

"Why do you persist in a job you believe unimportant?"

"Why does anybody?" she countered defensively. "Why do you?"

"My job is to help people. If they'll let me," he said. "Husband?"

"No."

"Boyfriend?"

"No."

"Equivalent?" the doctor asked, peering over the top of his legal pad. Upon seeing her puzzled expression, he added: "Girlfriend?"

"No, thank you."

"Siblings?"

"No."

"And your parents?"

Adriane blinked. "None that I know of."

He raised an eyebrow. "Do you mean you were adopted or your parents are no longer alive or–" He leaned forward in his chair. "What exactly do you mean?"

"Answer B. No longer alive." Adriane knew more was expected of her, and she took a deep breath, tried to decide whether she was willing or even up to this. She surveyed the office effects around her more closely: a black rotary telephone; a brass-plated banker's lamp with a small chip in its green glass shade; a framed, yellowing diploma from the University of Maryland School of Medicine dated 1949. Adriane thought, *GI Bill.* Thought, *This guy probably pines for the* old *electroshock days.*

"My father shot his face off," she allowed, leaving out the details: that he was a gambler who owed a lot of money; that at the time she thought mobsters killed him, because it seemed impossible he could desert her. That she was fourteen.

"And your mother?" he asked, moving right along. "How did she die?"

"Same," replied Adriane, surprised he didn't pursue the father angle, which seemed to her a rich vein.

"Speak plainly, Miss Gelki. I beseech you."

"What part of *same* don't you understand?" asked Adriane. She flicked another bug from her leg. "Did you know this couch is crawling with fleas?"

The doctor set aside his legal pad and pinched the bridge of his nose.

"We have gotten off on the wrong foot, Miss Gelki," he said. "There's a credibility gap between us. It's up to you to repair it. I don't have the energy."

"Gap?" she asked. "It's all true. Okay, so my mother took pills, but it *was* the same hotel room, though ten years later–"

"Get your act together, miss!" Dr. Harris slammed his hands on the desktop and pitched forward in his chair, which made a startling squeal. "And come back next week ready to *work*!"

Adriane checked her watch as a way of avoiding the doctor's intense stare. They'd used only twenty of their fifty-minute session, so she'd gotten off easy in a way, and yet she worried about the gleeful emphasis he'd given the word *work*.

He did not escort her to the front door, which was okay with Adriane. She passed through the fusty living room quickly, though not without taking notice of a gaudy tasseled lampshade and a chintz sofa coverlet; perhaps these were the trappings of a Mrs. Harris or maybe there was an "equivalent" in the old doctor's life. Adriane might turn the question back on him next time, if he put her on the spot again.

It was dark by the time she arrived home, and she took her dog for a brisk walk in the cold. Afterward, she gave him a smoked pig's ear, his favorite treat, then poured herself a Manhattan from the pitcher she kept in her freezer.

"What a day, Barry," she said. Together they sprawled on the couch and looked through the newly arrived issue of *Martha Stewart Living*. Adriane kept an eye out for good recipes and other usable tidbits of advice, which *Martha* was always full of. If only last month's issue had included a piece on how to take the MMPI.

The phone rang, and Adriane, inveterate screener, waited for her machine to pick up. It was her newfound partner in abandon. Except Shelley hadn't made the mistake of asking an undercover cop for money, so the judge had dismissed the charges against her.

"What up, ho?" she chirped in that sometimes charming, sometimes annoying British accent of hers.

Adriane tossed her magazine on the piano, took a step toward the phone, but hesitated. She really wasn't in the mood to divulge anymore today, so she continued to screen the call. Undeterred, Shelley waded into a detailed message describing her latest sexual exploit. You had to admire Shelley's self-assurance, not just with men, but with answering machines; she had no problem chattering into the void.

After sliding into their old booth, her boss Garrett asked for a vodka martini, and Adriane ordered the same. Flexible about cocktails, she considered herself, like H. L. Mencken, "ombibulous."

"You two haven't been in here for a long, long time," said their waitress, Calida, a wispily tall émigré from Madrid.

Actually, Adriane and her boss hadn't come to happy hour in four years, not since their brief, ill-fated fling. She smiled wistfully as Calida walked off, then whispered to him, "I can't believe she *remembers* us!" It felt strangely gratifying, in a sentimental way, and Adriane found her eyes grow moist.

"Look, as I said, I don't want to do anything to upset, well, *anything*," Garrett began, "but you've been seeming–out of sorts. I thought you might need to talk."

She sighed. "That's what my shrink says."

"You're in therapy?" he asked, boyishly wide-eyed. "Good for you!"

She flinched from his enthusiasm. "I don't really belong there."

"Are you kidding?" he said. "After everything you've been through? I should probably look into a little therapy myself," he added, eyeing the tapas buffet.

"Yeah, well, unfortunately my therapist thinks I'm a pathological liar."

Garrett blinked. "Really?"

"I even told him, you know, about my parents, and he wouldn't believe me."

Garrett was one of the very few people who did know about her parents. "He's supposed to believe you, I'm pretty sure."

"Well, I'd fudged a few answers on a standardized test." She sighed again, morosely. "He's way too dependent on those test results."

"Why don't you find a better therapist? Shop around."

"That's not an option."

She explained about the court order, which may not have been a wise detail to share with one's boss, but her need to reveal herself to him was a habit Adriane had never managed to break. It always felt good, in a painful, scab-picking way.

"You flashed a cop?" he asked, his normally lax facial muscles becoming taut with moral confusion. "Was that–really–*necessary*?"

"It was *fun*," she insisted, clicking the salt and pepper shakers together. "It was the most alive I've felt since . . ." She glanced at him with a trace of longing.

"You're probably getting this therapy just in time," he decided.

"Hey!" she snapped, stung by his remark. "Whose side are you on?"

Calida silently delivered their drinks and disappeared again.

"I'm on your side," he said. "Do you want me to go with you next time, to corroborate your story?"

Adriane imagined showing up to psychotherapy with her boss, the former object of her illicit seduction, as a way to impress upon Dr. Harris that she was honorable. What an appalling thought! She began to laugh, so loudly that Garrett squinted with concern.

"I really *am* on your side," he said.

She finally got her laughter under control and nodded gratefully, because she knew in her heart it was true. She reached for her martini. "Bottoms up."

The week passed quickly, and on Wednesday evening Adriane brooded over the next day's appointment with Dr. Harris. She kept hearing her boss's voice, offering to "corroborate" her story, and clenched her jaw. Abandoneers never asked for corroboration!

She approached the tall bookcase in her living room and crouched before the bottom shelves, where she kept back issues of magazines–*Harper's*, *Football Digest*, an erotic journal called *Nippleodeon*. Reaching for the 1992 boxed set of *Martha Stewart Living*, she extracted the November issue: "Ten Stuffings Worth Our Thanks." When the magazine had first arrived, on a gray Saturday four-plus years ago, Adriane planned to make the recipe featuring apricots and cashews, but events of the day intervened. She now flipped through the issue and found, lodged in the magazine's center, the document she would bring to therapy in order to prove herself:

Barry ambled over and sniffed the yellowed piece of paper.

Her mother's suicide note.

It would speak for itself.

After work the next day, Adriane stopped at home to walk and feed Barry, then dutifully drove to her session. She rang the doorbell to Dr. Harris's apartment, and he buzzed her in. As he had the previous two weeks, he waited for her at the top of the stairs, wearing a different but equally frayed tweed jacket. His ears appeared to have grown even larger.

"Are we ready to be more forthcoming?" he asked, leading her through the living room. Adriane took it as a rhetorical question and kept mum, distracted in any case by a framed sepia wedding portrait standing on an end table. From her distance, she couldn't tell if the photo was of the doctor and his bride or possibly his father and mother or someone else altogether. And now, already in the office area, he motioned her toward the orange couch as he shuffled to his post behind the large oak desk. His swivel chair squeaked as he sat down.

"About last week," she said. "I've brought documentation."

He raised a shrubby eyebrow as Adriane reached into her purse for the note. She smoothed it across the lap of her jeans, then looked up at him. "Maybe this is too abrupt," she said. "How are you?"

"How am *I*?" he asked. "I'm fine, thank you. Please, proceed."

She stood and brought the note to him. "It has to do with my mother's suicide."

"I see," said Dr. Harris, taking the page from her. He cleared his throat, as though planning to read aloud, which in fact he began to do.

To Adriane, Only Daughter of Mine,

Today has been a near-perfect day.

After you left for work, I awoke and ate a grapefruit. Then I practiced my Schubert–the B-flat sonata that always gave you so much trouble. Practiced with no earthly goal in mind, no impending recital, recording, or master class, simply practiced–*sending notes into the air as though freeing birds from their cages. You always seemed to think of music, or at least practice, or perhaps following in my footsteps, as the cage–though I suppose all that is my fault, too.*

Well, anyhow, I played through the piece twice. Then, for old times' sake, walked over to Louie's and savored one of their mocha ice cream rum drinks. I sat at the bar by myself, the conversations echoing around me. I've always liked Louie's, but the acoustics, as you know, are not optimal.

Someone had left behind a sports page, and I glanced at headlines recording one pointless conflict after another. With so much conflict in the world–real and often unavoidable–why should people contrive yet more and call it sports? Why should they waste their time, money, and feeling on the outcome? In your father's case, I believe he had difficulty making distinctions between actual life and its simulacra. A terrible influence you were on each other's adolescent natures. I always found your closeness untoward and, I might add, hurtful. I know I've intimated as much over the years, but saying it plainly, at last, seems more truthful, and it is only through the truth that one can be forgiven. You yourself seem not to need forgiveness, as was made clear on that otherwise lovely day at Pimlico, so I won't burden you with mine. Perhaps you might someday grant me the favor of yours, but I am not, as it were, holding my breath.

I am soon to rejoin my husband and will have put such niggling, peripheral concerns behind me. You'll find the deed for the adjoining plot in my safe-deposit box. Everything's paid for and taken care of, your father assured me, so there should be no problems. I would have picked a swanker hotel in which to wind things down, but this was the hotel your father chose, after all.

Good luck, kiddo–you'll need it!

Your mother,

Deirdre de Havilland Gelki

P.S. Thank you, that was *a pleasant afternoon at the track. We'll always have Pimlico!*

P.P.S. Please keep the piano in tune, even if you rarely play it. You can trust Mr. Hemmerdinger on all maintenance issues. I believe you're due for a complete re-felting.

Dr. Harris unwrapped a lozenge from the candy dish. Adriane watched him expectantly. He approached and handed her a blank sheet of paper and a pen.

"Please write the following words quickly and without thinking." He returned to his desk, picked up her mother's note, and dictated: *"Today has been a near-perfect day."*

Adriane shook her head in amazement. Would he carbon-date the paper next? Resignedly, she copied down the sentence.

Dr. Harris then collected her handwriting sample and compared it to the original. Studied them for a good minute. Eventually, he looked up. At some point tears had found their way into his eyes.

"Monstrous," he seemed to murmur. "Simply monstrous." And then louder: "Why would you keep such a caustic document?"

Adriane shrugged. Actually, hearing them read out loud, the words sounded less indicting than she'd remembered them.

"It seems significant that you've held on to this." He continued to clutch the original note. Using his free hand, he now patted his brow and cheeks with the handkerchief from his breast pocket. "Please excuse me for having doubted you."

Adriane felt her throat tighten at the sight of the doctor's tears. It caught her by surprise, how badly she must have wanted him to believe her. "Okay," she said.

"I've been doing this for so many years," he conceded, "and your test scores–"

"Don't worry about it."

"How have you–*survived* this long without therapy?"

Adriane blushed and lowered her eyes.

"You should consider coming beyond our brief stint." He glanced again at her mother's note, which trembled in his grasp. "I can reduce the fee, if need be."

Adriane nodded tentatively. She was still getting used to being believed. She watched him hold her documentation–her Certificate of Damage–then turned her gaze toward the doctor's own diploma hanging on the wall.

"What do your initials stand for?" she asked, as though this were a relevant consideration in choosing a therapist.

"Beryl. Phillip." The doctor smiled, almost dopily–the first smile she had seen on his face. His teeth were dingy and crooked; maybe that's why he didn't do it more often.

"You have a nice smile," she said, trying to make him feel better about it, but maybe, she feared, the lie was too obvious. The last thing she wanted was to reopen their credibility gap. His face reddened, and he swiveled in his chair away from her, still clutching the suicide note, and seemed to gaze out the window, waiting for her to speak.

So, it was going to be *that* kind of therapy. The Woody Allen kind. Adriane pushed off her shoes, raised her legs onto the couch, and closed her eyes. Still pleased to have won him over, she hoped to keep that good feeling going, and if it meant coughing up a few more truths, she could probably see her way clear to doing that.

Scrunching deeper along the couch, she lay her ankles across the far armrest. She felt awkward about reclining, but this seemed the standard posture in movies, and she wanted–as long as she was striving for Dr. Harris's approval–to get it right. Her hand came across a small rent in the couch's nubby fabric and she could feel the cushioning within. Someone, possibly a mouse, had gouged out a small chunk of foam. She poked her finger inside.

"I was a prude all through high school," she began. "I wouldn't give my mother the satisfaction of criticizing me on that score. And I'm still barely experienced, if you want to know. I hear you people care about that kind of thing. But she does have a point–about me and my dad being maybe too close. Not physically–we're not talking movie-of-the-week, but the *feeling*. I mean, he did love me more than he loved her."

Which I liked, thought Adriane. And then, she considered: Perhaps the insight only counted if she said it out loud. Therapy seemed in this way like confession, or so she imagined. Self-awareness was not enough; you were supposed to own up to your problems and have them witnessed.

"I liked it," she said, "that he loved me more than he loved her." She glanced over at the doctor to detect a response, any sort of response at all, and he seemed to offer a subtle, nonjudgmental nod.

Maybe, Adriane thought, *this won't be so bad*. She'd already found herself sharing more classified information than she'd ever shared with her boss, though not as much as she'd confided to her Gentle Listener. But there was something more satisfying, she decided now, about divulging herself to a physical person, a professional–even if doing so kind of put her abandoneering experiments on hold. Adriane settled deeper into the couch, pinched a bit of foam, and wondered how much Dr. H. would be willing to come down on his hourly rate.

"I *liked* that my father loved me more than he loved her," she repeated. "So the more she resented me, the more it meant he had, right? Maybe that's why I never moved out. You know, to keep that feeling alive." She wondered if the doctor appreciated such wry self-analysis. "I mean I *really* liked that feeling," she said once again for good measure. "From when I was ten, he and I would watch football on TV, and we had this whole Sunday ritual."

She described the hours upon hours spent watching NFL football. Later, in the spring, her father would pick her up from school early and they'd go to the track. Also the many, many poker games; Adriane would just watch, but that was more than her mother was allowed.

"That thing in her note, about thanking me for Pimlico? A few months before she died, she wanted to go to the track. She'd never been, and I really didn't want to take her; it stood to ruin some very pleasant memories for me. But she insisted: *Let's go to Pimlico! Call in sick. Let's go*. This was the first time she'd suggested we do anything together in I don't know how long. It was suspicious. I reminded her that people *gambled* at Pimlico–she was dead set against betting of any kind–but she shrugged it off this time and dressed up like it was Easter. She even put on a pair of white gloves. I mean this wasn't even the Preakness. This was some weekday afternoon. We were in the grandstand surrounded by drunks and washouts. She didn't seem to care. She kept asking things like, *Is this where you and your father liked to watch?*"

Adriane remembered one of the races coming to a finish–that exhilarating burst of dust, leather, and sweat as the horses passed. *They're so beautiful*, her mother said, and Adriane rejoined, jealously: *Yes, they are.*

"Let's bet on something," her mother suggested. "How do you decide which horse to bet on?"

Adriane buried her face in the racing form and mulled over their options. Her father had always liked exactas and tried to pair a favorite with some medium long shot that grabbed his imagination. Adriane tried explaining some of the math to her mother but soon felt embarrassed, as though she were describing a sex act.

She picked a front-runner, a four-year-old named Dandy Long Legs, and paired him with Homemade, who'd posted very fast practice times on turf. Ten minutes later, she'd turned her mother's ten-dollar bet into a little over three hundred bucks.

"She was stunned. She thought it was alchemy. A couple races later, I picked a second exacta, and then there was no shutting her up. *Now I understand the whole appeal*, she kept saying, in a way that sounded, you know, a little patronizing. But when she started referring to my handicapping as a 'talent,' that's when I started to get pissed off and said we should leave. I mean, come on, I know what is and isn't a talent.

"In the car, she asked me why I thought my father lost so much money. Not in the harping, judgmental way she used to ask him. She just really wanted to know, which confused me to no end, but I told her he was an addict, because that was the truth. She said she hoped I could avoid that in my own life, and I was trying to figure out how I should take that, when she added something that seemed so over the top, so eff-ed up, I totally lost it, Doc. We'd just turned off the freeway, and she said she'd been giving the tension between us a lot of thought, and then she said, *We all make mistakes, Adriane*–she never called me by my name, and she said–*I want to forgive you*.

"When you think about it, that's kind of a strange way to put it, you know? Like there was a *but* coming. As in: *But I can't*. Anyway, that's not what I was angry about. And, believe me, I was spastic angry. I swear to you, Doc, I almost rear-ended the car in front of us. I told her I had no idea what she was talking about;

there was nothing for her to forgive. I may have been screaming. *Don't you dare forgive me*, and so on. She just stared straight ahead at the road, and we dropped the subject completely.

"After that, for the next few months, we quarreled a lot less, and she made an effort to be pleasant, but in that way . . . Oh, in the way people can put themselves out when they know it only has to be temporary."

Adriane looked down at her stomach and saw a small pile of foam crumbs, which she'd plucked from the couch's wound. Except for the throaty moan of a hot water pipe, buried in the walls somewhere, the room remained quiet.

"Doctor Harris?" she asked after a long pause. "I've always kind of wondered. Do you think that time we went to the track . . . do you think she was deciding right around then . . . you know . . . was that the day she decided?" Adriane glanced over at him. "To settle her accounts or something? Put her affairs in order? What do you think, Doc?" He continued to face the window, still holding her mother's note, but he seemed to have nodded off, his chin resting against his chest.

I put him to sleep? She felt suddenly idiotic. *Pouring my guts out?*

"Hey!" She clapped her hands. "Sigmund Freud! Nap on your own time."

She strode toward him, leaned across his desk, and tried to draw the note from his grasp. But he wouldn't let go, and the force of her pulling spun him in his swivel chair, and when he stopped in front of her he pitched forward, his head hitting the desktop with a solid knock.

Adriane looked at the pale scalp glowing through his bald spot and felt the blood drain from her own face as well. His wrist felt cool and papery. She reached for the telephone, stuck her finger in the rotary dial. It took a moment for her body to remember how to use it. She called 911.

"Nature of your emergency?" asked the tinny voice of a switchboard operator.

"I don't know," whispered Adriane. "Death?"

She'd seen only one dead body: her mother's, lying across a hotel bed, her suicide note–the very note that Dr. Harris now held–on the bedside table next to an array of empty miniatures. The investigating officer had asked Adriane to identify the body, its skin a waxy yellow, which the doctor's here lacked, but maybe that was coming.

Adriane could hear the scrabbling of computer keys over the phone. "Medics are on the way," said the operator. "I'm transferring you to a nurse; don't hang up."

A moment later a young-sounding man came on the line and asked Adriane to describe what happened.

"Nothing happened!" she said suddenly defensive. "Dr. Harris just keeled over!"

"Is he breathing?" The nurse asked, his voice nearly cracking with puberty. "Place your finger under his nose."

Adriane did as she was told, wedging her finger in the narrow space between the doctor's upper lip and his desk, but couldn't distinguish any possible flow of breath from the tickle of his mustache. "I don't know," she said. "He's so frail." She withdrew her finger and noticed a smear of blood on it. *Good God*, she thought, *my yammering killed him*.

"Do you know CPR, ma'am?"

"Actually, no!" The phone felt slippery in her hand, and she felt irrationally afraid of dropping it. *Ma'am?* she thought.

"Are you alone?"

Adriane swallowed. "Yes."

"That's okay, ma'am. I'll talk you through this situation. I want you to lay him down on his side. Are you strong enough to do that?"

"Lay Dr. Harris on the floor?" Adriane put down the phone and pulled the slight man from his chair, spread him out under the window, and arranged him on his side as gently as possible. She could see now that he had suffered a nosebleed–when he'd hit his head? Blood had collected in his once-gray mustache, rejuvenating it with color.

"Now what?" she said into the phone.

"Open his mouth and make sure his tongue or anything isn't creating blockage."

She got down on her knees, pried apart his chapped lips, then his discolored rows of teeth. She looked inside. His tongue, small and pale, lay curled asleep. She plucked a half-dissolved cough lozenge from the cave of his cheek.

"Nothing's blocking his throat, but I still can't tell if he's breathing!" she said, the phone tightly cradled under her chin.

"Can you feel a neck pulse? Just like at aerobics class."

Adriane had never taken an aerobics class. She began pressing her fingertips against the sides of his slack, cool neck, then hurriedly loosened his bow tie. Tried the neck again. "I can't tell," she lamented. "I don't know what I'm doing."

"Are you okay with trying some mouth-to-mouth?" the nurse asked.

"I have a choice?" she said, steeling herself.

As instructed, she shifted the doctor onto his back, pinched his nose and pressed her mouth over his–the kiss of life, wasn't that what they called it? But when Adriane heard the rattle of her breath in his windpipe, all she could think of was the whoosh of a crematory burner igniting. She would sometimes hear this sound in her dreams or even when closing her shower curtain. It haunted her at the most unexpected moments. Her mouth trembled around the word *monstrous*. "Monstrous," she croaked, barely above a whisper.

She hovered over the doctor's dry lips and tried pushing another breath down his throat. The phone medic was saying something tinny and distant from the floor, so she picked up the receiver. "When is the ambulance coming?" Adriane cried with anger and wiped the doctor's blood from her cheek.

"They're almost there. Let's try some chest compression," he said. "Put both hands over his sternum and press down, like almost two inches, rapidly."

Adriane did as she was told, and immediately on the first thrust she heard a sickening crack that sounded like a snapped branch. "I think I broke a rib!"

"That's okay. Keep going. Then give him another two breaths."

Adriane heard a second crack and then a third. The doctor's chest became more and more sunken. Was she thrusting too hard? Angry at the doctor for abandoning her? If only she could ask him! A fourth crack. Before she could administer another set of breaths, however, she turned her head, reached for the waste paper basket, and threw up. Tears leaking out of her face, she wiped her sleeve across her mouth and pressed it against the doctor's once more and tried to stop crying long enough to transmit another pair of breaths.

The entrance buzzer jolted her, and she sprang to her feet and ran to the front hallway, pressed a button to open the street door, and shouted: "All the way up!"

She saw the heads of two young men bounding up the stairwell, and she waited for them in Dr. Harris's living room, pointing mutely toward the back office. They raced past her, carrying a folded stretcher, equipment jangling from their vests like sleigh bells. They positioned the stretcher in the middle of the office and sprang open its legs. Adriane tried to keep out of their way, stumbled back against the orange couch.

The taller of the two men dropped to the floor. "Shallow, but he's breathing," he said and turned to Adriane. "You break these ribs?"

"Yes," she said timidly. "They said it was okay."

On the count of three, the two medics hoisted Dr. Harris onto the stretcher then strapped him on. Within seconds, they were carrying him out of the apartment. Adriane grabbed her coat, turned off the living room lights, and closed the front door. Then followed them down the stairs. Outside, it was cold and dark already. The doctor, she noticed, still clutched her mother's note, and it disappeared with him into the ambulance.

"Mercy Hospital," the driver told her, "if you want to follow."

She watched the ambulance drive off, its lights flashing, and tried to remember now if the doctor ever mentioned anything about a Mrs. Harris. Adriane had meant to ask. She returned to the vestibule of the old building. Regarded the gray rectangle mailbox, which read, inconclusively: HARRIS. Still, something should be left. Just in case. She rustled through her purse for a scrap of paper and a pen. Against the building's brownstones, whose rough surface made her handwriting look like that of a child, she composed a note, then squeezed it into the crack of the mailbox door.

As she sat in the ER admittance lounge, Adriane watched a large pair of automated doors open with a *whoosh* whenever someone passed from the hospital's periphery into its core. She resolved to enroll in a CPR class. Everyone, apparently, ought to know CPR. And maybe she should look into aerobics as well. In the waiting area, she had plenty of time to obsess over whether she could have done anything differently; would Dr. Harris be okay if only she'd noticed earlier? She began wondering when exactly in their session he'd lost consciousness and which parts of her story he had heard. What about Adriane's football ritual with her father? Or that earlier part about how she'd taken such perverse pleasure in her mother's resentment? Had Dr. Harris a professional opinion about those things? Her truth seemed afloat in some kind of uncomfortable limbo. Trapped, maybe, in the orange nap of his office couch. She hadn't even gotten to the part about having her mother cremated! That cemetery deed–there *had* been problems with it, after all. Adriane sat mesmerized by the automated doors, waiting for what, and for how long, she did not know.

There did, in fact, turn out to be a Mrs. Harris. Later that night, a balding woman, wearing a sad amount of rouge, entered the ER waiting area with a *whoosh* and quickly managed to find Adriane.

"You were his five o'clock?" the woman asked, consulting her watch. Despite her stooped posture, she maintained an almost regal bearing.

Adriane needed a moment to recognize herself described in terms of an appointment. Mrs. Harris continued to look at her wristwatch and said she'd been visiting with her husband the past few hours. "He's had a stroke," she explained.

"Will he be okay?" Jittery from soda and vending machine candy, Adriane heard the smallness of her own voice.

"Yes, he *will*," said his wife, with a familiar tinge of jealousy. "After some time."

Instantly Adriane made the imaginative leap of placing herself back in his care. She dabbed a sleeve to her face and felt an embarrassing light-headedness and an overall expansiveness of body and spirit. The benefit of confession, she was starting to see, came from transferring part of one's burden to another person. It didn't matter whether the doctor, in their next session, would try to rationalize her behavior; she wasn't angling for that. He could say, "Yes, what a monstrous thing you did, denying your mother's last wishes" or "What a monstrous thing, sniping at your mother's compliment; are you unable to recognize a simple kindness?" and that would be okay. Adriane had done those monstrous things and more. He could even say: "Yes, you *are* a monster, Adriane Gelki. We certainly have our work cut out for us." He would give her the *tools*. The support. They would work on it together, long and hard. She would seek his forgiveness, and he would find a way to grant it. This supplication, the self-flagellation involved, well, Adriane could just imagine what derisive points her friend Shelley might have to make about the process. But Shelley needn't know; she and Dr. Harris were never likely to cross paths. The whole therapy procedure was cloaked in confidentiality, wasn't it? Doctor-patient privilege. And it was indeed: A rare privilege had been conferred upon Adriane. Feeling dizzy with relief, she found herself reaching for the elderly woman's shoulder, but Mrs. Harris flinched and withdrew.

"You have a little dried blood in the corner of your mouth," she said and handed Adriane a tissue before adding, "I guess now he'll take my advice and finally retire."

"Oh," said Adriane, whiplashed anew. "That's . . . He was so good though."

"Thank you for notifying me." Mrs. Harris smiled tightly, then fished inside her purse and returned Adriane's message and–

paper clipped beneath, as though they were pieces of a related correspondence–her mother's suicide note.

The elderly woman then hurried off, with a final *whoosh*, and Adriane read over the words she'd left for whoever might find them:

> *Dear Mrs. Harris (or equivalent),*
>
> *Your husband collapsed during our time together. He's on his way to Mercy Hospital, where I am headed right now.*
>
> ~~*I'm sorry.*~~
>
> ~~*I'm so sorry.*~~
>
> *I'm sorrier than you'll ever know.*
>
> *Adriane Gelki, patient*

4. polkas and capers

summer 1997

At lunchtime, Adriane set out to meet her friend Joan. It was a damp summer day, and the Brooks Brothers crowd from the brokerage firms headed to and from their restaurants, while the secretarial class sat at the edge of the large fountain at Hopkins Plaza, eating their sandwiches or chicken Caesar salads in foam containers, trying to avoid the spray whenever the wind shifted. Adriane waited at their usual spot on the north side; even though she was an assistant director, not a secretary, and Joan had recently made vice president at her company, they both saw themselves as fountain people.

"What's the deal with that dress?" Joan called out from twenty feet away. "This is the third time you've worn it in a week."

"Twice!"

"But you never wear dresses," said Joan, smoothing her own as she sat.

"I know," said Adriane, defensively. "Maybe that's why I like it."

Joan always worked in a dress or skirt, typically featuring a modest side vent to elongate her squattish legs, which made her insecure. She had intelligent eyes and the kind of simple decent looks that often went unappreciated in this world. Herself, Adriane's physical insecurities focused on her upper arms. But for some reason, in this new dress, silk and sleeveless, she felt beyond all that.

"Has Greg seen you in it?"

Mouth full, Adriane shook her head.

"He seems very taken with you," Joan reported.

"We've only been on two dates! There's a huge margin of error."

"You, on the other hand, sound not so taken."

"He's cheerful, smart, and kind," Adriane allowed. "And he has a soft mouth."

Joan began snapping her fingers in front of Adriane's face and asked, "What are you looking for?"

"Huh?"

"You keep looking over my shoulder."

"No, I don't," said Adriane.

Joan shook her head. "Just promise you'll try not to hurt Greg's feelings."

"Why'd you set us up if you think I'm such an ogre?"

"I don't think you're an ogre," replied Joan, as though the question weren't hyperbole but had actual face value.

"I mean, if you're so worried about him falling into the wrong hands, you could have asked him out yourself."

"I told you. I'm not his type."

This seemed a suspiciously self-effacing way to put it, and Adriane wasn't sure if it masked thwarted desire on Joan's part or was just her coy way of saying *he* wasn't *her* type. Whatever *type*

Adriane herself might be, well, she just hoped someone could like her in spite of it.

"What *are* you looking for?"

"Nothing," Adriane insisted, crumpling her empty lunch sack. But in fact, she had been keeping an eye out for the Frenchman, who at that very moment was walking across Hopkins Plaza, headed straight toward them. The gracious swagger of his shoulders underneath his suit jacket put Adriane in mind of a Thoroughbred racehorse.

"So! You bought the dress!" he said, spreading his arms wide as though to take in the full effect. "I was correct, yes?"

Joan raised an eyebrow and looked at Adriane's outfit with renewed suspicion.

The Frenchman introduced himself–his name, it turned out, was Luc–and extended his hand to shake, more of a squeeze really. He turned to Joan and asked, "Did she tell you the story about this dress?"

"There's an entire story?"

"She was admiring it in a shop window. I, a passerby, remarked how well it suited her. And I was correct, yes?" He asked if the women had eaten lunch yet.

"We just finished," said Joan, closing the lid to her foam box.

"Come join me for a glass of wine then. There's a lovely café right over here," he said pointing toward his left.

Joan glanced at her watch and then at Adriane, who was staring back at her, trying to send out an encouraging vibe.

"Sure," said Joan. "Why not?"

Leading them to an outdoor table, he held out Joan's chair and then Adriane's. The courtesy made sitting down almost balletic–far more complex than doing it alone–and Adriane wondered if this was just the sort of gate-keeping ritual designed to tell true ladies from the likes of her.

"The onion soup here is excellent," the Frenchman said, as he sat.

"We already ate lunch," Joan reminded him.

"He wants to humiliate us!" Adriane announced playfully. "You think we're going to eat melted cheese in front of a stranger?"

"You can master it, I'm sure," he said with a wink. "You are very graceful."

Adriane wondered if he meant *you-both* or simply *you-her*. No one had ever observed her grace before.

"Please try a small amount," he said. "You needn't finish."

Joan insisted she was too full, but Adriane decided to be a sport.

He ordered in French without looking at a menu or a wine list, and within two minutes, an ice bucket was set up at his side and shortly after that two crocks of onion soup were set before him and Adriane.

"What allows you to enjoy a leisurely bottle of Pouilly-Fuissé at lunch?" she asked before taking the first perilous spoonful of soup. She hoped to get him started on a long monologue so she needn't talk as she ate. She pierced the top layer of cheese and tried to cut off a small bite without dragging up the entire crust.

"My family holds a caper concern."

"Those little rabbit pellets that fall out of sandwiches?" said Joan.

"You're a caper tycoon?" Adriane immediately put in.

"The worldwide caper market," he said seriously, "is lucrative. And what do you do, Adriane?" he asked.

"I, too, am a caper tycoon." She smiled and managed to shuttle another spoonful of soup toward her mouth.

"An astounding coincidence." He smiled back. "And you, Joan?"

"Cable TV," she said. "VP of marketing."

Adriane was admiring his suit: All the pinstripes matched up across the seams, even at the pockets; Adriane didn't know suits could do that. A dozen pinstripes across each proportionately perfect shoulder.

"There is nothing like a beautiful woman eating soup," he declared.

"What a cheesy line," said Joan, and the Frenchman graciously smiled at her pun.

Adriane blushed, her limbs suddenly warm and fluid, like melted Gruyère. She *was* doing well with the soup, had never eaten onion soup so gracefully; she credited his watching her, as though his gaze had exalted her, imbued her with powers. Unless, of course, it was a special cheese or something.

"You've barely touched yours," Joan pointed out.

The Frenchman took a sip of broth, then lit a cigarette and leaned back in his chair. "My capers have earned awards three of the last five years."

"Are there big differences between capers?" Adriane said.

He scowled, and she immediately regretted overbantering.

Joan finished her glass of wine and, reaching for her purse, took out a piece of nicotine gum.

"I will undertake to show you," the Frenchman announced. "You must come *chez moi*. We'll conduct a test."

"A caper tasting?"

"Yes. Tomorrow evening." The fountain changed patterns, shot up to its fullest extension, and a light mist drifted their way, dampening Adriane's face. She and Joan exchanged an edgy glance.

Tomorrow was Saturday, and Adriane had a date planned with Greg, their third.

"I can't tomorrow," she said.

His brow arched with amusement. "You are, how you say, 'seeing' someone?"

A filament of cheese tethered her spoon to the soup bowl. "Nothing too serious."

Joan shot her a scolding look.

"And you, Joan, do you have *un petit ami*?"

"No such luck," she said, and continued to gnaw at her gum.

"Please visit me Sunday afternoon, both of you," he said. "After you are done with church." He raised one eyebrow teasingly, implying that he himself was not a churchgoer. In the warm air, droplets of condensation had collected along the wine bottle's throat.

"We don't even know your last name," said Joan. That was just the kind of common-sense wisdom she was full of and for which Adriane depended on her. Usually Adriane counted this quality among the blessings of their friendship, but just now she felt more irritated than anything.

"Here is all my information." He handed his calling card toward Adriane, making her lean forward a little to reach it.

They parted company soon after.

"Call me," Joan murmured to Adriane, as they left the café.

On her way back to her office, Adriane meandered along the perimeter of Hopkins Plaza, looking into shop windows. She paused to admire her reflection a couple times. Since encountering the Frenchman the week before, her self-worth had seemed to rise, and today's lunch kicked it up another notch. Beforehand she'd assumed her charms were the kind to go completely unnoticed by men as suave and well-to-do as he. That this long-held assumption could be disproved so abruptly seemed as bizarre, as unliberated as it was delightful.

She watched Greg saunter back from the bar, carrying a pitcher of Löwenbräu and two plastic cups. He poured for both of them and then topped off three old women in dirndls who happened to be sharing their family-style table. He surveyed the dance floor, his forehead damp from having polkaed the past hour. Mostly with Adriane, but when she got tired, he finished out the set with a few of the blue hairs. He clinked his plastic cup against hers.

"Did you know," she shouted over the general hubbub, "Thelonious Monk used to play in a polka band?"

"Who?"

The band began their next set, and he took her hand and pulled her toward the dance floor. He was a good polka-er; it surprised Adriane that anyone in his twenties would even know how. When he'd taken her here to Blob's Park a couple weeks earlier, for their first date, she'd assumed he viewed the place with the same ironic distance she did–but maybe not.

He whisked her along now, her feet barely making sensible contact with the floor and she told herself, *Just don't look down, don't think about what you're doing.* In this way she could enjoy herself, but if she imagined what she must look like, Adriane became self-conscious and stumbled.

She was sweating now, and after a few more dances, he solicitously guided her back to their table against the mirrored wall. "Should I get another pitcher?"

"Not just yet," she said. She knew he was just being attentive and generous, but the idea that he might have a drinking problem gently tapped her on the shoulder. She reviewed his alcohol consumption from each of their three dates, trying to form a reasonable conclusion. Well, their second date had been a movie, so that skewed the average. But it was important to discover these things early, Adriane decided, even though she was a fairly heavy drinker herself.

A few moments later, an extremely elderly woman in a red dirndl and black shawl began inching past their table. She used a cane with a large rubber plunger at its base. And her husband, presumably, who seemed almost as frail, guided her elbow. The woman paused in front of Adriane and looked directly at her, leaned a little closer now and began to touch the edge of her own mouth right next to a small web of veins. Adriane thought the woman might be trying to tell her she had a little beer foam on her lip, so she rubbed in the corresponding spot. But suddenly the woman startled, and her clouded eyes widened.

"Oh dear, excuse me," she said. "I thought I was looking in . . . in a mirror."

"Say what?" mumbled Adriane.

The woman began to mince again toward an exit, the "Beer Barrel Polka" wheezing in the background. Adriane turned to her date and asked, "Can we leave?"

Being the obliging young man he was, Greg agreed and drove her home.

Parked now in front of her apartment building, they were making out, and she marveled again at how soft he felt–like kissing a ripe peach. She pulled back to study him, and traced a fingertip around his mouth, comparing the two textures, skin then lip–soft and softer. He would probably age well.

She said, "I can't believe that woman thought she was looking in a mirror." The way she'd just helped herself to Adriane's face; it felt like a violation.

"Maybe you look like she did," said Greg. "I mean fifty years ago. Maybe you're how she looks in her memory."

This observation was so obvious and of so little help, Adriane found herself blaming him a little for the incident. She stuck her finger in his mouth and then a second one, sliding them across his tongue.

He took hold of her wrist and pulled her fingers out, wet with his saliva, and kissed her knuckles. "May I," he asked, "maybe come up?"

She liked this boy. Cheerful, smart, and kind. And it had been a long time since she'd put her fingers in anybody's mouth; it was not something she did all that lightly. But if she invited him upstairs, she reminded herself, they'd be crossing a frontier, with all of its expectations and presumptions–not just his, but her own, and Joan's too, no doubt–and was she ready to take that on, she wondered.

"I'm a little tired from all that polkaing," she said at last. "I'd better go to sleep."

He sighed and looked out his windshield. "What are you doing tomorrow?"

"Tomorrow?" She leaned her head on his shoulder. "I have plans." There was an awkward silence, which she felt compelled to fill. "I'm going to a caper tasting."

"Those little rabbit pellets that fall out of sandwiches?"

Kind of an unattractive thing to say, she noted, and then remembered Joan had used the same line. Maybe he already knew about the caper tasting.

"Yes, those. Apparently there are important distinctions," she said with newfound authority. "If one knows what to look for."

"You know what to look for?"

Instead of answering, she kissed him one last time, tabling for now the fact that she hadn't invited him upstairs or to the caper tasting. She wondered how much Joan had already blabbed about the Frenchman and how much Adriane was expected in turn to volunteer; whether this moment represented a test of her integrity. She felt uncomfortable mentioning Luc, though she felt uncomfortable not mentioning him either, and so he took up an invisible space between her and Greg, who now gazed at her and confessed, "I'm growing very fond of you."

"And I you," she'd replied, in that awkward Elizabethan way she spoke when nervous. "I'll call you tomorrow evening."

"After your caper tasting."

"Yes," she said and leaned in for a last good-night kiss. "After my caper tasting."

As she rode the dingy elevator to her apartment, Adriane pondered her evasiveness. She *was* going to a caper tasting, after all. And Joan would be there. It was all completely innocent when looked at from a certain angle.

Inside, she found Barry where she'd left him: lying in front of soft-core porn on TV–which seemed to soothe him–surrounded by his stuffed toys. He approached Adriane, sniffed the traces of Greg and Löwenbräu.

"Okay, my friend, time for a walk." She reached for his leash and the Maryland Public Television tote bag she used to smuggle him in and out of her no-pets building. "Let's be productive."

Later, after they'd crawled into bed, Adriane reached for the phone and called Joan, who picked up after the third ring.

"I'm sorry, did I wake you?"

"That's okay. How was your date?"

"Surreal." Adriane told the part about the elderly woman and the mirror.

"Yikes," said Joan. "I can see why you're depressed."

"I'm irked," Adriane corrected. She pounded a knot out of her pillow and said, "So, Joanie, are you up for this thing tomorrow?"

"Oh, God? Do we have to?"

"I can't go without you!" said Adriane, wondering if indeed she could summon the nerve should it come to that. Luc's caper tasting seemed like just the sort of moderate engagement with risk she'd lately been wanting to condition herself toward.

Joan sighed. "He's so creepy."

"Really?" Adriane didn't see it herself, but then she probably had a higher threshold for eccentricity than Joan. "All the more reason I need you to come with me!"

"Are you going to wear your special dress?" Joan teased.

"Maybe I'll buy a dirndl," muttered Adriane, and pictured again the old woman from Blob's, gazing at herself in Adriane's face. To be appropriated for a senile stranger's mirror: Now *that* was creepy.

Adriane awoke eager for the new day. Barry stretched and wriggled out of her grasp, then curled into a ball and began to slurp at himself.

"Don't let me interrupt your personal time," she said, tousling his neck.

He looked at her guiltily then leaned closer to lick her face.

"No, thank you," she said and rolled out of bed. After taking him for a long walk followed by breakfast and reading the Sunday papers, she proceeded to try on every piece of clothing in her closet. Since the Frenchman had already seen her one nice item, she tried to determine the next best outfit and ended up jury-rigging something presentable out of navy slacks and a button-down top. With her dog watching, she stood in front of the mirror, opening and closing the third button of her blouse, and finally decided to leave it open before she completely loosened the threads that held it.

She then set out toward the Inner Harbor, walking the dozen or so blocks.

Joan, who lived in Federal Hill, would be coming from the opposite direction; they'd agreed to meet in front of the Frenchman's building. As it happened, they converged at almost the same time. Adriane arrived first but could already see Joan approaching–her sandals' three-inch heel slowing her down a little–and Adriane felt a growing peace and calm as her friend neared.

"You look nice," said Adriane, who could not help but notice that despite Joan's dismissive attitude toward the caper event and capers in general, she'd gone to the trouble of wearing a freshly pressed skirt and a rather sheer blouse. Maybe she felt the elevating call of the Frenchman's gaze as well. He probably had that effect on a lot of women; Adriane shouldn't begrudge her friend a taste.

Adriane led the way through the building's revolving door and handed Luc's calling card to the receptionist, who–maybe she was imagining this–cast them an overly familiar glance before picking up the phone and announcing their arrival.

"Please follow me," he said, and escorted them to an elevator beyond the main bank of elevators. Inserting a key in its lock, he then held its door open and bid the women good day as they stepped inside. Adriane pressed "P," the only other button besides "L." The ride was smooth and quiet. There was no Muzak version of "Bridge Over Troubled Water," for instance, and Adriane decided this was one of the true benefits of being rich, the ability to eliminate all kitsch from your life.

"So have you and Greg," Joan asked as they ascended, "slept together yet?"

Adriane blinked; what a strange and possibly undermining moment to ask such a question! Was Joan developing an interest in their creepy French friend? Or was this emblematic of a more general rivalry? Adriane shook her head vaguely, and the two women stepped into a bright foyer dominated by a large oil painting, in bold, almost fluorescent colors, of a dwarf devouring his own foot.

"Uh-boy," said Joan, removing her sunglasses.

At the foyer's far end a door opened, and their host now stood at its threshold, wearing a pair of large black-framed glasses and a turtleneck, even though it was June.

"You are early," he declared and smiled condescendingly. "That is all right. I am nearly ready." He kissed Adriane on both cheeks, then did the same with Joan, before turning to face the painting. "You like this?"

"What, um, does it mean?" Adriane asked.

The Frenchman merely laughed, and she could kick herself for sounding so Baltimore. He led the women into an immense loft; lustrously polished walnut floors and twenty-foot high walls on which hung contemporary oils of bold color and chaotic theme much like the dwarf eating his own foot, but somehow tamed and contained within their simple stylish frames.

Outside the room's floor-to-ceiling windows lay the gentrified Inner Harbor and the grisly port beyond. Even the wretched Domino Sugar sign, when framed by the Frenchman's civilizing picture windows, became its own piece of ironic art.

At the room's far end, a telescope rested on its tripod, and

Adriane couldn't help but notice it was pointed not heavenward but down toward the street.

"So what do you think?" asked the Frenchman. He reached into a huge built-in refrigerator and pulled out a bottle of champagne, a brand she didn't know. He unwrapped and popped it in what seemed a single fluid motion.

"It's very . . . grand," Joan said. "Do you live here alone?"

"Completely alone," he said cheerfully and handed each woman a flute of champagne. He began to arrange a row of crystal bowls along a stainless steel countertop.

Against the far wall towered some sort of media center, with four separate monitors and various amplifiers and recorders and players. Adriane pictured the Frenchman scouring all the networks for news vital to the caper industry. He looked handsome and stylish in his big glasses.

"Do you have any pets?" she asked him.

He *pffft*ed out some air between his lips in a dismissive manner and began filling each bowl from a different jar of capers.

"No cheating," he said and shooed them away.

Adriane approached the windows and looked at the tiny people below. She peeked through the telescope and watched a woman striding across the street toward the building's entrance and tried to imagine Greg observing Adriane as she had entered the same building moments before, as she had ridden the elevator and entered the Frenchman's apartment–her quasi boyfriend Greg watching a sort of movie of her actions today. Would she be ashamed for him to see it? she wondered. And was that how she should gauge the right- or wrongness of her behavior? Certainly if they were, say, married, she might have granted him such "movie rights" to her life. To do so now seemed premature, even silly. And yet she found herself unable to dismiss the question. Her thoughts turned to the champagne, which was damn good.

"Let us begin."

Luc spread some capers from the first bowl onto three triangular toast points; he held one out for Adriane to take into her mouth. Not unlike communion, she supposed, and obliged him by leaning forward and opening wide. But when he tried to offer Joan one in the same way, she waited for him to place the morsel in her palm.

"You are looking for six things," he told them. "Ripeness, texture, obverse or initial taste, predominant flavors, acidity, and converse taste or finish."

"That's a lot of things," mumbled Adriane, her mouth full. The sample tasted like capers.

"Now try to hold those ideas in your mind," he said, topping each glass then handing out a new toast point. The capers on this one were a little larger than the previous sample and they seemed more split open, or bloomed, she thought, adopting his rhetoric. They tasted like capers, as well.

"Which do you prefer?" he demanded.

"I don't know," said Adriane. She glanced at Joan, who was already washing her toast point down with champagne. Her friend had an elegant neck, a feature Adriane had never noticed before. Swallowing champagne was a good look for her.

She felt at a loss for some witty comeback and as far as forming a knowledgeable opinion, she was starting to feel out of her league. "The second one seemed more, I want to say, *bloomed*."

"Because it is half-rotted," he lamented. "That caper is garbage, from Algeria."

Adriane was quick to say, "The first caper was definitely better."

Luc was already dumping the Algerian capers down the drain. "Now that we have established a baseline," he said, "try the next sample."

The third sample tasted like capers.

She kept searching her palate for something, anything that might qualify as a valid perception. "The aftertaste on this one is very different from its initial taste," she said.

"What do you mean, *different*?"

"Well, at first the tang is very fresh, piquant, exciting, but the aftertaste–"

"What's wrong with the aftertaste?"

"I don't know. A letdown?"

Luc turned toward Joan and demanded her response.

"Possibly even a little bitter," she said, her mouth slightly puckered.

The Frenchman scowled then popped his own toast point into his mouth.

"Where's your rest room?" asked Joan.

He pointed her toward a hallway at the far end of the loft. She excused herself, and the clunk of her heels echoed in the silence that hung between Adriane and her host. Three-inch heels seemed a little excessive, Adriane thought, for a Sunday afternoon caper tasting. Herself, she had worn penny loafers. Well, perhaps it would seem she wasn't trying as hard.

"You are clearly not a caper person," he told her, after Joan had disappeared.

"Probably not," she admitted. She began to wonder how something so tiny could loom so large on this man's landscape.

"That is all right," the Frenchman went on, topping her champagne again. "You did not really come here because of your interest in capers."

"I didn't?" She smiled her most winning, flirtatious smile.

"Please, sit." He gestured toward the couch. "Let us be frank with one another."

She wondered if the French were by nature "frank"; she would have to look that up when she got home.

"We have established a rapport, you and I; there is a *frisson* between us. Does it offend you that I should say such a thing?"

"No," she said, plucking nervously at the thread of her blouse's loosening button. "It doesn't offend me."

He nodded thoughtfully, a little disappointed maybe. "You said you have a beau?"

"I'm dating someone. It's vaguely defined."

She imagined Greg able to see her on the Frenchman's couch having this conversation, and she felt another flicker of shame, and then anger, over the idea. Didn't she have any privacy?

"What does he do?"

"He's a researcher at the Library of Congress."

"Ah," said the Frenchman. He removed his large glasses and studiously sucked on one of the stems. "He lives in Washington?"

"No, here. He commutes."

"Ah," said the Frenchman again. "I suppose it's cheaper."

"I find him to be a very nice young man," she murmured Elizabethanly.

Luc merely smiled, and Adriane blushed at the implied critique of her passion.

"You seem like a woman who is confident in her own sensuality," he went on. "Who sees it as a frontier between the mundane and the beyond."

"Well, I wouldn't go so far as the Marquis de Sade," she said.

"You have read the Marquis?"

Adriane had flipped through a few chapters on a rainy Memorial Day weekend at Ocean City.

"The very fact that you have bothered to read him is a testimony to the openness of your erotic spirit."

He sucked now on the other stem, and Adriane wondered if he even needed the glasses to see or whether their main purpose was oral gratification. Both stems were faded and pocked from the acids in his mouth.

There came the echo of a toilet flushing and soon the *clip-clop* of Joan's heels as she emerged into the light of.the main room. She glanced at the elaborate entertainment center to their left. Luc rose and insisted she take his seat on the couch. He in turn sat cross-legged on the floor, as though warming himself by a campfire, despite the availability of other chairs. Adriane needed to use the bathroom herself, but didn't want to leave Joan alone with him–not if he still had flirtatious declarations to make.

After a moment of awkward silence, he reached for an almond from the crystal bowl on his glass-topped coffee table and said, "Adriane and I were just discussing the Marquis de Sade."

"Swell guy," said Joan; it was a little unclear whether she meant the marquis or Luc. She crossed her legs and reached into her purse for a piece of nicotine gum. Adriane knew Sade lay beyond the pale as far as Joan was concerned.

"That's quite the electronics store you've got there," said Adriane, pointing to his audio-video equipment.

Luc perked up. "I do like my toys," he confessed.

"You watch much sports?" asked Adriane, figuring there had to be some safe common ground in that.

But Luc shook his head. "However, I do watch a lot of film. Are either of you buffs of film? Yes? Do you like Truffaut? Godard? We French are addicted to film. It is ingrained in the culture."

"So you're a buff of film?" Adriane said, trying not to make too obvious fun of him.

"I've even created my own humble efforts. Just as a hobbyist. I can show you a videotape," he continued. "It's a kind of performance art piece I've been working on."

He approached the collection of four TVs, and Adriane imagined herself ensconced before them some Sunday during football season, keeping up with all her wagers and sharing a tumbler of Manhattans with her host, or maybe even some more of this very nice champagne.

The Frenchman hefted an extremely phallic remote control and flicked on all four monitors plus various other black boxes. Up came a home video of a naked woman missing most of her right arm; she took her place on a pedestal and folded her other, good arm behind her back in some semblance of the *Venus de Milo*. At least she was faking the second missing arm, thought Adriane, relieved to deduce the woman hadn't become an amputee just for this project.

"I should caution you," the Frenchman said, "the piece is somewhat blue."

"Blue-dirty or blue-sad?" Adriane asked. She found herself crossing her legs now, mostly because she really needed to use the bathroom. It seemed like an even worse moment to leave Joan on her own.

The Frenchman smiled gently, studying them both a moment. "Blue-dirty."

"As long as it's not blue-sad," Adriane declared, meeting her friend's forlorn stare. So the guy was into porn; she hoped it would at least be one of those whimsical pornos, like that Bond spoof she'd once rented, *On Her Majesty's Secret Cervix*, or some such nonsense.

On two of the monitors, the Frenchman now ambled into frame. He studied the model pretending to be a statue and then wheeled a tall stepladder next to her. Climbing to a superior vantage, he unzipped his pants. A third monitor focused now on his uncircumcised penis. Adriane was starting to get a queasy feeling about this. Joan, she noticed, was putting on her sunglasses.

There was no live sound, but a dubbed recording of Satie piano music. The composer, Adriane recalled having read somewhere, had championed the idea of "music as furniture."

"This is just a rough edit," the Frenchman apologized, glancing between Adriane and the monitors.

On screen, he now began to relieve himself over the model, who stood entirely still and managed even not to blink. Luc, in preparation for his role, must have drunk several bottles of Perrier. To her surprise, Adriane had begun to sink into a hypnotic calm over this footage, but now on the fourth monitor there played a close-up of the model's torso, and Adriane couldn't stop fixating on her; not the woman's stump, but the intact arm, with its fairly noticeable batwing, at least as fleshy as Adriane's own. Joan, who'd already stood to leave, paused now, riveted by some other, perhaps equally appalling, screen epiphany. The Venus's squat thighs maybe, which were now occupying most of the third screen.

"So what do you think?" the Frenchman asked.

"I really don't know much about art," Adriane murmured, distracted by a trickle of sweat rolling down her spine. She continued to watch the model's upper arm. The rest of her was not especially fetching either; not hideous, surely, but not the sort of girl most people would call pretty, not if they were being honest. Her main qualification seemed to be her stump.

"Have either of you," Luc began tentatively, "ever thought about appearing in film? Adriane? There's an *Annunciation* that hangs in the Uffizi you'd be perfect for."

"Flattering as that sounds," said Adriane, getting up to follow the *clip-clop* of her friend's heels, "we have to go."

"I'm afraid I have offended you." He smiled bashfully but knowingly and then showed them to the elevator. "I apologize if this was not to your taste," he said, as the elevator door opened. Before it closed, he'd already stepped back inside his apartment.

Adriane reluctantly caught glimpses of her flickering reflection in the revolving door. Outside, neither woman looked at the other.

"Well, that was a bust," said Adriane. "Want to watch the O's game?"

"No thanks," said Joan, staring at the pavement and folding her arms in front of her. A long, quiet pause; the silence between them started to feel a little creepy.

At last Adriane said, "Shouldn't we talk about what just happened?" She could use a little of her friend's wisdom and moral clarity about the whole thing. "Don't you think that old idea of beauty, or whatever, being in the eye of the beholder, doesn't that feel inadequate? I mean, one has the right to a responsible beholder, yeah?"

"Let's you and I," Joan proposed, "never talk about today again."

"There have to be some *standards*, some *baseline*–"

"Look, Adriane. This was one of the most degrading experiences of my life."

"Of your whole life?"

"Yes! And to be honest, I blame you."

She turned and walked away, growing smaller with each step, while Adriane watched from in front of the building, feeling a slight tug. She glanced down and saw she'd been pulling at her blouse's loose thread. When the button fell off, she put it in her pocket and began her own walk home.

That evening, as she and her dog got into bed, she thought about calling Greg as promised, but she put if off, because the thought of all she would have to omit overwhelmed her. It was an awful lot not to tell. Maybe she'd call him tomorrow from work, but that seemed hard to imagine as well.

She picked up the phone and tried Joan's number but got a busy signal and wondered if her friend was recounting the day's events to Greg at that very moment. Maybe they were commiserating, Adriane mused. Commiserating about *her*. A disturbing idea. She tried not to let the thought upset her, but it was only natural to care about such things.

5. what would thelonious do?

summer 1997

Now that Adriane had finally removed her mother's urn from atop the piano, she tried playing music again. Not the persnickety sonatas that had been the mainstay of her mother's modest career and which Adriane, despite years of lessons, never developed an ear for–but jazz. And not just any jazz, either. Monk, lately she'd been listening to a lot of Thelonious Monk. He'd made beautiful music by deliberately hitting the wrong notes. Adriane was convinced there had to be some kind of life lesson in that.

In the evening, after a quick dinner, she'd settle in front of the piano and chart out the changes to "Brilliant Corners," "'Round Midnight," "Epistrophy," pressing the replay button on her CD remote whenever she'd butt up against a particularly tangled chord. Barry lay by the pedals. Each time she struck the same flat-fifth tone cluster, he let out a brief yowl.

"Hush, sweets," she told him. Fortunately her walls were thick and the air conditioner made all kinds of distracting groans and whines. She practiced every available hour, because that's what Monk had done.

Before going to sleep, she'd lie in bed, reading about Monk's many quirks: his hat fetish, the little shuffle dance he'd do onstage while his sidemen soloed, his cheerful misanthropy. *"When anybody says something that's a drag,"* Monk told one interviewer, *"I just say something that's a bigger drag. Ain't nobody can beat me at it either."*

Adriane would chuckle admiringly at this attitude. Between his music and his life, Thelonious Monk seemed to personify *abandon*, a philosophy Adriane was still trying to cultivate. She approached Monk the way one would a guru. Why *couldn't* a '50s black jazz legend be a role model for a twenty-eight-year-old white girl on the cusp of the new millennium? Heredity meant nothing here, as far as Adriane was concerned; in fact, she was counting on it. She certainly felt no particular attachment to her own. And neither of her parents was alive to object. They were both suicides; hell, a suicide couldn't very well complain about being replaced as a role model! She loved her father, Adriane did, and her mother somewhat less, but for sure both her parents had been messed-up cats.

When Adriane had built enough repertoire to last an hour, she decided to find a venue. Not some yuppie enclave like the Belvedere Hotel. Didn't want middle-aged divorcées requesting Neil Sedaka or requesting anything at all really.

One Saturday evening, she smuggled Barry out of the building in her Maryland Public Television tote bag, then attached his leash and began walking him up Charles Street. He peed on a couple of his favorite signposts, then glanced back at her in surprise as they continued north beyond their usual route. To go for a walk of any real length in Baltimore in August, a person really had to want to get somewhere. Even after seven P.M., the day's gummy heat still rubbed your face and baked the soles of your feet. A city bus exhaled its carbon cloud in front of Adriane and Barry as they passed Union Station. A few minutes later, they finally reached North Avenue and hung a right. Long ago a nightlife hub that had fallen into neglect after the riots of '68, North Avenue was supposedly on the upswing. The Mayor's Office of Neighborhood Enhancement, Adriane's department, had recently approved new streetlamps, each with its own decorative banner of Eubie Blake. The newly renovated school administration building gleamed in the mercury vapor twilight, but as it was Saturday night, there were no bureaucrats hustling home. Hardly anybody out at all, and Adriane was easily the only white face in sight. She became aware of the click of Barry's nails against the concrete sidewalk.

Each passing block became more and more deserted. Soon she started coming across boarded-up windows. Apparently the neighborhood was still recovering. If she'd been black and alive in '68, would she have rioted, too? She tried to picture herself lighting a Molotov cocktail and hurling it into a Woolworth or some other ofay exporter of capital from the community.

As Adriane passed one building, she paused to consider the bumper sticker plastered over its plywood windows: WHAT WOULD JESUS DO? They were everywhere lately, those bumper stickers. Meant, she supposed, to guide the reader out of a personal dilemma toward the higher road, the challenge seemed unrealistically lofty. Jesus never had to decide whether or not to default on his bookie, as Adriane's father had; never had to determine the right Valium rehab program, time and again, like her mother. If people were going to choose a role model, Adriane concluded, they should really pick a more practical one.

Between gaps in the plywood boards Adriane could make out blurred human movements. If she wasn't mistaken, at that very moment she was standing in front of a crack house. The city had become famous for them. Hey! Adriane wasn't *judging.* Her man Monk once lost his cabaret card because he wouldn't explain why he and Bud Powell were sitting in a car that had a packet of heroin in it. After his sixty days in jail, he was banned from playing in New York for six years. *Well, fuck 'em!* Monk mostly kept to his room for those six years, practicing, denying the world his gift.

"Just say something that's a bigger drag," thought Adriane, trying to peek through the gaps in the plywood. The hunger to create and the hunger to destroy. She'd always figured people were drawn to one over the other. But maybe you could have a taste for both.

"Hey, baby."

She turned around and saw a gaunt brother of indefinite age, wearing a Jiffy Lube baseball cap and a tattered Orioles jacket. He seemed to be sucking on a Slim Jim.

"You lost?" he asked.

"Do I look lost?" she said as nonchalantly as possible.

"Yeah." The man chuckled, crinkling the cellophane as he slipped it lower along the Slim Jim. "Most definitely."

Maybe, Adriane decided, he could be helpful. "So, are there any, like, bars around here that have a piano?"

The man reached into his back pocket and produced a switchblade. Barry startled when it snapped open. Adriane glanced over her shoulder, just to see if anyone else was around, but there wasn't. Just an overflowing garbage can with a rat scuttling around inside, which, surprisingly, Barry didn't notice. Maybe the garbage stench masked the rat.

"I think I seen a piano about six blocks more," the guy said, pushing up the rim of his Jiffy Lube cap with the tip of his knife. He proceeded to carve off a small piece of Slim Jim. "Your dog like meat?"

He crouched before Barry and held out the morsel between two fingers like a cigarette butt. Barry let out a low growl.

"Look like you got a racist dog there."

"Maybe he's scared of the knife," said Adriane, eager to move on.

"You sure it ain't you that's scared of the knife?"

"I could do without the knife."

"You white chicks and your paranoid fantasies," he said, dropping the meat on the sidewalk in front of Barry, who decided it was okay now to wolf it down. He then sauntered up to the man and–Adriane had never seen her dog do this before–mounted his leg and began to hump it.

"What the fuck?" said the man.

Barry's eyes were half closed and he seemed lost in thought.

"Get him the fuck–"

"Hey, Barry, come here!" she called, tugging his leash; but he'd attached himself to the man's leg and wouldn't let go. Her dog was in a trance state beyond the reach of her voice, and he moved his hips with blissful compulsion. "Barry quit it!"

"Get him off before I cut him!"

"Barry, now!" said Adriane and gave the leash an extra big yank that tore him from the leg and sent the man staggering for his balance.

"Dog's got some serious mentality."

Adriane tried to shrug her shoulders. "At least he seems over his racism."

"Yeah, all right, then," said the man, passing Adriane and continuing in the opposite direction. "Catch you later."

"Nice talking with you," she said, picking up her stride.

She wanted to check out this place he'd mentioned, but some other night, she told herself, hanging a right homeward, her knees shaking. *Don't feel like it tonight*, she decided, walking briskly, trying to not smell the garbage.

Drag, she exhaled.

Adriane thought about attaching her keys to a small can of pepper spray, but resented being put on the defensive–liked her *old* key chain, man, shaped like Maryland. The following Saturday, she summoned up the nerve to venture north once again.

She took a slightly different route, past other boarded-up windows, but avoiding the Jesus crack house. More people were out this time, sitting on their steps, trying to catch a breeze, and a young girl asked to pet Barry, who behaved himself, except for trying to lick the girl's knees, which made her giggle. The girl walked back into a form-stone row house that was missing half its windows. For how long had those windows been gone? wondered Adriane, dismayed to think about that girl paying for someone else's recklessness.

They kept walking and soon afterward came across a small street-level saloon. She peeked through its window and saw a pair of elderly customers sitting at a booth, an upright piano against the far wall.

She opened the door and a bell rang, a small bell attached to the doorjamb like a shopkeeper's bell, a convenience-store bell, not the kind of sound you'd expect at a nightspot. Slipping into the air-conditioned room, she tied Barry's leash to the radiator's foot and made him lie down. The saloon was long but narrow, with a low ceiling that reminded Adriane of a rumpus room. The walls were dotted with postcards, mostly from Pennsylvania Dutch country. Adriane approached a vinyl-rimmed bar patched with silver duct tape. A stout middle-aged woman with a medium-cropped Afro emerged from the back, blinked in surprise at the sight of Adriane, and said, "May I help you?"

"I'm looking for a place to play some Monk tunes," Adriane said, glancing over at the piano. "Are you the owner?"

The woman behind the bar nodded. "I don't have an entertainment budget."

"That's okay. I'm not looking to get paid."

The owner smiled at Adriane, a curiosity. "You could set up a tip glass."

"No thanks."

Money, that universally acknowledged motivation, having been renounced, there passed an awkward silence between the two women. Finally the owner said, "You know Monk almost played here once."

"Really?" Adriane looked around her, astonished and hopeful.

"In Baltimore, I mean. He had a weeklong gig lined up."

Adriane nodded cautiously; it seemed she was expected to know.

"Well," said the owner. "I'm Roberta. There's the piano. Go try it out."

Adriane took off her coat and sat before the old upright Knabe. A couple of its white keys were stripped of their finish, and the low F-sharp rattled, but overall the strings held their tune, plus Adriane couldn't afford to be choosey. She started to play "Well, You Needn't." Barry yowled when she struck that flat-fifth tone cluster, and the elderly couple in the booth laughed at that, applauded politely when she'd finished.

"Do you know 'Sweet Georgia Brown'?" the gray-haired man asked, rising out of his chair, holding a couple bills in his hand.

"I'm sorry," she said. "I don't take requests."

"Oh, okay," said the man, sitting back down, stuffing the money into his pocket.

Adriane felt bad. She could have just said she didn't know "Sweet Georgia Brown," but then he might have kept suggesting titles. Better to nip the whole thing in the bud. She decided to play "Ruby, My Dear," something mellow and conciliatory.

Midway through, she heard the bell above the door tinkle, and then a low growl from Barry. A man muttered a few words and the door closed. Adriane kept playing and finished her audition set.

"That was fine," Roberta said. "But if you come back here, you can't bring your dog. You cost me a customer."

"So, I can come back?" Adriane asked.

The owner laughed at Adriane's eagerness. "Of course, you can come back. Those are great tunes."

"Okay," she said. "I'll come back tomorrow with my charts."

"Tomorrow's Sunday. I'm open Wednesdays through Saturdays."

"Wednesday," said Adriane. "I'll come back Wednesday."

She untied Barry from the radiator and began the walk home, feeling satisfied about the whole evening.

They soon passed a corner building whose marquee read THE GREAT BLACKS IN WAX MUSEUM. She hadn't noticed that earlier: a whole museum full of role models. Well, a lot of people needed them, not just Adriane. Too bad there were no windows, just a solid wall in front, because she wanted to peek inside.

The Baroness Pannonica de Koenigswarter had lived in Weehawken, New Jersey, with thirty-two cats. A famous jazz patron, she'd taken Monk under her wing, became a kind of mother figure for him. He seemed to collect mothers, Adriane read with admiration and envy. Mothers to spare! The baroness often chauffeured him to gigs in her Bentley, which must have been sweet indeed.

Adriane thought about that Bentley now, driving her Checker Marathon along North Avenue.

"This 'hood's not so menacing, is it?" muttered her friend Shelley from the passenger seat. With that British accent of hers she acted like she could get away with saying anything, and Adriane was mildly offended on the neighborhood's behalf.

"You white chicks and your paranoid fantasies," she murmured.

"Since when did you grow such big ovaries?" asked Shelley.

Adriane parallel parked and, feeling a little hypocritical in front of her friend, attached a massive lock to the steering wheel.

They crossed the deserted street and entered the saloon with a tinkling ring. It being a Wednesday, there was only a single customer, a pale brother sitting at the bar nursing a tropical drink. Adriane settled Shelley at a table not too near the piano. Wanted the moral support but didn't need her friend breathing down her neck.

Leaning against the bar, Roberta said, "I see you brought some business with you. What're you having?"

Shelley ordered a pair of Budweisers and two shots of Jack Daniels, then turned to Adriane and asked, "What about you?"

"I'm good," sighed Adriane.

Roberta laughed, then realized Shelley was serious. Although getting drunk was probably a counterproductive way to celebrate remission from intermittent-recurring MS, Shelley had her own ideas about abandon.

"Have a mai tai," the pale brother urged. "On Ricky."

"Too many vitamins," said Shelley. "Come join me anyway, Ricky."

"I'll stop by later," said the man, whose face, now that Adriane looked at it closer, seemed to have suffered bad burns. "Sobbin' to my bartender here."

Adriane opened the piano lid and positioned her hands across the opening B-flat major of "Nutty." She played the song through then launched straight into "Criss-Cross" for some serious dissonance.

After she'd paused, Ricky clapped loudly. Shelley let fly a piercing whistle. Adriane was glad they appreciated the music, but the applause embarrassed her.

"Do you know 'I Can't Get Started'?" asked Ricky.

Roberta leaned across the bar and murmured, "She doesn't take requests. She's eccentric."

This thrilled Adriane enormously; not only did she not have to explain herself, but she was already developing her own quirky reputation. She decided to play "Misterioso," after which it was time for a little breather.

She joined Shelley at the table, and Ricky came over then, too. Bought a round of mai tais. Said he played a little blues guitar himself and wondered if Adriane might want to jam one night.

"Sure," she said cautiously. She preferred to think of herself as a solo act, but it seemed cold to refuse to play the blues with a man who'd suffered third-degree burns.

"You got real nice technique there," Ricky said, toasting her.

Adriane cringed; Monk wasn't about technique after all. "There's a 'but' at the end of that, isn't there," she said, staring at him.

"Naw, no, well . . . You could let it swing a bit more, you know. Relax with it."

A bitter pill; he was calling her uptight. "Yeah," she said, chugging her mai tai. "I dig." Though even just saying that, she probably sounded less like Monk than Sammy Davis, Jr.

Adriane returned to the piano, tried to loosen up a bit, but Ricky's words weighed on her, and she felt self-conscious, so she cut the set short, told Roberta she'd be back again soon, if that was okay.

"Anytime you want," said Roberta.

"Hey, Ricky," said Shelley, loose as you please, that Shelley, even without any alcohol in her. "See you around."

"Bring your guitar some night," added Adriane, trying to sound relaxed about it. But she was a little rattled by the idea, worried she wouldn't be able to hang with him.

The two women climbed into her Checker, then drove back to the relative affluence and safety of Mount Vernon, which did nothing for Adriane's insecurity about being a poseur. Hell, she *was* a poseur, there was no escaping that–but at least she wanted to be a good one. She wanted to do it justice. She regretted going public too early.

After smuggling Barry downstairs for a quick pee, she sat down to practice for a couple hours. She heard herself hitting Monk's "wrong" notes with painstaking accuracy. Resting her head on the piano lid, she wondered how she would ever swing. This, after all, was central to the whole enterprise: losing the uptightness inherited from her mother. She'd been a corkscrew of uptightness, her mother. So many things had vexed the woman. Little things like talking on the phone or opening mail. The existence of newspapers and television. Headphones. Computers. Digital remastering. Rap and rock. More personal things, too, like her dwindling recording royalties. Her husband's gambling. Her husband's death. Widowhood. Addiction and rehab. And Adriane herself. Adriane had often vexed her mother, sometimes by accident–many other times on purpose.

Long before the woman's suicide, Adriane's mother really was the *anti*–role model.

Before going to sleep, Adriane read about that gig Monk almost played in Baltimore. He and the baroness were driving in her Bentley through Delaware when they stopped at a motel so he could get a glass of water. The manager found him unnerving–maybe it was that brooding stare–and called the cops. By the time they arrived, Monk was already back in the car and could not be persuaded to step out of it–his fortress, his womb–so they beat on him. Beat on a musical genius for drinking a glass of water. *What kind of a sick fucking world*, Adriane wondered, tears now clinging to the bottom of her chin, *a sick fucking world do I live in*?

She practiced five hours a night for the next two nights (canceling her Friday poker game) and most of Saturday; finally stopped after dark and walked Barry around the neighborhood. Fed him and ate a bowl of soup for her own dinner, then decided to give Roberta's another go.

"I wish I could take you with me," she told her dog. It pained her to leave him behind, and she wondered how it affected him, whether he felt deserted, which was the last feeling she'd ever want to inflict on any living creature. "You know I always come home, don't you?" she asked him. She set out a pig's ear for him, even though she knew he wouldn't touch it until she got back. He absolutely refused to eat alone.

After driving north, she had trouble finding a spot in front of Roberta's, so she parked a couple blocks away. As she walked through the humid heat, she mused how nice it would be to have her own baroness drive her to gigs. What a great perk. She bet Monk really appreciated that. Not just the chauffeuring but also the attention and the sweet goodwill of it.

Adriane expected to see at least a few customers, but when she opened the door, releasing the chime above her head, the place was empty. Well, it would give her a chance to ease back into the public eye.

It was hot inside. Roberta came out from the back and said hello. "Ricky dropped by last night with his guitar," she said. "He was sorry to miss you."

"Oh, I wasn't feeling well," Adriane said guiltily. "I hope he'll try again." She accepted Roberta's offer of a drink.

"On the house," said Roberta, pouring. "Sorry the a/c's busted."

Adriane asked something she'd been wondering. "There don't *ever* seem to be many people in here, Roberta. How do you stay in business?"

"Oh, you know, the place is paid for. My folks opened it in the forties. They made me promise to keep it going. It's just force of habit more than anything."

"Didn't you ever want to do something else?" asked Adriane.

"All the time. But my father, rest his soul, begged me. How's a person meant to defy that?" She smiled and shook her head. "Besides," she added, "what else am I supposed to do with an English degree from Oberlin?"

"That's supposed to be a nice school," said Adriane.

"Where'd you go?"

"Peabody. My mother taught piano there, so they let me in. I thought if I went, it might please her, but it didn't, and I dropped out after a year."

The bartender smiled again, more ruefully this time. "Sounds like you went for the wrong reason and you quit for the wrong reason."

Adriane was caught off guard. She didn't know such blunt criticism could be delivered without rancor.

"They were impulses more than reasons," she argued, but in her heart she knew Roberta was right. It felt disorienting–a little scary but also uplifting–hearing a stranger point out something about you with such effortless clarity.

Adriane downed her drink, walked to the piano, and sat down. Started to play with her right hand the melody to "Blue Monk," gradually adding phrases with her left, in no particular urgency this time. Formed the harmonies when it suited her, changed a couple of them as she went. The piece had a nice stumbled-upon quality that her playing had been lacking; she liked making up her own wrong notes. It would be nice to remember what she was doing, but she kept going and figured the notes would come to her again or something better would instead. She gave the more dissonant tone clusters an extra flick of the wrist, like she was splatting them against a wall.

She played through most of her song list in this new way, extending the solos into a distant horizon, viewing the music now as though at ground level, strolling through it like it was a landscape, a swamp maybe. She played, not so much in a trance as in a state of relaxed attention, waiting to be pleasantly surprised by whatever she came up with next. It was a damned satisfying way to play, and so she didn't want to stop. Two measures into the bridge of "'Round Midnight," she just barely heard the bell above the front door tinkle, but she continued to play without opening her eyes, and even when she felt the cold metal of what had to be a gun prodding the side of her neck she continued to play, because she didn't want to have to think about what might happen after she stopped.

"Leave her be," Roberta's voice was saying. "I've got the till right here."

"Where's your purse?" a reedy voice asked Adriane.

"I don't have a purse," she said, still playing. "I don't have any money."

"Then lie down on the floor over there."

Adriane kept playing, trying not to rush the tempo, when she felt the man reach for the piano lid. She pulled her fingers out of the way just before he slammed it shut–an echoing report that made her heartbeat splat.

"I said lie down on the floor."

She reluctantly opened her eyes. The man was pointing his gun at her and trembling, shaking even more than she was. His lips were badly chapped, and he plucked them with gritted teeth, like he was trying to eat his own face.

She shook her head before opening her mouth. "I don't take requests."

"Don't what?"

"Forget about her," said Roberta, waving a cigar box. "Here's the cash."

He sneered at Adriane before limping to the bar, where he

grabbed the box. Spilling the money onto the counter, his voice croaked, "That's all?"

"This isn't Harborplace. You better go before someone sees you."

The guy leaned against the bar shaking his head. "Go when I'm ready."

"Why risk it?" argued Roberta. "Why put your future in jeopardy?"

The man grunted, glanced over his shoulder toward the piano.

"Take a taste," Roberta suggested. "To go."

"Yeah," he said, eyeing the bar now. He chose an unopened bottle of Frangelico, which she bagged for him.

Limping back over to Adriane, he waved his gun at her. "I'm coming back, when I don't have to be somewhere. Gonna have some requests."

As soon as the door shut behind him, the bell above ringing daintily, Roberta raced over to lock up. "That is *not* the way the police recommend you handle this kind of thing! That's a good way to get shot!"

"Brother's got a heavy drug problem," Adriane mumbled.

"First of all, he's not a brother. Man's a Samoan, I think." Roberta stood behind the bar now, pouring bourbon. "And second of all, he sure as hell ain't *your* brother."

She brought a glass over to Adriane, set it on top of the piano lid and returned behind the bar. Adriane sniffed her drink then gulped it. Opened the lid and began playing again. It wasn't coming back to her, though, that nice flow she'd enjoyed. Her fingers were shaking too much. She made a fist and punched the keyboard. She could still feel her heart dancing in her chest. She slammed both fists down.

"Don't break my piano."

"Sorry," mumbled Adriane.

She closed the lid again and thought about Monk's knuckles, how the police had beaten them as he hugged the steering wheel. He would not get out of the Bentley. The cops beat his knuckles with nightsticks, while the baroness screamed: *Spare his hands, his musical hands!* Screamed with impotent rage, while Monk, for his part, continued to hold on. They were his hands, after all. Those hands he had put through so many years of practice. He wasn't going to let go, if he didn't want to.

Adriane wondered whether that robber would make good on his threat to return, and what she'd do when he did, if she was around, which, she vowed to herself, she'd make a point to be. This did not mean she had a death wish.

Not necessarily.

6. pillow talk

fall 1997

Adriane dreamt her dog was having a dream–the kind of urgent whimpering nightmare that always made her wonder what he was dreaming *about*, what was going on in his mind, his heart, and she wondered this now in her own dream–when suddenly she heard a yelp and woke up. Barry looked at her with soulful confusion. Then coughed–once, twice, and on the third try something warm and wet and rubbery popped out of his mouth and into Adriane's outstretched hand. In the nightlight's feeble glow, she could barely make it out: a human ear. She touched the left side of her head, and where her own familiar, twice-pierced lobe once dangled, there now oozed a warm sticky hole. Barry whimpered and tried to lick her wound. Adriane stared in bewilderment at her shame-faced bedmate, waiting for him to explain. *Am I awake?* she wondered.

Turning on the bedside light, she felt a clench of nausea at the sight of her bloody bed.

She was awake.

She staggered into the bathroom and lay the ear on her counter, then rifled the drawers for some gauze, trying not to glance in the mirror. She found a bandage and wrapped it tightly around her head. Her shoulder felt slick with blood. After carrying her ear into the kitchen, where she placed it in a sandwich baggie with some ice cubes, Adriane called a cab. *I am simply doing what needs to be done,* she told herself. *I can break down later.* Then threw on some clothes and phoned her most steadfast friend.

"Can you come watch Barry please?" asked Adriane.

"What?" murmured Joan, half-asleep. It was three in the morning.

"I need someone to keep Barry company. He's beside himself," she said, looking at her dog, who lay on the couch now, gazing back at her and whimpering.

Adriane heard muffled words on the other end of the line, as though her friend had covered the mouthpiece.

"I have to go to the hospital," Adriane thought to add.

"What happened!" asked Joan, suddenly alert. "Do you need me to take you?"

Adriane quickly briefed her, said a cab was coming. "Who's over there?"

"He bit your ear off!"

"He didn't mean to," said Adriane. "Who were you talking to?"

Her cab was already pulling up to the building.

"It's Molly," said Joan. "We can discuss this later."

"Molly from poker?" Adriane couldn't believe it. She tried switching the phone to her other side, where she usually heard better, but her ear canal was sloshing with liquid. When she pressed the phone tighter against her head she felt a twist of pain and a warm, viscous trickle down the side of her neck. "Molly of Monique and Molly?"

"Not now. I'm coming right over. I have the keys here somewhere."

"You're gay?" Adriane began to feel faint. "Since when?"

"Adriane, now is not the time!"

Outside, her cab honked, a muted underwater sound. Adriane stood in front of her living-room window and waved. The cab honked again.

"Go already!" said Joan. "I'll be right over."

"You're leaving now? Joan? Hello?" But her friend had already hung up.

Adriane turned to Barry and wrapped a comforting hand around his snout. "Everything's going to be fine." She kissed the top of his head, the soft fuzzy spot between his eyes, then headed out, clutching the baggie that contained her ear. She leapt into the waiting taxicab and noticed the driver–bearded, burly tough guy–staring at her in the rearview mirror.

"That's a ton of blood," he said, his voice soft and mushy in her head. "Who did this to you?"

"No one," said Adriane. "Mercy Hospital, please."

"I'd leave the motherfucker, whoever he is," the cab driver said a little later. He wore a black kerchief tied around his head. Adriane adjusted the Ace bandage wrapped tightly around hers. Felt tiny stabs of pain, as though she'd slept on a pillow of nails.

"The shit that goes down this time of night," her cabbie went on. "The shit people do to each other. People who say they love each other. Don't be a victim."

"I won't," she said, dizzy. "I'm not."

"You got to promise me you'll respect yourself."

Adriane nodded.

He shut off the meter and turned to face her. "I need you to say that."

"Okay. I'll respect myself." She overpaid him and bolted into the emergency room. Catching the eye of the admitting nurse, Adriane held up her bagged ear, waving it like a deli-counter ticket.

The nurse's jaw dropped, and she immediately phoned someone. Within moments, she led Adriane to a gurney around the corner and had her lie down. Gently propped up her head. "We're putting in a call for Dr. Robley–he's our plastic surgeon," said the nurse. "If anyone can save that ear, hon, it's him."

"They might not save it?" Oddly this hadn't occurred to her.

"I'm sure they will. Did you bring your insurance?"

The nurse wrote down Adriane's personal info and asked to borrow her ID card to make a photocopy. "Did you want to file a complaint?"

"What? Do I . . ." stammered Adriane. "No, you all seem very professional."

"I mean with the police. There's an officer here now on account of we've had two cases already tonight." She added, in response to Adriane's confused stare, "Of domestic violence."

"It's not like that. I just want to get my ear fixed and go home. They might not save it?"

"You shouldn't go back, hon."

"I'm not in danger. It was probably my fault anyway." Adriane felt a fresh wave of blood rush to her wound. "Could I have a pain pill?"

"It's not your fault. They always want you to think it's your fault–that's the psychology of it–why we keep coming back. I know something about it."

Adriane looked into the nurse's concerned eyes, felt unworthy of her sympathy, but neither did she feel up to hearing the woman's story. "My dog bit my ear off."

"Don't cover for him, dear. He's not worth it. You're young. You're pretty. You'll find someone who'll be good to you."

"He is good to me," she said. "Tonight was just a horrible, ironic accident."

"Why don't you talk with Officer Domantay for a moment while we get everything prepped for you. I'll bring something for the pain," the nurse said. "Something *good*." She disappeared deeper into the ER, then returned to deliver a pair of light blue pills. Adriane gulped them down.

Soon a tall police officer approached. Handsome, in that world-weary way Adriane prized. The soothing surf of a two-way radio issued from his hip. He crouched next to her. His eyes widening, he seemed to repress a cringe, and Adriane glimpsed a future in which men would look upon her with terror and pity.

"I know this is difficult," he began.

She nodded mutely, dreading all the presumptions he was about to make.

"We can petition for a restraining order. We can find you temporary lodging, hook you up with social services. You can rebuild your life, your self-esteem. You need to understand, we live in a society where no young lady has to suffer physical abuse."

"That's . . ." Adriane said despondently, "that's my favorite kind of society."

"You're in shock," he allowed. "Maybe you're not ready to deal with the seriousness of your situation. At least take my card. And keep it hidden from your . . . partner." He put his card in her open palm and wrapped her fingers around it before walking away.

My partner, thought Adriane, wiping a sniffle on her sleeve. As she lay on the narrow hospital cot, she wondered if Joan had made it to the apartment yet and whether she'd brought Molly with her. Barry did not like having to share attention; it made him anxious and depressed. Joan knew this. So hopefully she had the good sense to come alone. Adriane's face slackened; tears seemed to be falling out of her head. Everything, everything felt . . . wrong. Strained, so strained: their friendship these past few months. As though Joan had set aside a part of herself that was no longer available. Adriane, waiting for her to come around. But she hadn't, and now it was clear why. A secret. Secret from Adriane, at least. Neither of them lucky in love, but unlucky together. And Joan the more prudish–were women in general attractive all of a sudden? *What's so great about Molly? She's not even a good poker player*, thought Adriane, temper rising, as she rolled along a hallway and into the operating theater, where four androgynous figures in sea-foam-green scrubs danced in and out of a bright light. *Not a good poker player at all*, she thought, *though lucky in love, apparently. Just like the saying. Lucky!*

"We've been seeing a lot of this kind of craziness," said a man–the surgeon?–and he began to examine her bagged ear.

"I know what you're going to tell me, Doctor." She couldn't bear another lecture about self-respect and bad choices. "Why don't I ditch him? Get on with my life. That living without him would be better than living in fear." As she was helped onto the operating table, Adriane grew more and more worked up. "But he loves me, Doc, I know he does. And I love him, more than anything. And it's our home. What goes on in our home is our business. People think they have a duty to interfere. Everyone's an expert on love! They think they understand. But I'm happy. *We're* happy. I won't desert him."

"Actually," the surgeon's craggy twang, Midwestern, intruded, "I was going to suggest you have him put to sleep."

Adriane blinked, wiped her cheek. "But–"

"This is obviously a dog bite. A clean one, but still, it's not from a knife. He bit all the way to the intertragic notch. Let's take a look at that head of yours, miss."

He uncoiled her bandage, then pointed out the wound's features to his colleagues. Immobilized Adriane's head.

"Will you be able to save it, Doctor?" she asked, fearful again now that her anger had ebbed.

"We'll certainly try."

The prick of anesthetic, but no discomfort after, just a gentle tugging sensation, like a nagging reminder about some personal shortcoming she'd put off addressing. She drifted in and out of consciousness; hardly noticed the passage of three hours.

"Hopefully this'll take," the surgeon said. "If not, we may have to harvest cartilage from a rib." The procedure sounded biblical and invasive. "Is there somebody at home who can look after you?"

"Yes," she lied. Well, Joan would be there, but only for a while. "Doctor, am I going to be," she had trouble getting it out, "repulsive to other people?"

"With luck, the scarring should be minimal," he replied with clinical authority. He gave her some antibiotics and more pain pills–which she gulped down on the spot–told her to make a postop appointment for the next day. "Don't get it wet."

A cab dropped Adriane at her doorstep. Break of dawn. She let herself into the apartment. Found Joan asleep in the big chair. Barry curled on the floor. Immediately he woke up. Scampered toward her, tail between his legs. Groveled at her feet; he remembered. The events of the evening. Not a dream after all.

Joan stirred, murmured: "That's some bandage. Your ear okay?"

"They think it will be. Barry did a very neat job of it."

"Do you need anything?" Her friend's voice muffled through the layers of dressing.

"We'll be fine." Adriane tossed her coat onto the piano bench.

"I wish you had let me take you to the hospital."

"Barry needed you more," said Adriane, pride getting the best of her. She sat on the couch. Asked bluntly: "Why didn't you tell me?"

"Because," said Joan, "I didn't think you'd be very understanding."

"I'm in shock is all. I can't believe it's come to this."

Joan sighed. "I know you're in pain, but could you be a little less nasty?"

"I'm not even in pain," Adriane insisted, though she was. She slumped against the armrest. Barry at her feet. "Since when did you become a lesbian?"

"I don't like that word. It's lazy and full of assumptions about personal things. About what's going on in my heart." She spoke softly, and Adriane tried reading her lips to help make out some of the words.

"So you're *not* a lesbian?"

Another sigh, deeper this time. "Me with Molly, it just feels right. Be happy for me." She tucked her hair behind her ears–both ears, shapely and intact–with a delicate poise Adriane had not before registered in her friend's movements. Side lit by the dawn. The profile of her head and neck, the edge of her face, glowed softly.

"You look beautiful," observed Adriane.

"I'm in love," said Joan, with a contentment Adriane suddenly found enervating.

"Well," she mumbled, "thanks for looking after Barry."

Joan rose from the big chair. "Are you sure you don't need anything else?"

"We're good," said Adriane, but when she stood had to steady herself against the couch. Her friend took an elbow, helped guide her to the bedroom. At the door, flicked on the light and gasped. Half the bed was stained red. A few small puddles still glistened. Adriane took pleasure in her friend's distress. *You see what I've been through?*

Joan sat her down on the ottoman and began stripping sheets. The mattress pad badly stained, too, Joan replaced it with a thin blanket. Gathered the bloody linens and put them in the hamper. Then made the bed anew. Asked, "Where's a clean nightgown?"

Adriane nodded toward the dresser. "Bottom drawer."

Joan chose the flannel–pattern of melting snowmen–and set it on the bed. Turned now to Adriane. Spread the neckline of her shirt and gently lifted it past the bandage. Adriane wondered what sort of impression her bare shoulders might be making. But Joan seemed focused on the nightgown–bunching the hem of it, then lowering it carefully over her bandaged head. Adriane let one arm be guided through, then two, then, unzipping her jeans, felt Officer Domantay's card in her pocket. *"Keep it hidden from your partner,"* he'd said. *I have no partner*, she thought. *Not even the kind of partner who would cut off my ear.*

She stood now and placed both hands on Joan's hips and peered into her eyes, trying to fathom the depth of her friend's secret life. Whatever was going on in her heart. Looked to see herself in there, reflected. Wondered: *What about ME? Why didn't you turn to ME? What's wrong with ME?* In each pupil: a bandaged blob that was her own head–the size of a Q-tip. She felt herself lean forward, watching for the Q-tip to grow. But her friend drew back and turned aside her face, as though she'd assumed Adriane was trying to kiss her, which she *wasn't*, but the rejection stung all the same. Adriane sighed and rested her good ear on her caretaker's shoulder. Nodded against soft neck. Let spill the dregs of her longing, its sad mix of envy and nostalgia: "What's wrong with me?" Aloud this time.

"You've just had a rough night," said Joan and gave Adriane a tame, consoling hug before leaving to go spread some newspapers on the kitchen floor. Returned with a plastic bowl for the bedside table.

"In case you can't make it to the bathroom," she said. "I'll check on you at lunch and walk him then."

"Thanks, Joanie. You're a good girl," said Adriane. Then felt compelled to add, in a moment of conviction but less so common sense, "She doesn't deserve you."

A mild scowl from her friend, who said, "Get some rest," then tiptoed out.

Things between them would remain strained for now. Even further, it looked like. And was Adriane to blame for that? Probably yes, but damn-it-all why did everyone else get to be an expert on love and not her? Why *not* her? Maybe she wasn't an expert on *all* of it–like *finding* love and *keeping* love or even–she thought of that soft-mouthed boy she'd never called back–*deserving* love. But surely an expert on yearning for it. At least that. As pale morning brimmed through the blinds, she lay down, her remaining companion watching her from the floor.

"Come on up," she told him. "If you fall off a horse, you have to get right back on. Isn't that what they say?"

He started whimpering again. She climbed out, picked him up, placed him on the bed, got in after. Once settled, she patted a spot next to her chest, but Barry chose to lie further down.

"Don't you want to sleep closer to me?" she asked. "I forgive you." She stroked, enticingly, the pillow by her shoulder, but Barry stayed put. His natural preference, Adriane remembered, had always been to curl up at her feet. She'd trained him to sleep with her arms around him. But that had never been his idea of the proper arrangement. All he ever wanted was to be a dog.

7. adriane and the montreal bagels

spring 1998

Not so crazy, thought Adriane; this date wasn't so crazy after all. She and Phillip were making out on his sofa, shirttails ayank, her tongue exploring inside his mouth, when suddenly he pulled away and demanded: "What's that odor?"

"Odor?" asked Adriane, trying to detect it, praying that it wasn't coming from her.

"Rather like fish," said Phillip.

"They served fish on the plane," Adriane confessed.

"You chose airplane fish?"

"It was okay. Orange roughy." She added a playful growl: "*Rrruff.*" Smiling queasily, she reached for her weekend suitcase. "I'll unpack my toothbrush."

"I'm sorry," said Phillip, rising from the sofa. "This isn't quite how I pictured it."

"What?" asked Adriane. Her hearing in one ear was just a bit off.

"Our little visit." He trailed a hand through the air, a disturbingly broad gesture. "The romantic gestalt."

Adriane slumped against the sofa, reeling with betrayal, and clutched a pillow to her stomach. He had shown such promise when they'd first met! Just a month ago, at a wedding back in Baltimore. She'd caught the bouquet and he the garter, which he then eased onto her leg with such delicate titillation she later agreed to visit his Montreal apartment over the upcoming holiday weekend. Well, it was some sort of Canadian holiday; Adriane herself had to spend vacation time. Plus airfare. But still: It was an exotic tryst in a foreign country. A different language, kind of. And currency, kind of. Miles from home *for sure*. The whole project's frontier spirit had spoken to her. Now, this setback. Had he been drunk at the wedding? Maybe he'd never expected her to come. She wondered if he really was a research psychologist or if that was just a line to impress girls at weddings. Adriane felt around in the outer pocket of her suitcase, trying to remember if she'd packed pepper spray.

"I'm sorry about the disappointment," Phillip was saying. He rotated the McGill class ring on his finger, as though starting the painstaking chore of disassembling himself. "This sort of impulse rendezvous–the anticipation, the fantasy, well, they can overwhelm the reality."

He seemed to pause for her concurrence.

"If you like," he went on, "I can recommend a quaint inn."

"No thanks," she said, collecting her stuff. "I'll find a place."

Here, of course, was the problem with a first date in a foreign country: Not only did there exist the presumption of immediate sexual involvement, but also you couldn't just get in your car and go home.

Outside, snow had begun to fall and the evening wind pierced her new full-length coat. In the store it had looked warmer, and the sale price had been so slashed Adriane couldn't resist, even though it was several sizes too big. The overall effect might have been almost regal in a more festive color, but she'd bought it in black, and so it looked more like the coat from under which one might pull a brace of shotguns.

She tried to hail a cab, but the ones that passed her were full. *Hey, I've got luggage here!* Adriane announced to Canada in general as she rolled her weekender, its small wheels rutting periodically in the sidewalk seams.

On the lookout for a place to stay, she hoped for something with a little charm, maybe a b&b–that quaint inn Phillip had referred to; she probably should have listened to his recommendation. Now she was drifting further into some kind of business district, and after a dozen blocks of trudging against the wind and snow, the only likely contender she'd passed was an imposing high-rise luxury hotel called the Summit Arms. The doormen wore fancy livery topped by beaver-pelt hats. Even the receptionist sported a royal blue tunic with a golden tassel across each shoulder. It all looked very military.

"Do you have a special rate for people who are stranded after their dates have turned on them for no good reason?" she asked the receptionist, who politely shook his head.

On the twelfth floor now, she surveyed her expensive room, money better spent on a nice French dinner. Still wearing her enormous coat, she flopped onto the bed and stared at the phone, wanting to call home to share this latest anguish.

"Gelki residence," answered Joan, who was house-sitting for her.

"Hey, it's me, Mistress Gelki, checking in."

"Everything okay?"

"There's been a setback," Adriane confessed, fiddling with the phone cord. "He just totally turned on me."

"What happened?"

"He literally became a different person within a half hour."

"Well," said Joan, "it's not like you knew the original person."

"We'd talked on the phone!" Adriane cried, but then gave in. "You were right, Joanie. It was crazy to come up here."

Her friend did not argue the point.

"What's this fatal attraction I've developed for Frenchmen?" Adriane wondered aloud. "I mean, Phillip's Canadian, but he speaks French. And Luc was totally French."

"I don't know," Joan said impatiently. "I don't want to talk about Luc."

"I need to figure out an appropriate payback," said Adriane, twirling the phone cord around her finger. "Phillip doesn't own a car, so I can't slash his tires," she added, only half-joking.

Joan sighed. "We can't dole out payback every time life disappoints."

"Why not, Joanie? Why can't we do that?"

"Because it's childish. And paranoid. And delusional."

"Delusional?"

"It's pretending you have this godlike control of the universe. Plus it's immoral," Joan added. "It's totally immoral."

Adriane sat up in the bed. "Are you mad at me?"

"Not everything is about you, Adriane."

"You sound mad at me."

Joan sighed again. "I'm just having a blah day."

"What's wrong?" asked Adriane, shedding her coat. "Is it Molly? Is she over there now? Is that her I hear in the background? Just say yes or no."

"No, it is not Molly you hear in the background," said Joan. "It's the TV. Your dog's glued to some beach volleyball tournament. Those women are in pretty good shape, I gotta say."

"Would you put him on a sec?"

Adriane heard Joan carry the phone across the room and then call out: "He's on."

"Barry? Sweetie?" If she listened very closely, Adriane could hear him pant. "Are you being a good boy? Please be a good boy, Barry, and don't hump Joan. No humping, Barry. That's not what she's there for. No humping," she said again, louder this time. "Do you understand, sweetie? *No . . . humping!*"

"We understand," Joan said, back on the line already. "I'll make sure Molly knows, too."

"I didn't mean–"

"I know you don't want Molly over here. You've dropped enough hints."

"I just . . ." Adriane stammered, "it's just that Barry gets jealous when he doesn't receive enough attention."

"It's you who gets jealous. You've never been supportive of me and Molly."

"That's not true!" Adriane argued, though it was, it *was*.

"For the last six months, for as long as I've been seeing her–"

"You've been seeing her longer than that," said Adriane. "I've only *known* about it for six months–"

"You've never wanted anything to do with her," Joan went on. "And at poker, if she touches me, you roll your eyes at Shelley.

Or . . . Oh, what's the point! I don't want to fight. I'm sorry I said anything."

"I don't want to fight, either!" Adriane felt a pang of guilt. She wished she could be more supportive of Joan's romance, *in theory*, but it threatened her, threatened their bond, part of which had been built around their mutual misfortune in love. "We'll sort it all out when I get back, Joanie," she said, struggling to fill the awkward silence. "Thanks again for watching Barry. I won't forget your bagels."

Montreal was famous for its bagels, made in wood-burning ovens, and Joan wanted to surprise her girlfriend with a present, so she'd asked Adriane to bring some back in exchange for the dog-sitting.

"Don't go to a lot of trouble," Joan mumbled, but Adriane knew she was just saying that. Apparently six months–or six-plus months–was the "bagel anniversary," an important one.

"I'm happy to do it," said Adriane and vowed, "I will bring them."

The next morning, she woke up famished. Snow continued to gust against her twelfth-floor window; still, she couldn't bring herself to order a six dollar cup of coffee or a fourteen dollar plate of French toast from room service, even if they were just Canadian dollars.

She got dressed, squeezing into an underlayer of silk long johns, as though cramming a sausage into its casing, then jeans and a flannel shirt, a bulky cable-knit sweater, and finally her oversized coat. She trundled down to the lobby to ask where she could find the best hot-out-of-the-oven bagel Montreal had to offer. But the concierge wasn't there, so she wrapped her scratchy wool scarf twice tightly around her throat and set off into the blizzard.

Snow clearing machinery scraped and gurgled all around her, as Adriane made her way through knee-deep drifts on the sidewalk of Boulevard René Lévesque, past sleek office towers closed for the holiday weekend, and then up Chemin de la Côte-des-Neiges and eventually onto smaller streets, where she passed tantalizing signs for THE BAGEL CONNECTION, BAGEL WORLD, LA BAGEL-ERIE–all closed, either for the weather or the holiday or for spite.

Adriane should have asked Phillip to recommend the best place to buy bagels, but she suspected the whole idea of a woman eating food disturbed him. He probably wasn't the only man who felt that way: If they didn't fault you over the weight thing, they spurned you for the lingering aftertaste.

As she trekked, she passed the time wondering how she might wreak a little vengeance on him. If only he were a clinical psychologist and not in research, she could file some sort of patient complaint. You had to hit these people where they lived, she'd learned. The last guy who'd crossed her, Luc, was a food importer, so she'd sent him a letter, copied to the Food and Drug Administration, alleging that several random jars of his capers tested positive for botulism. Of course, she hadn't really copied the FDA, but she had designed some very convincing letterhead for her phony diagnostic lab. She imagined him ranting to federal bureaucrats, trying to clear up an allegation that had never been made, his face purple with frustration. If only she could come up with something as good for Phillip. *Retribution*, she reminded herself, *must be swift and proportionate.*

Not until she'd been walking an hour–head bent against the wind, which slapped at every exposed centimeter of skin; her ears, especially her left one, aching–did she come across a small brick storefront called simply EMIL'S, a glowing neon bagel in its window. The smell of wood smoke wafted from a rooftop exhaust fan resembling a large mushroom, melting the snow all around it. Salivating, she entered.

A thin man with salt-and-pepper hair, Emil himself maybe, stood behind the counter and invited Adriane to take her choice of seats.

"Are you all right?" he asked.

"I've been walking a long time," she said, wondering how awful she must look.

"Here, sip this," he said, handing her a cup of bouillon. "Complimentary."

The broth eased its way deep into the frosted cavity of her insides, unclenching her muscles and even melting loose a few tears.

"You seem distressed," said Emil.

"The cold always makes my eyes water. Could I have a bagel, please? Whatever's freshest. Nothing on it." She wanted the pure experience.

Emil soon returned with a large, golden-brown sesame-seed bagel, still hot. He set it in front of her, where it seemed to float like a small life preserver.

She picked it up and began nibbling at its crusty edge, prying off sesame seeds with her tongue, rotating it with trembling fingertips. Its warm simple presence, its very existence, touched her, after her long quest. Molly was lucky to have someone like Joan to ask someone like Adriane to bring something so wonderful back to her.

"Chérie," said Emil, handing her a napkin, "why do you cry?"

"This is the best food I've ever tasted," said Adriane, unashamed of her own tears. "I need four dozen."

She bought a dozen of the sesame, another of garlic, and a third of salt. Then waited a few minutes for a fresh batch of bialys to come out of the oven, and she put a dozen of those under her coat to keep her warm on the trip back.

"You were the only place open this morning," she said with heartfelt gratitude.

Emil smiled pleasantly and handed her his business card. "Come again please."

"I would if I lived here," she said as she stepped back into the snow.

"Tell a friend!" he called after her.

The sidewalks were more treacherous than ever. All the taxis seemed on vacation or snowbound. Or maybe they too were avoiding her out of spite. She suspected spite. When finally she burst into the hotel lobby, her bangs had formed icicles. Both ears were killing her. The concierge now stood in place behind his desk, and he grimaced when he saw her.

"Where have you been?" he asked.

"Out shopping." She kicked the slush from her thin rubber boots.

"You should've used the underground city. There's an entrance here at the hotel."

"An underground city?"

"It runs for kilometers," he said. "You need never have set foot outdoors."

"How clever of you people," Adriane said fuming. "That would've been nice to know."

"Can I help with anything else this morning?" he asked, adjusting his tassels.

"Is the airport open?" She thought she might head home early in case the blizzard got really bad. Plus, it occurred to her, she should get these bagels to Baltimore while they were still fresh. She imagined the look of pleasure and satisfaction on Joan's face, and a day early even.

When the flight home made a stop in New York, Adriane stepped off the plane to buy some aspirin; her head was throbbing and the landing had been hell on her eustachian tubes. As it turned out, the aspirin did nothing for her head, but it did upset her stomach, and the second landing soon proved even worse than the first. Trying to relieve the pressure, she manipulated her jaw so much, she feared it might have unhinged.

Adriane was the last passenger to rise. When she reached into the overhead bin to collect her fresh-baked loot, she touched only the cold fabric of her weekend suitcase. Not comprehending, she fluttered her hands around the storage space, expecting to hear the crackle of paper bags. She clambered onto her seat, peered inside, and gasped.

"Stop!" she croaked. "Everyone stop!"

The remaining few passengers paused by the exit to stare at her.

"My bagels are gone!"

"What's wrong?" A steward rushed down the aisle.

"Call everyone back!" Adriane said. "Someone walked off with my bagels!"

"Are you talking about those large paper bags in the bin?" the steward asked.

"Yes!"

"Oh dear," he said. "I believe they were thrown out."

"Thrown out?" Adriane said, a strobic pain moving across her forehead.

"When we cleaned the aircraft in New York I remember seeing

the crew dispose of something in the trash. I'm very, very sorry. What did you say was in them?"

"Bagels!"

The steward's expression softened with relief.

"Really good fresh ones!" said Adriane.

"Please see someone at our customer service counter. I'm sure they'll gladly reimburse you. You wouldn't happen to still have your receipt?"

"Reimburse me!" said Adriane, wrenching her suitcase from the luggage bin. "I need the bagels. I promised to deliver them."

Adriane staggered off the plane, distraught over this mistreatment, this abuse–and from a major American carrier, no less, to whose mileage program she'd been a devoted member since 1993. She set off in search of customer service. Kicking herself for having gotten off the plane in New York.

An airline representative, wearing a logo pin in his lapel, said, "We'll be happy to reimburse you."

Adriane pictured herself entering her apartment, empty handed, defeated–her friend's worst suspicions about her jealous nature confirmed. "You don't understand. Someone is counting on me!"

"I wish we could do more," said the rep.

"You *can* do more," said Adriane. "You *must* do more. Everyone's going to have to do just a little bit *more*!"

The rep said something about a free upgrade on her next trip to Montreal.

"Here's what I need from you," said Adriane. "A dozen sesame bagels, a dozen garlic, a dozen salt, and a dozen bialys. And they have to come from Emil's. And you should tip him."

"I don't see how we can arrange such a thing."

"Sure you can. You make big hunks of metal soar in the air."

"I'm going to get my supervisor; wait here just a moment please."

Adriane closed her eyes and exhaled audibly.

When the supervisor came to the counter, Adriane repeated her demands: "A dozen sesame bagels, a dozen garlic, a dozen salt, and a dozen bialys. Onion is acceptable, if Emil is low on any of the others. But they have to come from Emil's," she insisted. Emil was a decent, hardworking shopkeeper, open for business when everyone else in the city had forsaken her. "You should be writing this down."

The supervisor said maybe they could manage a free ticket for her.

Adriane looked at her watch. "When's your next flight?" she demanded. "If you're not going to replace my stolen property, you should at least send me back to do it."

"*That's* how you want to use your free ticket?" asked the supervisor.

Feeling warm and a little faint, Adriane unzipped the full length of her coat with a dramatic flourish, and something about this gesture must have intimidated the supervisor because he began quickly checking the flight schedule for openings. Within another few seconds he was printing out a ticket for a flight due to leave in three hours. She would have to spend the night in Montreal before the next available plane home, however, and the airline would not assume that cost.

"All right," said Adriane, pocketing the ticket. "But I want the heads of that cleaning crew on sticks."

"Pardon me?"

"I apologize," she mumbled hoarsely. "That was inappropriate."

She rolled her suitcase toward the gate area to wait.

On the flight back to Montreal, Adriane entered a languid daydream in which the airplane window had become an aquarium. Inside swam the cleaning crew of a certain major American carrier. Standing over them, Adriane sprinkled bits of fishmeal and watched them compete for it. Eventually Phillip floated into her dream and she was glad she'd saved some food. She sprinkled it over his head, and he swam to the surface and gulped down each flake, his little fish lips puckering with every swallow. Pucker, pucker, pucker . . . Luc the Frenchman swam into view at some point and so did the concierge; Adriane enjoyed doling out their portions as well. This went on for quite some time. Before she knew it, the plane touched down, and she was soon riding in a taxicab back to the Summit Arms, the only place in town she knew. The snow had let up, but nonetheless traffic moved at a spitefully slow crawl.

The receptionist seemed surprised to see her again, and while he was sympathetic to her tale of woe, there was no discount available for people returning to replace items lost on the flight home.

In her room, on the ninth floor this time but otherwise identical, Adriane instinctively wanted to call Joan. Joan, the more grounded, stable friend who provided Adriane a home base she could retreat to whenever one of her misadventures went awry. As they so often did. Awry, awry, awry. Six months ago, out of the blue, her friend had delivered the blindsiding news that she was in the throes of a romance–with a woman. And what did *Adriane* know about being the home base? She was totally *ill-suited* to the role. Everything was thrown out of whack. Starting with: Joan hadn't even discussed the possibility beforehand, just went ahead and did it. As though she'd decided to carve out a secret life for herself. Adriane discovered the secret by accident, and it stung. More than a little.

In part because she didn't like Molly, who seemed needy and histrionic, even more than Adriane.

She suddenly craved a drink, but when she opened the minibar and saw that a finger of Scotch cost twenty dollars, she shuddered and closed the door. She decided instead to have an anchovy pizza delivered to Phillip, and this made her feel better, but only for a minute. As retribution went, it felt more prankish than "proportionate," rushed instead of "swift."

The next morning she went downstairs to ask how to find Emil's through the underground city. A different concierge, so she was spared having to explain why she was back the very next day. He looked at the address on Emil's business card and said the tunnels didn't lead there, but she'd find bagels in the underground city itself.

"No, it has to be Emil's," she insisted. She was choosey, almost grudging, about her loyalties, but once declared, she could defend them fiercely.

Bundling up, she set off intrepidly once again into the snowscape. She trudged past The Bagel Connection, Bagel World, La Bagel-erie, all open today, all beckoning her with the wonderful smell of wood smoke and their toasty interiors. Bagel World in particular offered a seating area of big upholstered chairs gathered around a hearth; Adriane peered through the picture window at the klatch of comfortable young people in attractive wool sweaters and ached to join them, but she pressed on toward Emil's, who had been there for her when she'd needed him. She began to worry that maybe Emil would take today off instead and kicked herself for not having called ahead, but when she approached his shop and smelled the wood smoke wafting from the mushroom-shaped exhaust vent, she took a deep breath of relief.

Emil, God bless him, was open. *God bless you, Emil,* she thought.

"Back so soon?" he asked, bringing her a cup of broth.

Adriane told him the story. Even the stupid part about getting off the plane in New York; even the humiliating part about Phillip. And while she was at it, even the other humiliating if otherwise unrelated part about Luc. And, on a roll now, she told him about Joan, how her friend had carved out a secret life for herself and was mad at Adriane for not being supportive.

"And are you not supportive?" Emil asked. Standing on the other side of the bagel counter, he reminded her of that retired psychoanalyst she'd once patronized; maybe she could be similarly honest with Emil. He seemed sympathetic and nonjudgmental. Plus they were in a foreign country and the likelihood of any of this blowing back to her small circle in Baltimore seemed remote.

"She betrayed me," Adriane complained, still feeling the sting of it. "She should have told me about it when it happened, not let me just find out about it."

"Hmm," Emil murmured.

"I know," she admitted. "I know I'm being stupid."

She began to cry now, not the few glistening tears of the time before but a genuine snot jag. Emil handed her a napkin. He was so gentle, so sweet. After listening to her go on a while, he suggested she admit her jealousy and then maybe her friend would be able to reassure her. Also, if Adriane made more of an effort to welcome Molly, Joan might in turn pay more attention to their old friendship. Who knew, he said, Adriane might even enjoy the honor of becoming a confidante about her friend's relationship. But she needed to let her friend grow and to support this growth in the name of friendship, which made demands of people, like any job–the job of being a good friend.

He offered to replace her bagels for free, but she insisted on paying for them, and added a tip as well. It wasn't Emil's fault they'd been jacked. The man was a credit to his nation. He had single-handedly redeemed Frenchmen and other male speakers of French. Glancing at his left hand, she noticed, wistfully, a wedding band. Alas, she told him, it was true: All the good ones were taken. (Though the impracticality of long-distance romance had already been made clear to her.) She left his shop with a renewed sense of hope about human nature, even her own, and generally feeling better about everything.

The airport x-ray attendant raised an eyebrow as Adriane waddled through the adjacent metal detector, her coat bulging with four-dozen bagels, but no one searched her. On the flight back to Baltimore, the nonstop flight she'd originally been scheduled to take, she kept her coat on and her arms resolutely crossed over her prominent stomach, and she maintained a Secret-Service–like vigilance. A renewed hope about human nature was one thing, but she wasn't taking any chances this time. She continued to ponder Emil's sensible advice–he should be a psychologist–and Adriane knew she'd been slouching on the job of friendship, and she resolved to execute better.

As the plane landed, she felt a calm and well being this time–which continued throughout the cab ride to her apartment–the comfort of being back in Baltimore, back home, about to see her dog and her friend, and to deliver her friend's bagels, which felt like the discharge of a profound trust.

"Twenty-three dollars," the driver said, pulling in front of her building. As she reached into her pocket, however, she saw Molly stepping out from the lobby. Adriane quickly handed over some money and instinctively leaned back in her seat, as though she'd come across something she wasn't meant to. As though Molly's exit had been timed to avoid Adriane's return. Luckily, Molly didn't even glance toward the cab, just turned up the collar of her raincoat and soon disappeared around the corner–still, much of Adriane's homecoming joy had been dampened.

"Twenty-three American dollars," said the driver, and Adriane mumbled an apology as she replaced the wrong currency.

In the elevator ride to her floor, she told herself it shouldn't have come as such a surprise; the two of them probably found it impossible to keep their hands off one another! Adriane was just feeling sour grapes because her little tryst with Phillip had blown up in her face. She should be grateful her friend was willing to look after her dog, and just get over herself!

As she pulled her suitcase across the threshold of her doorway, Barry jogged up to her and excitedly sniffed the yeasty smell drifting out from under the hem of her coat. On the couch, Joan looked up, face half hidden by a tissue.

"How was the rest of your trip?" she asked then blew her nose.

"Montreal's one fucking winter wonderland!" Adriane declared. She patted her full belly with satisfaction and waddled over to the couch where she dramatically unzipped her coat and began jostling the four large paper bags so that bagels tumbled forth over Joan, like a ticker-tape parade. "Ta-da!" said Adriane, spreading her arms wide in the continued spirit of largesse and abundance. But when she saw Joan covering her head, her lap filled with bagels, loose sesame and poppy seeds speckling her hair, Adriane's gesture suddenly seemed harsh and belligerent.

She noticed now a few blooms of used tissue scattered across the coffee table. Her friend's eyes were red.

"What's the matter?" she asked, clearing a place on the couch to sit.

"Molly and I had a fight," Joan murmured. "She said– Oh, I don't want to talk about it."

"You can tell me," said Adriane, then waited silently, hoping not to seem pushy.

At last, Joan said, "She complained that I'm–I'm sexually–reserved."

"Oh, Joanie. I'm sorry." Adriane felt a pain in her stomach much like the pain she'd felt on Phillip's couch, but here was a case of actual love, and the pain of that–well, there could hardly be a comparison.

She reached to brush a sesame seed from her friend's shoulder, but Joan recoiled and said, "You're not sorry."

"I am," insisted Adriane. "I'm sorry you're hurting. I'm sorry she betrayed you."

"She didn't *betray* me; we had a fight. I'm *sad*," said Joan. "Just plain sad."

Adriane nodded, though her own feelings, which always seemed to overlap and contradict each other, were never just plain anything. But this was Joan's sadness and it could be plain if she wanted it to be. Together they began stuffing bagels back into their paper sacks.

Joan hefted one of the bags and observed, "You really cleared out the store."

"Well, these are great bagels. They made the whole trip. I'm going to fix us a couple right now."

"Were they hard to find?"

Adriane considered recounting the whole ordeal. It was a good story–nutty, even amusing–but would it make Joan feel any better to hear Adriane had gone to so much trouble? No, it would not, she decided. A good friend would leave out the gory details.

"They're everywhere in Montreal," she said. "They're growing on the trees."

She placed half a sesame bagel, with just a little butter, in front of Joan, then sat down to the other half.

Next they shared a garlic, then a salt, then a bialy. The two women ate together silently. Between courses, Adriane divvied some of the extras for her freezer and some for Joan's.

"How many for Molly?" she asked, as benignly as possible.

"I don't know. A dozen," said Joan. "I think she's wrong. I'm not all that reserved." She added, "Make that a half dozen."

After setting aside a half dozen, Adriane put each of the to-be-frozen bagels in an individual plastic bag. She then sucked out any extra air with a straw wedged strategically in the final open centimeter of each bag's zipper. True, defrosted bagels would lack that fresh-out-of-the-oven goodness, but this was the next best thing. She even prepped Molly's now in the same painstaking way.

"That's a good trick," admired Joan, her mouth half full.

Adriane put down her straw and regarded the multitude of bagels ready for the deep freeze, to be taken out later and thawed someday–singly or two at a time or even more, depending. Whatever she and her friend might need.

8. adriane and the fibroid tumor

fall 1998

Plump and pink, three inches in diameter, and floating in a mason jar filled with preservative: Adriane's newly harvested fibroid. Her first day back at City Hall, she displayed it on her desk. This was going to cause trouble–she could have guessed as much–and before long her boss called her into his office.

"Why would you even want to keep that?" he asked.

"It's like shrapnel," argued Adriane, who wanted credit for her suffering these past two weeks. She and her boss observed one another in silence.

Shaking his head, he said at last, "I'm sorry I couldn't stop by. It would have caused an argument. At home."

He sat behind his desk, and Adriane noticed his computer had one of those new stickers that read Y2K COMPLIANT. They were sprouting all across City Hall, as tech people made their rounds.

Someone had also stuck one to her boss's desk, though why a plain piece of furniture required millennial certification was something only a government task force would consider. She glanced at the framed picture of her boss's wife and young daughter, then turned her gaze to the view from his window and the recently opened babyGap below.

Adriane had thought she was long over him, over their awkward fling from more than one, two . . . She began to count on her fingers and realized: six years had passed! But her surgery had brought up old feelings. Major surgery it had been, the equivalent of a C-section. So much could have gone wrong: mistakes made, corners cut, care withheld. Hemorrhage, infection, coma, stroke; some of those things could yet happen. This had not been a lucky year and a half for her, healthwise.

"When May-Annlouise had fibroids," Garrett was saying, "she got that new treatment, where they just cut off the blood supply and–"

"You told me," Adriane interrupted. "I wanted it out. Out out out."

"Yes, well, you're young," he said, blushing. "And that myo-whatever's supposed to be more thorough. You made the right choice if you want children someday."

"Myomectomy," she said. To the degree she'd thought about children, Adriane had decided she didn't want any. Children, her mother had always taught her, were whom you blamed for your own unhappiness. It could be said Adriane's lack of regard for kids–in having her own someday or in caring about other people's overall–had once helped make the idea of an affair with a family man, well, thinkable. Since then she had certainly grown up a little, but just now she experienced the distinct sense of backsliding.

What if maturity were merely the thinnest veneer of socialization? She looked at her boss, his face aglow in the slatted sunshine from his office window, and felt an itch across her abdominal stubble. She was going through a second puberty down there. "I'm just glad the thing is out of me," she insisted.

"Please don't leave it on your desk."

"It's my desk."

He sighed. "Why must you always be so difficult?"

He cast the mildly paternal scowl he would give her whenever she was acting out–a furrow in his brow that she found perversely attractive and which she usually arranged to see at least once a day. Even when she was being scolded, her conversations with Garrett, alone in his office with the door closed, marked the highlight of Adriane's workday. She felt safe in his orbit, grateful to spend forty hours a week together, which was probably more than his family got to see him. He seemed to need Adriane as well, enjoyed the unspoken doggedness of her attention. Maybe theirs wasn't the healthiest emotional bond between two people, but it contained a kind of deformed beauty.

The next day, her phone rang, and it was Dru Pringle in Public Relations with an absurd request. His assistant was out sick, and some fourth-grade class needed a tour of City Hall.

"Fiona's sick?" Adriane asked. Fiona was about the only coworker, besides her boss, with whom she'd formed any kind of camaraderie.

"She'll be fine," said Pringle dismissively. "I need you to show these kids around, tell them about the inner workings here."

"Isn't fourth grade a little young for inner workings?"

"Well, they're gifted, from the Brandon Academy. I already cleared it with Garrett. He said I could have you."

That had an unpleasant ring to it, a hint of pimpery, and also, the nasty insinuation: *Garrett's done with you.* She watched her tumor floating in its jar and thought, out loud as it so happened, "Why don't you do it yourself?"

"I'm too important," said Dru Pringle, with no trace of irony. "They're in the lobby now. You'd better hurry and meet them."

"Yes, uh, okay," Adriane said and hung up. Putting on her blazer, she felt a tug across her stitches, one of her many layers of stitches. She had stitches along the inside of her uterus, stitches along the outside of her uterus, stitches in between those stitches, and stitches across her abdomen. For the next month at least, she was under orders to avoid heavy lifting and to check frequently for unusual bleeding, and she wondered now if she should take a quick peek. Though the bathroom was located just across from her desk, she decided not to spend the time; Dru Pringle had sounded impatient. She grimly began her march down the winding marble staircase toward the lobby. What did Adriane know about children, their world, their language, their customs? Hers was the esoteric, somewhat lofty realm of municipal public affairs. She had no idea what to tell kids.

She saw, standing off to the lobby's side, one, two, three, four . . . ten of them, chaperoned by a young teacher, younger than Adriane, but married and, by the bulbous look of her, knocked-up. The woman wore a fashionable maternity dress with a cashmere sweater and pearl stud earrings, sensible but supple loafers, and carried a conspicuously large handbag. She seemed to glance disparagingly at Adriane's blue jeans before introducing herself as Mrs. Coynes.

Adriane swallowed dryly. "Welcome to City Hall, the seat of city government," she said, hoping not to sound like a filmstrip.

In the pause that followed, Adriane could hear whispers and footsteps from across the rotunda.

Mrs. Coynes cleared her throat and said, "We're far along into our civics and government unit. Who can tell Miss Gelki what we've been studying?"

"We're learning about the three branches of government," volunteered one myopic little girl in a plaid smock. Even though she was standing at the back of the group, the rotunda dome shuttled her small voice into Adriane's ear with startling insistence. "Executive, judicial, legislative."

"We learned about the Constitutional Convention," said a slender, doe-eyed boy.

A taller, wavy-haired lad with a thirty-five-millimeter camera hanging over his cardigan announced, "We watched parts of *The American President*."

Adriane asked, of no one in particular, "Is that the movie where Michael Douglas keeps trying to order roses for Annette Bening?"

"Yes," the children said in unison, their voices reverberating.

"If only life here at City Hall were so romantic," she replied wistfully. "You're going to have to set aside your preconceptions." She then asked the teacher, "How long a tour did they promise you?"

"About an hour. More or less."

Both women studied each other nervously before Adriane glanced at her watch, which seemed to be standing still. She spanked the side of her wrist until she saw the second hand move but then it stopped again. She exhaled in frustration. The children, she noticed, were staring at her. A few of them held notepads and pencils, as though ready to ticket her.

Anxious to move the group out from the rotunda's echo chamber, she said, "I guess you all would like to see where the mayor works."

Everyone said yes, their voices caroming inside Adriane's head.

She led them along the curving marble staircase to the second floor of the north wing, and soon they entered the anteroom to the mayor's office. They gathered before his closed door, the city seal mounted upon it.

"This is it," said Adriane.

The boy who carried the thirty-five millimeter camera took a picture now of the closed door.

The mayor's secretary had managed to step out somewhere, so Adriane described the woman's workspace. "As you can see, it's Y2K compliant," she said, pointing to the stickers on the computer, the desk, and also the back of the chair. "Even though the millennium is over a year away, we're making sure everything is ready so there are no rude surprises here at City Hall." Referring to the triptych picture frame next to the pencil cup, Adriane said, "These must be her grandchildren. Oh, here she comes now."

As the silver-haired woman returned, she smiled at all the kids, a little less so at Adriane.

"Is Hizzoner in, Patsy?" Adriane asked.

His secretary explained that the mayor was in the middle of a meeting with representatives of the Baltimore Archdiocese.

"What's he like?" a large-toothed girl in a snowflake sweatshirt asked Adriane.

"The mayor? He's okay, I guess."

"He's a *very* nice man," interjected the secretary. "And a *wonderful* mayor."

"I'm *sure* he is," said Mrs. Coynes, adopting Patsy's spirited inflection.

The class regarded the city seal a while longer before Adriane said, "All right, then. Maybe we can try again later. Why don't we make our way over to the Mayor's Office of Neighborhood Enhancement, where I work?"

She led the troop up another flight of stairs, to the third floor, which had lower ceilings than the second or first floor and which did not even exist, she explained, until the building's renovation in the mid-1970s.

"Did you have to move your desk?" asked one of the kids behind her.

"I wasn't working here yet," she said, adding, "I was younger than you are now." Christ, how old did they think she was? "All right," she said, standing before her cubicle. "I give you the Mayor's Office of Neighborhood Enhancement. We help neighborhoods put together special projects like concert series or maybe you remember the Painted Screen Door Slam from a couple winters ago? As a walking tour, it would have worked better in the summer when more people have their screens up; we might try it again though. On North Avenue, which used to be a happening corridor for nightlife, we hung streetlamp banners of Eubie Blake, who was a pioneering jazz musician born right here in Baltimore. Um, let's see. The Korean-American 'Bulgogi Nights' festival–we were very involved with that. . . ."

The kids stared at her blankly, and Adriane checked her watch, still frozen, then pointed to Garrett's door. "That's my boss in there, the Director of the Mayor's Office of Neighborhood Enhancement, Garrett Hughes. Let's see what he's up to, shall we?"

She tapped on the door, and when that didn't get an answer, she rapped with the ham of her fist.

"Yes?" grumbled Garrett.

Adriane ushered the ten tourists and their teacher into the room.

Garrett put his hand over the mouthpiece of his phone. "Can I help you?"

"Yes, you can! This is Mrs. Coynes and her fourth-grade class. They're studying the Constitutional Convention and the three branches of government and have watched parts of *The American President*. Could you tell them a little bit about, like, when you're not sending me roses, what you do here at City Hall?"

"Maybe you could stop by on your way back, when I'm not on the phone?"

"Please," she whispered.

He conferred on her that mildly paternal scowl she craved, then told the person on the other end of the line he'd call back. It was probably just his wife anyway.

"Fourth grade!" he said with sudden, circuslike gusto, and began to coax information from the kids, including their names and ambitions. Beyond the usual choices like veterinarian, these included "diplomat or maybe spy" and "sitcom writer." Maryjane, the large-toothed girl in the snowflake sweatshirt, wanted to be a physicist. The Asian kid had set his sights on architecture. The boy with the camera planned to be a thoracic surgeon like his father. There was a future investment banker in the bunch somewhere. And the doe-eyed boy named Jeremy admitted, while fiddling with the zipper of his parka, that he wanted someday to be mayor. Adriane had never heard so much raw aspiration revealed at one time, and she felt a little embarrassed by it.

"Great!" Garrett told the mayoral hopeful. "We need new

blood. Otherwise, you see, government can fall into a rut and become just about perpetuating itself. We need to continually remind ourselves of our larger mission as stewards, helping people, and leading society toward a better future. So welcome aboard, Jeremy, you've come to the right place."

Her boss would make a good father. Was *already* a good father, no doubt. As he chatted up the students from the Brandon Academy–the room's mood climbing steadily, like a funicular–Adriane let herself drift into a nostalgic reverie about their brief affair. He'd been recovering from an injury, his leg bound in a cast, his face bruised the color of Tropical Swirl sherbet, but hardest hit: his confidence and self-worth. And in her small ways, she had nursed him back to wellness. At a time when his wife remained distant and angry, Adriane had offered herself to this man she admired and even, truth be told, adored. She remembered the tapas restaurant where they'd retired for happy hour, his crutches leaning against the bar as he waited for her to return with a small plate of food. She bought him a martini and later helped him into her car. He seemed, at least for a little while, deeply appreciative of her. It was intoxicating, this personal appreciation, and with his melodious baritone now wafting in the background, she managed to conjure up the faintest trace of it–a dangerous fantasy. She'd been good for so long; what a shame to lean off the wagon now, though she couldn't help herself. In the hospital, drifting under the anesthesia, she'd supposedly called out his name.

Her eyes still closed now, she felt his fingers splay across the wing of her shoulder and was startled to notice him gently ushering her out of his office.

"Have a wonderful visit," he was telling the group. "You're in great hands with Ms. Gelki, here."

She heard his door click, and the mood, not just hers but the group's, seemed to lurch downward. Adriane tried to prop it up by invoking her boss's name. "It was Garrett's idea to create the North Avenue banners," she said, dabbing the moist corner of her lips with a tissue. "They were made from a lightweight nylon and there was plenty of back and forth with the printer over the four-color registration, let me tell you. This is where I sit," she said, pointing a trembly finger toward her desk.

"What's that?" asked Jeremy, the aspirant mayor in the downy parka, as he held up her mason jar.

"Oh, that," said Adriane. "That doesn't really have anything to do with municipal government per se. It's more of a–paperweight."

"But what *is* it?" asked the myopic girl, peering up close against the jar.

"Just a tumor," Adriane said with finality, knowing her boss would not approve of this conversation.

"Like cancer?" called out a child from the back.

"Kind of, but this type isn't cancerous. It's called a fibroid and it's really just a blob of cells deciding to do their own thing, which regrettably serves no biologically useful purpose."

"Did it come out of you?"

"Yes, it was surgically removed. From my stomach. Which cost a lot of money, because I went out of network."

"Do you mean your uterus?"

"Yes."

"People," said Mrs. Coynes, "our biology unit isn't until next month."

"My mom has fibroids," offered one kid.

"Most women who get these," Adriane couldn't help pointing out, "are older than me."

"How old *are* you?"

"Alan," cautioned Mrs. Coynes.

"I'm thirty," said Adriane, swallowing dryly. "I just turned thirty."

"This one looks like an alien," said the myopic girl, and immediately a couple other children agreed.

"It does look like an alien, doesn't it?" said Adriane, perking up suddenly. She was glad someone else thought so. "That small flappy part resembles a mouth, I think."

"Let me see!" demanded the boy who wanted to be an architect. "Is it alive?"

"I think it needs a blood source to stay alive," Adriane said. "But, hey, you never know with aliens."

Their faces brightened as each kid got a chance to hold the mason jar. A couple of them tapped on the glass and talked to it.

"All right, Maryjane, let's put down the paperweight," said Mrs. Coynes, trying delicately to wrest Adriane's tumor from the large-toothed girl. "Miss Gelki's been very generous with her time. We don't want to keep her from her work."

Miss! Adriane caught that. This Coynes ingénue, Adriane could see, was suddenly in over her head. Suburban princess, she probably wanted to hightail it out of there, get back to Towsontown Center, where she could concentrate on picking out the right Laura Ashley wallpaper for the twins' room. She didn't know from fibroids, not to mention hemorrhage, infection, coma, stroke. And if she ever did have to wake up from a major surgery, there was that husband in the picture–some Johns Hopkins University professor or titan of industry–looking out for her.

"Keep me from my work?" Adriane locked eyes with the young teacher. "Are you kidding? This is a bloated civil bureaucracy. I've got all the time in the world. I didn't know these kids could handle the *real* tour instead of the fairy-tale tour."

"Well," began Coynes, "There might be a limit to–"

"All right then, who wants to know about city government? The political machine? The pageantry and atrocity of democracy in action?" Already she was feeling better, energized.

"I want to see the machine," said a tiny voice.

"You can't actually see it," said Adriane, "and it's nowhere near as big as it used to be, but it's there in the background. Let's go look at the City Council chambers," she said, leading them toward the south wing.

"Does anybody know what H. L. Mencken, the irascible sage of Baltimore, had to say about democracy?" No one raised a hand. "He called it 'the art of running the circus from the monkey cage.'"

A couple of students laughed, and Adriane congratulated herself for the well-chosen quote. She called over her shoulder: "Where's the kid who wants to be mayor?"

The doe-eyed boy in the parka raised his hand.

"What's your name, slim?"

"Jeremy Pierce."

"Okay, Jeremy. What stepping stone did you have in mind? Are you going to be a state's attorney first? Or a City Council member. Let's get you elected to the Council. You're a Democrat, aren't you, Jeremy?"

"I don't know. My parents are."

"You bet you're a Democrat, because this is Baltimore." She began walking backward now as she spoke; it was easier than craning her neck. And she had to project rather loudly to be heard over the clomping of so many feet. "You need to run as a Democrat, so you need the party's support to launch a successful campaign. Not only that, but one of the powerful incumbents in your district, Council Member R., wants you on his slate. Fortunately R. has an opening, and he likes you, Jer, the two of you see eye to eye on many issues of the day, and he wants you to be elected."

"What about voting?"

"Relax, Jeremy! This one's pretty well sewn up. That is unless there are *two* powerful incumbents in the district and they've grown to hate each other's guts and have decided to each run his own slate. Then things will get *really* interesting! Fundraising through the roof! Sack loads of direct mail to every voter in the district. A barrage of radio message ads, maybe some cable, like during a Baltimore Blast game. Do you watch indoor soccer, Jeremy? What do you think your message might be?"

They passed Dru Pringle going the opposite way, and he gave her a narrow look over his shoulder. Adriane smiled and waved as though she were on a parade float, before refocusing her attention on Jeremy, who seemed at a loss. She looked into his doe eyes and offered, helpfully, "Crime. What's your position on crime, Jeremy?"

"Against."

"You're hard on crime, but not too hard, you know what I'm saying? You probably supported amending Maryland's three-strikes law to a four-strikes law–which shows you're tough, but merciful–never mind that the City Council doesn't make state law. You might consider developing a position on taser guns and rubber bullets that'll make sense to the public without pissing off the Fraternal Order of Police. How about the schools? Voters are always complaining about the city school system. You have no idea, right? People, raise your hand if you've ever gone to public school."

A girl with braided pigtails, one of which was stuck in her mouth, raised a hand.

"Yes, blue cord dress," Adriane called out. "What's your name?"

"Chloe."

"Chloe, what was your public school like?"

"Not so nice," she seemed to say.

"Okay, Jer, what are you going to promise to do about the public schools?"

"Pay teachers more money," he said, smiling toward Mrs. Coynes.

"Good answer; you've just clinched six thousand votes from the Baltimore Teachers' Union. But where's this money going to come from? Baltimore's city property tax rate is already twice the county's. Most of the rich people are worried about crime and fled to the suburbs years ago. Something to ask your parents about."

Adriane wasn't trying to sound cynical; she just felt these kids should get the unvarnished look at city government that they couldn't get at school; plus she didn't want her tour to pale in comparison to the tumor.

Jeremy furrowed his brow.

"That's a tough one," Adriane consoled him. "We'll come back to it. What if you're in a really tight race against–" She pointed to the one girl in jeans, a peace sign patched over each knee–the kid who wanted to be a sitcom writer.

"Tara Nichols."

"What if Tara's breathing down your neck? She's got a perky wholesome image that won't quit, and she knows every Catholic in the district. It's going to be a squeaker. How are you going to help your slate, Jer?"

"Maybe she isn't as goody-goody as everybody says."

Adriane's face lit up. "I like where you're going with this, Jer, and if you've got something juicy on her, you might use it. But here's an easy way to shave two or three percentage points off her vote: a little something we in Baltimore politics call the Name Game."

"That may be too advanced for them," said Mrs. Coynes.

"You just get yourself a phone book, okay?" Adriane went on. "And find someone in the district named, say, *Tama* Nichols. And you pay to have her file her candidacy, plus give her a little something extra for her troubles, and voila: Tama Nichols's name appears right above Tara Nichols on the ballot! Ready to siphon off Tara votes, just like a tapeworm."

"Hey," said Tara Nichols. "Unfair!"

"Well, Tara, you could have found someone named Gerry Pierce or Jerzy Pearce to nominate; too bad the filing deadline has passed. By the way, that was smart, Jeremy, waiting till the last moment to register Tama. Maybe Tara will see the light now and drop out of the race. Especially if you can think of some sort of contract job or patronage position to dangle in front of her."

"What's a patronage position?" asked the myopic girl in the plaid smock.

The Asian architect raised his hand. "Is it like when you pick your friend for the kickball team?"

Adriane paused. "That's . . . not bad."

She led the group now into the empty council chambers.

"Okay, here we are," she announced. "The Sausage Factory."

Coynes cleared her throat. "Who can tell Miss Gelki the rules of parliamentary procedure for a roll-call vote?"

"Why sausage?"

"It's an old saying about making laws." She proceeded to describe at length the recent passage of a zoning ordinance for a newly proposed cultural-and-shopping development then asked the class what that had to do, if anything, with the biohazard disposal plant that had managed to attach itself to the same piece of legislation.

No one had any answers. "I don't know," said Chloe.

"Exactly!" said Adriane. She was getting a kick out of watching Coynes nervously click the clasp of her oversized handbag. "Let's just say someone's taking care of his favorite supporters."

The children looked at her, puzzled.

Adriane turned to Coynes and asked, "Have you covered conflicts of interest? Cronyism? Corruption?"

"That's wrong," piped up doe-eyed Jeremy, before his teacher could answer.

"Yes, Jeremy," said Adriane. "It is."

She told them about Zolly Chernofsky, the once-brilliant City Council president who went to jail for taking bribes from a sludge-hauling company and who now had colon cancer, which then led quite naturally into a sober discussion about irony, which Coynes tried to interrupt several times, but Adriane managed to keep on point.

The tour continued like this for another twenty minutes. To Adriane's surprise, the kids were an insatiable source of questions, and they seemed to look up to her as a political insider, like James Carville or Arianna Huffington. One kid even asked if she ever appeared on CNN.

Finally the teacher proposed with almost desperate urgency: "Shall we swing by the mayor's office once more before we have to leave?"

"Sure," Adriane allowed. "Couldn't hurt."

"What's he *really* like?" asked Gray, the future diplomat and/or CIA agent.

"He's complex," Adriane answered this time, as they trooped

back to the north wing. "He can be charming, but he's not without his moods. He's . . . I'll give you the scoop after you meet him. I want you to form your own impressions first."

Patsy, the mayor's secretary, saw them coming and picked up her telephone. "Mrs. Coynes's fourth-grade class from the Brandon Academy has dropped by again. Do you have a moment?" She hung up and looked toward the group. "The mayor will be right out."

The tall door swung open, and the mayor, his most optimistic grin scrunching his eyes tight, strode briskly into the anteroom, extended a shirt-sleeved arm forward, and took hold of Adriane's hand.

"Mrs. Coynes," he said. "Thank you for coming. When I was a freshman at the University of Maryland, I thought about becoming a teacher, but I decided the workload was just too darn hard! My hat's off to anyone who takes it on. Guiding young people. And that extends to private schools, not just the city system. Noblest profession–calling–I can think of. If only I'd had more advance notice of your visit. I'd've cleared some time."

Throughout this little speech, he was pumping Adriane's arm, and alternately smiling at her, the children, and the wall clock, whose frame, she only half-registered, had been certified with a Y2K sticker. She was in such shock, such unnerved humiliated shock, that she could only murmur, "Thank you."

No one stepped in to correct him. Whatever brief window there might have been had passed. Mrs. Coynes, the architect, the large-toothed girl, Jeremy–all of them smiled stiffly. The boy with the camera seemed too stunned even to snap a photo.

The mayor's smile, Adriane noticed now, seemed a little crinkled, as though he sensed maybe he'd screwed up, but if so, the window for repair must have seemed closed to him now as well.

He asked the children, "Anybody here considering a career in government when they grow up?"

Jeremy gingerly raised his hand.

"Terrific," said the mayor. "We need new blood." He glanced one last time at Adriane and said, "I hope you'll come again soon."

"Thank you," said Adriane. "We will."

"Our future is in your hands," he said, and let go of her hand. He turned to his secretary and said, "Hold my calls, Patsy." Then he retired to his office, the tall door closing softly behind him.

After a moment of embarrassed silence, Mrs. Coynes asked if anybody needed to use the bathroom, and most of the kids waved. The teacher looked expectantly toward Adriane, who blinked before realizing she was being asked to lead them. As they left the mayor's waiting area, she thought she saw Patsy smirk.

No one spoke as they filed through the hallways and up the spiraling stairs to the third floor. Adriane tripped against the top step, but managed to catch herself. Gawky she felt, laden with the shame of adolescence. She might occupy an adult's body and move in an adult's world, but largely unnoticed and now it would seem, utterly without importance. On the flow chart of City Hall, truth be told, her job and the mayor's lay far, far apart; no huge surprise, really, that he wouldn't recognize her. And what about the flow chart of her life? she wondered. Would she ever be important in this world? To whom? And for what?

Most of the assistants in her section had gone to lunch, and the common area seemed deserted. Their desks, she noticed as she tromped past, all seemed to have been plastered with Y2K COMPLIANT stickers since she'd last checked, but her own work space had yet to be certified. Apparently her capacity to function in the approaching millennium was not a priority around here.

Adriane leaned a steadying hand against her desk and pointed to the bathroom doors a dozen yards away.

Coynes took charge. "Everyone meet back here in three minutes. If you don't need to go, stay with Miss Gelki." She turned to Adriane and added, "Is that all right?"

"Sure, sure," murmured Adriane. How quickly she'd been demoted from pundit to babysitter.

Most of the girls followed Mrs. Coynes into the women's room. A few of the boys explored the men's room next door. That left Adriane with Jeremy the mayoral hopeful and also the investment banker named Robert Toogood and Chloe, who was sucking on her braid and who had not expressed any career ambitions earlier.

"This job was supposed to be temporary," Adriane told them. "I've been here seven, no, almost eight years–about as long as you people have been alive."

"We're nine," said Robert, but Adriane barely heard because she was staring at her desk trying to figure out what looked wrong about it, besides the lack of Y2K stickers, speaking of which, truth be told, she didn't even know if she'd live to see the new millennium, and–

"Where's my paperweight?" she demanded.

"Paper what?" Chloe mumbled over her braid.

"My tumor!" said Adriane. "Who took it?"

The three children looked at each other.

"Maybe one of the bathroom kids did," Jeremy suggested, a little too helpfully.

Adriane swooped to a crouch in front of him and thrust her hands deep into his cargo pockets. Wide eyed with terror, he jerked away and knocked a heavy stack of file folders off her desk. Adriane, hands still in his pockets, almost fell on him, found herself pulling back to stay upright. Felt her stitches twang, her body a harp, being plucked with a crowbar. Inside: a rupture that was to cost her another hospital visit, two weeks bed rest, and, as her surgeon would soon nag her, the likely formation of scar tissue that could permanently damage her uterus. Meanwhile, inside Jeremy's pockets, her hands grasped a bunched-up ski cap and a few loose coins on the one side, and on the other an empty soda can and an embryonic blob of gum.

"There it is!" said Robert Toogood, pointing to her desk. From her new angle, Adriane could see the jar, behind her pencil stein. She removed her fists from Jeremy's pockets, pressed smooth the flaps.

"Sorry," she said with a groan. "Sorry, sorry, sorry."

He looked at the floor and fiddled with his parka zipper.

"Don't be scared of me," she said gently, trying to ignore the throb in her loins. "You're going to be mayor," she reminded him. "And then, if you're still mad at me, you . . . you can have me fired."

In her current frame of mind, Adriane considered this scenario plausible. Likely even. She hoped young Jeremy at least got some solace from it, because it sure discomforted her. And would he be a better mayor, she wondered, for having met her? Or would there come a time when he'd issue some shocking policy decision whose roots, if one but knew how to trace them, would lead back to this day. She brushed the down of his cheek with her thumb, drew a fingertip lightly across his lips, a kind of this'll-be-our-secret gesture.

To her astonishment, he seemed to relax under her touch. He smiled with something like forgiveness then put his arms around her and squeezed. Adriane found herself returning the embrace and squeezing back. Over the boy's shoulder, she saw her boss standing in his doorway, looking down at them.

"Adriane?" he asked. "Everything all right out here?"

"Fine," she said, holding on to the boy.

"You sure you don't need me for anything?"

Her boss was scowling in that paternal way, but at the moment this expression–or was it his tone of voice?–seemed patronizing to her. The idea of retiring to his office and listening to his advice or criticism or even consolation just for the pleasure of his attention felt perverse–bad perverse–not to mention fruitless and possibly the very last thing she needed right now.

"No, thanks," she told him.

Garrett raised an eyebrow, then retreated into his office and closed the door.

She hugged the boy Jeremy to her tightly, and then tighter still, which put pressure on different parts of her gut, as though she were sliding from one level of pain into another.

Children, thought Adriane, awakening to a desire already beyond her reach. *Maybe I should have some children.*

9. the godmother

summer 1999

At poker, right in the middle of a hand, Joan and Molly announced: "We're thinking about starting a family." Molly said the words and Joan merely nodded, but Adriane heard it in unison.

"You mean, like, becoming parents?" she asked.

Joan and Molly both nodded this time. They'd been an item for about two years already; still, Adriane wasn't the only one at the table shocked by this news.

"Really?" asked Monique, Molly's dour ex, who'd only recently returned to Friday night poker now that she had a new girlfriend to bring along. Lesbians, Adriane had noticed, now held a majority at the table.

"Are you going to adopt?" asked Tamara, the new girlfriend.

"Can't we *please* see the river?" muttered Shelley, whose impatience usually signaled she was holding a great hand.

Molly flipped over the final community card, while saying something about willing sperm donors. "Or we might just buy some. There's a sample bank with a long client list, and they hook you up." She was wearing a Hello Kitty tank top that featured a rainbow and the words IT'S A BEAUTIFUL DAY. For the life of her, Adriane couldn't tell if this was meant to be ironic.

"How long have you been thinking about this?" Monique demanded. Maybe the issue had never come up when she and Molly were a couple–or come up and been dispatched in such a way that this announcement held radioactive significance. Adriane, too, found herself sitting forward in her seat. Complications from fibroid surgery had reduced her own odds of ever conceiving, and so she'd become increasingly alert to all related subjects. Trying to feign nonchalance, she tossed a sliver of Camembert on the floor, near Barry's snout, while continuing to listen.

"Don't get defensive," Molly told her ex.

"We only started talking about it recently," said Joan. "We're floating a trial balloon here. What do you guys think?"

"I think it's wonderful," said Tamara. "I think you should go for it."

"Me, too," said Fiona, who'd been quiet until then.

"Me, three," Adriane called out suddenly. "I've got dibs on godparent."

There was a brief silence, during which Molly checked her hole cards, as though she'd forgotten them, which maybe she had; she was a distractible player. "That's thoughtful of you, Adriane–"

"But *not* how it works," snapped Shelley, as she folded her hand in disgust. "Do you even know what being a godparent means?"

"Sure I do. It means I get to spoil the baby rotten. I get to take her to the zoo and the park and to every G-rated theatrical release.

If there are scheduling conflicts with any of you, our plans take priority. And if I buy her the same clothes as you guys, you have to exchange yours. Plus I get to buy her savings bonds and teach her poker. And also if, um, both parents"–here she nodded toward Joan and Molly and lowered her voice slightly–"were to meet an untimely end, then I would assume custody and raise the baby as my own."

People seemed to be cocking their heads slightly as they looked at her.

"What?" Adriane protested. "I called it!"

"Well, here's the thing," said Molly, raking chips toward her, because, it so happened, she'd sucked out a flush on the river. As she leaned forward, her hair draped smoothly around her face, despite the humidity. "My sister and brother-in-law, they have three kids. And, it's just that I'm *their* godmother, and I'd always figured that when I had kids, well . . . My sister and I are very close."

"They live in a nice small town," said Joan, "and Brenda teaches home economics, and her husband is an insurance broker, and Molly says they have a really big backyard."

"What town?" Adriane asked. "Have you ever met them?"

"Salisbury," said Joan defensively. "We're going next weekend."

"For five or six days," added Molly, who always demanded a lot of Joan's time.

"Their yard's not that big," murmured Monique.

Adriane had always thought of Salisbury, Maryland, as just a speed trap between Baltimore and Ocean City. "People still take home economics?" she asked.

"It's so sweet that you'd want to do this." Molly leaned across the felt and squeezed Adriane's hand. "If we weren't already going to ask my sister–"

"And *nothing's* definite yet," Joan added.

"Okay, okay," said Adriane and began dealing the next hand. "I didn't mean to turn it into a whole *thing*."

Though of course now it *was* a "whole thing." The next morning, Adriane kept picturing the weird stare people had given her, and Shelley, brutally honest Shelley, demanding: "Do you even know what being a godparent means?" Adriane envisioned the role as a kind of side entrance into some semblance of family life, which she had long gone without, but there was a lot more to it than that, apparently. Bylaws, perhaps, secret handshakes and such. So she did what she usually did whenever faced with a gaping deficit in her life–she sought to surround herself with printed matter.

At the Enoch Pratt Free Library, its main location an easy walk from her apartment, Adriane cast a Boolean net across her subject. Though this turned up surprisingly few titles, she was nonetheless able to check out *The Godparents' Handbook*, as well as *Godparents: A Tribute* and, because she'd never read it before, *The Godfather*. She brought home these low-hanging fruit and began nibbling them. Two facts emerged almost immediately: Adopting an orphaned child was actually *guardianship*, which might or might not be assigned to the godparent but in any case required a legally binding will and a court's approval. And the other big thing was godparenting typically involved *God*, preferably the Christian one. Some denominations had more rules about it than others, but the crux seemed to be about promoting a child's religious education and when you weren't doing that, saying prayers for the child.

"Where's the chapter on savings bonds?" she asked her dog, his snout warm across her thigh.

Adriane had pursued her own unconventional relationship with God some years back, but they'd grown apart, and she wondered now if it would be necessary to try to patch things up in her campaign for this position. On the other hand, she had read a broad variety of religious texts over the years, so if breadth and academic interest were valued, she might score some points there. She felt oddly confident she'd make a fantastic godmother, if only the rules could somehow bend to accommodate her own existential misgivings.

Sunday afternoon, she decided to visit Joan and Molly. Not to push her agenda–she told herself she wouldn't bring it up, at least not directly–but she needed to get out of the house for a while. She packed Barry into the car and off they went. The ballgame at Oriole Park was starting soon, which tacked fifteen minutes onto Adriane's trip to Federal Hill–she could have walked there already–and made finding a parking space near Joan's town house a trial of its own.

Her friend answered the door, holding a sheaf of pages. "Come in," she said. "I was just screening applicants."

"Where's Molly?" asked Adriane, pleasantly surprised to have Joan to herself for a while.

"Monique and Tam had an extra ticket to the game. We flipped for it."

Without needing to be asked, Adriane poured Barry a bowl of water and helped herself to a beer. Normally, she'd drink it from the bottle, but when she saw the Hello Kitty mug in the drain board, she just had to fill it with alcohol. She joined Joan at the dining table, which was covered with papers loosely organized into two stacks: NOS and MAYBES.

"Molly and I have slightly different taste in sperm donors," said

Joan. "I kind of like this guy." She handed over a five-page document. "He's supposedly very popular."

Adriane scanned some of the listing's highlights:

Donor profile: 25SH889 . . .
Ethnic origin: French, Dutch, 3/16 Navajo . . .
Blood group/Rh: O Negative . . .
Donor lab results: Chlamydia–negative; Hepatitis B–negative; Hepatitis C–negative; Tay Sachs–n/a . . .
Religion: Atheist
Special talents: "Weight lifting; Ultimate Frisbee; I write a little poetry, mostly villanelles. . . ."

"Damn! It's just like personal ads," said Adriane. "Except now we're really cutting to the chase."

"Tell me about it," said Joan, getting herself a beer.

"Is it good or bad that he's an atheist?" asked Adriane.

"I'm okay with it, but Molly wants to see some profession of faith."

"You think that's genetically significant?" asked Adriane, setting the dossier aside.

"Molly can be a little irrational."

"This her mug?" Adriane raised it in a toast.

"Her new thing. You should see the panties. Don't get me started."

Joan rarely said anything disparaging about her girlfriend, and Adriane took tremendous, if guilty, pleasure in those confederate moments. She had learned, however, not to add any criticisms of her own–which would be untoward and because nothing could make Joan leap faster to Molly's defense. Besides, Adriane knew her friend well enough to understand "don't get me started" had been said with only a mock-exasperation meant to convey that Molly's charms, quirky and untranslatable, far outweighed her flaws.

So, changing the subject: "Whose womb were you planning to use?"

After taking a slug of beer, Joan replied, "That we have not yet decided."

"You've been curious about the whole maternity thing, right?" Adriane tried to picture her friend pregnant. As a look, she could probably pull it off very well. Since falling in love, she had that beatific glow, which pregnancy would only enhance. And even before Molly, Joan radiated the wholesome calm of the well adjusted, though at this particular moment, she seemed fidgety and surprisingly wan.

"I haven't told my parents," she confessed.

"About having a baby?"

Joan nodded. "They love Molly, of course, but they sort of treat her like my 'special friend' and not, um, a 'spouse.'" Joan made little finger quotes around both these terms. "They may not be as happy about this idea as the Slezaks."

"Your parents will be happy for you. They'll be great about it," Adriane said confidently. "So, you two are 'spouses' now?"

"We're feeling pretty 'spousal,'" said Joan, regaining some of her glow. "By the way, we're going to Salisbury right after work on Friday, so we're going to have to miss poker."

"I want to be godmother."

Adriane stood abruptly and began pacing around the dining table, trying to piece together some kind of spontaneous argument. "You used to say I wasn't supportive enough of you and Molly, and

I'll grant you that. But isn't wanting to be godmother totally supportive?"

"Yes, it's supportive–"

"It's the epitome of support!"

"True, but–"

"Her sister already gets to be aunt."

"Yes, but–"

"Aren't I good enough to be part of your family, Joanie?"

"Of course you are." Her friend raised an eyebrow. "Is that what this is about?"

"Not merely." Why reduce this desire of hers, a desire Adriane had yet to fully grasp herself, to so simple a diagnosis? It did neither of them credit. "Just please keep an open mind while you're in Salisbury. That's all I ask." Adriane rinsed her empty beer bottle and set it on the counter, washed the Hello Kitty mug, returned it to the drain board, and put the bowl in the dishwasher. She woke her dog. "Come on, Barry."

Adriane left hopeful that she'd bought her candidacy a little time but still insecure about her readiness for the position, should she be called upon to serve. And so, Monday evening after work, after she took Barry for a long walk then settled him in front of the TV, Adriane drove herself to the mall. She hated the mall, but it had a big bookstore. Few things beat the pleasure of flipping through new books, hefting a prospective purchase, weighing its knowledge in your hands–a ritual full of promise. *Why*, she wondered now as she headed for the aisles, *didn't bookstores have shopping carts?*

Alas, she found just two, very lightweight, titles of any relevance (*What to Expect When You're Expecting a Godchild* and

Godparenting for Dummies) and so, her printed-matter craving still unmet, she began thumbing through volumes on adoption and assisted fertilization, and after she'd chosen a couple of those, she moved on to general child-rearing books, which she figured she'd share with Joan and Molly. Not as a bribe, exactly, but the gesture couldn't fail to demonstrate her interest.

The following Friday, her boss walked by her desk as Adriane was reading *Godparents: A Tribute.* Not bothering to conceal its cover, instead she asked him, "Does your daughter have godparents?"

He shook his head and said, "Hasn't even been baptized."

"Oh," said Adriane, trying to recall if she'd read any exceptions about that. Surely somewhere; even the Wicca got in on godparenting. More direct to her area of concern, she asked, "Do you think I'd make a good godmother?"

Garrett's jaw tightened and he glanced at his shoes, and murmured, "I think May-Annlouise might be uncomfortable with that."

"Not for *your* child!" Did everyone assume she was that pushy, meddlesome, and selfish? It always caught her by surprise how suddenly a conversation could go so badly. "For someone else's child."

"Oh, sure," he blurted, turning a wavy shade of purple, "for someone else's."

This exchange put her in a foul mood. The world, according to Adriane's growing suspicion, found her unfit for her new ambition.

Rather than search for Joan and Molly's replacements, she canceled that night's poker game, feeling unfit in any case for human company. At home, she poured herself a Manhattan and continued reading *Godparents: A Tribute*, from which she learned that Renaissance Florentines typically based their choice on financial and political alliances, and sometimes enlisted multiple godparents–as many as thirty. Now there was a fallback idea: Perhaps Molly's sister would be open to a joint arrangement. As to financial alliance, Adriane could offer to underwrite the cost of insemination; she could help sort through the paperwork of screening a viable candidate. Could, in effect, sponsor the sperm. There were a lot of practical and symbolic ways she could try to be helpful.

Early Saturday morning, she read testimonials from godparents and godchildren and parents about their children's godparents. To hear these people tell it, god-relationships seemed the ideal affiliation. Better than actual parenthood, it offered mutual love and appreciation with none of the judgment and psychodrama. Nor, Adriane supposed, any of the chronic anxiety she would have surely felt watching her own genes' twisted bloom. Godparenting would employ none of her biological nature and only the cherry-picked highlights of her nurture.

She learned that Gordon Parks was godparent to Malcolm X's daughter, as Telly Savalas was to Jennifer Aniston. Adriane pictured a young Jennifer Aniston–pre-tabloid, pre- *Friends*, prepubescent–riding around on Kojak's shoulders, both of them sucking lollipops, her little hands grabbing at his bald head–it seemed to Adriane a blissful image.

On page 156, she came across a checklist of qualities the author deemed essential in a good godparent:

1. *Enthusiasm for the godchild.* [Yes, Adriane had that.]
2. *Spirituality.* [Had some, but it needed work.]
3. *Sense of morality, ethics, decency.* [Check, check, check.]
4. *Optimistic attitude.* [Working on it.]
5. *Loyalty.* [In spades.]

6. *Responsibility.* [Ditto.]
7. *Patience and empathy.*

Adriane hoped impatient empathy was still acceptable but vowed to work on both. Overall, she felt the list reflected well on her and dog-eared the page. She continued to immerse herself in readings, as though cramming for an exam, and by dinner had even cracked open *The Godfather*, not the most practical of the texts she'd brought home, but immediately absorbing. Before long, she found herself enthralled by Puzo's underworld, where social outcasts rallied round their Family, a crime syndicate to be sure, but a clan nonetheless, held together by ironclad bonds and ferocious allegiance. Despite authorizing some truly repugnant behavior–that poor horse, after all, was a civilian–Don Corleone got to impart sagacious bon mots, such as: "Friendship is more than talent. It is more than government. It is almost the equal of family. Never forget that." The Godfather made it a point of personal pride to give his own godchild whatever he needed or wanted. And when she read how Sonny Corleone, as a boy, had brought home Tom Hagen, the little Irish orphan, and how Don Corleone sheltered the orphan and raised him as his own and eventually made him consigliere even though Tom wasn't Sicilian, it brought a tear to her eye. She fell asleep sometime after midnight, fully dressed, with the book open on her lap. And when she awoke eight hours later, the book was still there, pressing her stomach.

Before she'd even brushed her teeth, she called Joan's cell phone.

"What's up?" asked Joan, who fortunately sounded awake.

"Just wondering what's going on in Salisbury."

"Not much. We're heading out to church in a little while. Maybe take the kids over to a friend's pool later."

In Baltimore, Joan sometimes attended the Unitarian church, where in fact they'd met seven years earlier–at a book-group discussion of Salman Rushdie's *The Satanic Verses*. Chosen in solidarity against the ayatollah's fatwa (not the original ayatollah and the original fatwa, but his successor, who reaffirmed the fatwa–or the "paperback fatwa" as Adriane liked to think of it) the actual book turned out to be too long for most of the group, or so they explained when they next saw Adriane and Joan, the only two members who'd shown up that night.

"Do they have a Unitarian church in Salisbury?" Adriane asked now.

"I don't know," murmured Joan. "That's probably not where we're going today."

It would be very like Joan, obliging girl, to attend some alien church out of politeness to her hosts. To adopt their customs, lean into their gravitational pull. "Just promise me this, will you?" said Adriane. "Don't ask Brenda to be godmother until you guys have had a chance to hear me out. I'm putting together a compelling case."

Actually this case was still gelling in her mind, but it seemed built around the notion that she offered certain gifts–not just actual presents or even her willingness to chair the sperm search committee–but she'd gleaned a few things about life, its challenges, and its slippery struggles that a child or certainly a moody teenager someday might appreciate. Gifts that were currently going to waste.

"I can't promise," whispered Joan. "I don't know when she wants to bring it up."

"Can you speak louder?"

"Not really. Look," she said, "it might not even come up on this trip."

"She's totally itching to bring it up. I can tell. You've got to stop her."

"Joan!" someone, it sounded like Molly, called out in the background. "Do you want bananas or strawberries on your waffle?"

Was Molly making Joan's waffle or was Brenda? What kind of people put bananas on their waffles? Joan must have covered her mouthpiece, because Adriane couldn't hear the reply. Returning to the phone, her friend said, "You're getting carried away. We'll talk when I get back. I gotta go."

"That might be too late! Once Molly asks, I'm out of the running. It's not the kind of deal people rescind. It's a sacred bond. And I'm not getting carried away, I'm enthusiastic! That's, like, the most important thing!"

"You're exhausting," said Joan and hung up.

Adriane looked around her apartment and felt the walls closing in around her. She'd managed to piss off her friend, who never hung up on people, it wasn't in her nature, yet Adriane had driven her to it, which was not a good way to leave things at this crucial juncture. She started to call back, wanting to end on a more cordial note, but stopped in mid-digit, afraid Joan would not appreciate hearing the chirp of her phone again so soon. Adriane should try later. She brushed her teeth and drank some coffee, but lacked the patience to read her newspapers. Even at this early hour, Adriane could tell it was going to be oppressively muggy, the kind of weather that could swell a normal dose of the Sunday blahs into gravid gloom and overwhelm her feeble a/c. A day that required motion, the breeze of an open car window.

"What do you think, Barry? A little drive in the country?" Maybe Sandy Point State Park or some other beach this side of the bay. She packed a thermos of water, a blanket, and the newspapers, and after escorting Barry on a quick walk, the two of them climbed into her car. Not the most reliable transportation, a 1963 Checker Marathon, but she'd changed the oil recently and put in new coolant, and she was feeling optimistic about the old heap. It could get them to Sandy Point and back. They headed down to the beltway, then further south on Route 2, past Severna Park toward Annapolis–Barry's snout analyzing the winds with the same hopeful hunger Adriane brought to bookstores.

They switched to Route 50 now, driving east into the rising sun, the hum of tires, wheels, of movement filling her car and her head, and before she knew it, they were coming up on the exit for Sandy Point. Hardly a half hour had passed, and she wasn't ready to stop driving. Glinting on the horizon, the Chesapeake Bay Bridge came into view, inviting her to cross. To feel the satisfaction of straddling vast waters and reaching the other side of something. So she paid her toll and rolled onward and upward, marveling at the ingenuity of a structure like this, its balanced tension, its millions of rivets, each one, if you looked at it close, probably no bigger than an infant's fist, but together a concert of great strength and accomplishment. The bay itself was dotted with sailboats, and this enhanced her mood as well. In fact, she was feeling something very akin to an "optimistic attitude," and midway across she even let out a brief holler of jubilation. She decided to continue on to Salisbury. Hell, they were almost there already–another hour, tops. With luck, she'd arrive before any deal had been closed and would make her case in person, charm all parties involved–*reason* with them, as the Don might say–convey her sincerity and aptitude. Molly could watch her play with the sister's kids: board games, maybe catch. Adriane would demonstrate a skill set others had failed to appreciate in her before, domestic powers she'd only recently imagined herself.

As they drove deeper into the Delmarva Peninsula, Barry savored the rising farm smells, in particular the sweet-and-sour mash of chicken crap.

She would call Joan from Salisbury; surely her friend would soften up and invite her over when she learned Adriane had taken the trouble to drive out there. Adriane remembered that summer afternoon three years earlier–pre-Molly–when she'd wrangled field-box seats for Joan's parents, visiting from Chicago. The White Sox put on an eight-run fourth inning that delighted Mr. Lummis no end, and Adriane was glad to have delivered such an entertaining game for him. He laughed at her jokes and her instructions to poor Mike Mussina, who was getting shelled on the Oriole mound. Mrs. Lummis, also an exuberant fan, bought Adriane several humongous beers and more Polish sausage than she'd ever eaten at one time. Then they all staggered back to Joan's town house and played Scrabble, Joan and her mother on one team, Adriane and Mr. Lummis on the other. (He arranged their tray of letters to spell "lionize," for which she found the perfect and only spot on the board.) That was a good day.

She wondered what Molly's family would be like and whether Salisbury had a minor league farm team they could all go watch play. She kicked herself for not having thought to pack a toothbrush and change of clothes, just in case she was invited to stay the night–of course when she'd set out, Adriane needed to remind herself, she hadn't known she was going to Salisbury.

Ninety-three minutes after leaving home, she and her dog rolled into town. She was pleasantly surprised to find a quaint business center, kind of historic and intimate, and was further pleased to find in front of the hardware store a regular old-fashioned phone booth with a printed directory dangling under its stainless steel shelf. She dug some coins out of her ashtray and tried Joan's cell, but got the voice mail. They were all probably still in church, Adriane reasoned. She didn't leave a message and decided to look up Brenda's house and be waiting for everybody when they returned. It wasn't until she began leafing through the phone book, however, that the hole in this idea emerged. There were no Slezaks listed, and the more Adriane thought about it, Slezak would have been Molly's family name; her sister was surely the sort of wife to take a husband's name, and what that might be, Adriane had no idea.

So she thought about meeting up with them at church. How many of those could there be in a town this small? But the answer to that, she discovered in the Yellow Pages, was *a lot* (even a Unitarian). Though it was probably not the sort of tactic an aspirant godmother ought to employ, she ripped the church page out of the phone book and folded it into her pocket.

Ducking inside the hardware store, she bought a town map and, so she wouldn't show up at Brenda's empty-handed, one of the potted orchids sitting by the cash register. She then returned to her car and began plotting the coordinates for one of the Catholic church sites–figuring that was a good place to start. Five minutes later, she and Barry pulled into its lot. She parked under a shady tree and told him to wait in the car. As she walked across the gravel, she heard the muffled major chords of a choir. Peeking through a small window in the back door, she saw an assembly of men, women, and children, their backs toward Adriane as they stood facing the stage. There did not seem to be a white person in the room, and Adriane felt a disorienting jolt, as though she'd arrived late to a party, the only person wearing a costume. She shielded her eyes and squinted back toward the parking lot sign and saw she'd pulled into the African Methodist Episcopal Church. Up the road on the other side of the street, she could make out a spire, the church she'd been aiming for probably. She lingered, though, a little less sure about this idea of crashing a service. Also the music held her–what was it about gospel music, maybe that major third in the baseline, always promising to resolve toward something sweet and satisfying. If her local Unitarian church had a choir like this, she might even be tempted to return.

She jogged back to her car, then drove the quarter mile to St. Ambrose's. Pulling into its asphalt lot, this time she noticed the sign. Someone had posted an aphorism: "Don't use a period where God would use a comma." She'd always suspected that God, if He existed, would be a stickler for grammar. The windows were too high off the ground for her to peek into, and her wariness about entering the chapel had only grown in the past couple of minutes. She really hadn't dressed for it. It was almost noon, however, so she figured she'd wait in the parking lot. A row of air conditioners thrummed from a brick annex, and above them, the windows displayed a series of finger paintings: of the manger, an ark cresting the briny deep, and something that may or may not have been the head of John the Baptist. She gave Barry a drink of water from the thermos cup.

Soon, parishioners began their leisurely exodus from the service, pausing out front to shake hands with the priest and each other, moving forward in kinship clusters of three, four, occasionally more. A path was cleared to let through a very elderly woman in her wheelchair, steered with confident steadiness by an Adonis-like figure very likely her grandson, and Adriane slumped against the warm seat of her car and exhaled hoarsely. *I am nobody's daughter*, she brooded. *Nobody's mother, nobody's sister, nobody's aunt, nobody's niece.* As she watched the ongoing parade of congregants, she continued to list relations whose benefit she did not enjoy. Who was going to push her wheelchair out of church, if she ever decided to start attending again?

She drove back to the hardware store and tried calling Joan, who still hadn't turned her phone on. Unsure what to do–after all, Sunday services were probably ending all over town, as well–Adriane decided to explore the residential grid, in the hope of spotting Joan's Subaru. It was a feeble plan, but she was running out of bright ideas. She'd start close to "downtown" and radiate outward. She and Barry passed a number of charming Victorian wood-shingled homes and, as they branched out further, brick ranches with short chain-link fences and jungle gyms, the occasional Big Wheel, skateboard, or scooter left trustingly parked on the sidewalk. She crossed out each block on her map as she covered it, Barry at her side, panting from the heat. The orchid seemed to be holding up just fine. It was a good choice of present, and Adriane felt glad she hadn't stopped at a regular flower store for a bouquet that would have surely begun wilting by now. She wondered what the home of a home economist looked like. Would it be filled with prototypes of classroom assignments? Hand-stitched cozies for the toaster and blender? A refrigerator stocked with nourishing, if not particularly glamorous, foods? As she drove, she found herself thinking about bean casseroles and turkey meatloaf, and her stomach began to grumble.

Paused at a stop sign, she saw on her left a baseball field and a kids' T-ball game–bleachers packed with parents and siblings. They cheered the next batter's hit, cheered when the shortstop picked up the ball, cheered when he threw it toward first base, and cheered when the first baseman caught it, even though the runner had long since tagged safe. Even the players daydreaming in the outfield were singled out for cheers. To the side of the bleachers, a young woman sat on a picnic blanket, giving haircuts to a pair of identical twin boys.

A car horn beeped, and Adriane glanced in her rearview mirror and saw she was clogging the way. She pulled over to the curb and let the other driver pass, then set off again into the neighborhood. At ten miles per hour, her Checker chugged like a tugboat. If she ever did become a godmother, she would have to get seatbelts installed, she decided; those infant car seats didn't just anchor themselves.

Adriane circled back to the pay phone and tried Joan's cell again, but still got the voice mail. And so she continued her compulsively slow drive, and as the afternoon crept on, the air began filling with the smells of charcoal cookouts. Passing one backyard, Adriane gazed, and Barry sniffed, at a shaded picnic table crowded with platters of chicken. Her car seemed to be steering itself, a satellite orbiting this galaxy of suburban family leisure. At one point she saw a Subaru wagon, dark green like Joan's, and Adriane accelerated toward the driveway, but when she pulled alongside, saw a Delaware license plate. She slowed her car to a complete stop, just to double check.

From somewhere in the distance, she heard a faint soprano call out, "Marco." It seemed to come from the other side of the street. "Polo," chimed another childlike voice, and Adriane could see, through the crosshatching of a chain-link fence, the leviathan outline of an aboveground swimming pool. Her spirits swelled at the recollection of her friend's afternoon plan: taking the kids swimming at a neighbor's. "Marco?" came the tiny question. "Polo!"

She turned off the ignition, and her Checker chugged into silence. "Stay," she told Barry, then strode across the quiet residential street toward the brick, ranch-style house, an old van parked in its driveway. She wondered whether she should ring the doorbell, then decided to case the scene discreetly first. Not glimpsing any adults in back, she nonetheless opened the galvanized latch and let herself in for a better look–("Marco?" "Polo!")–and wondered again if she should knock on the front door–("Marco?" "Polo!")–or maybe she could just ask the kids ("Marco?" "Polo!"). She was mouthing the words as she heard them, that ancient call and response dredged up from her own childhood memory–sneaking with her father into the Sheraton's rooftop pool, on the east side of town, past the prison, where she would play with whatever children happened to be staying there. A pickup game of Marco Polo. Never the same kids twice.

A metal stepladder led up one side of the oval pool–how many thousands of gallons did this thing hold, she wondered–as the call and response seemed to grow more rapid. She peeked over the edge and saw two young Aryan-looking tykes swimming amongst a flotsam of toys, the girl wearing an underwater mask, its attached snorkel dangling loosely to the side as she called out "Marco," and a boy in cutoff shorts, frayed like the fingers of a jellyfish, trying to keep out of reach ("Polo!"). He was cheating, answering "Polo" only after he'd put more distance between himself and the girl.

"Marco!" the girl said again. And this time Adriane answered, along with the boy. That was part of the game: There could be multiple Polos taunting a single Marco–it was all coming back to her. The two children looked up at her, and the boy quickly called out, "Mom! There's a lady in the backyard!"

Popping up from beyond the far side of the pool: a woman

wearing a string bikini, sunglasses, and hair curlers large enough to be lemonade cans.

"What?" she demanded, striding closer. Her shoulders glistened with oil.

"I was just looking for Brenda's family," said Adriane, pausing hopefully. Maybe the universe of Salisbury pool owners was tight, always crossing paths in the chlorine aisle of that hardware store. "Her husband sells insurance. Do you know them?"

"No, I don't know them," the woman said. "Why would I know them?"

Adriane backed down the ladder, barking her knee on one of the rungs. She winced and took a couple steps toward the woman. "Her maiden name is Slezak."

"Don't you come into my yard and talk to my kids."

"Hey, lady," called the boy's voice. "Put 'em up."

Adriane glanced behind her and saw both children leaning over the pool's edge, training enormous water cannons on her, the girl sighting along the barrel through her fogged goggles.

"Okay, you win," said Adriane as cheerfully as possible, and raised her hands. "I'm unarmed. Not even wearing a wire."

"What the hell are you talking about?" asked the mother, who didn't get that her kids had turned this tense moment into a game, which Adriane was only too glad to play along with. *Parents*, she thought with a sigh, *can be so obtuse.*

"I'll tell you guys everything you want to know," she said. "Who sent me. How you can get to them. We ought to be able to make a deal. We're all reasonable people here, with interests to protect. I have friends who could be very useful to you and your–your spice trade–"

The blasts struck her shoulder blade and the back of her head, knocking her a step forward. It was like being hit with water balloons–cold, wet, and more startling than painful. The shots left her instantly drenched.

"Good one, guys," she said, reaching behind to pluck the sodden T-shirt away from her back. This only prompted a new volley, which propelled her farther, as though the children were hosing a leaf down the driveway. She continued limping toward the gate, and after about a dozen more steps was finally out of range. She heard the children laughing. Her knee, she noticed from the water's sting, was bleeding.

"I'm calling the police," said their mother.

Adriane accelerated her limp and got in the car. Barry licked the wetness from her neck as she started the engine. They drove quickly back to the main street and stopped by the hardware store pay phone one last time.

Come on, pick up, Joanie, but the cell phone was still off.

Maybe the cops were looking for her already. Her car would be conspicuous enough. Adriane's visit seemed at an end; there was little recourse but to skip town before she got herself into serious trouble. She found her way back to Route 50, then headed west.

For the next twenty minutes, her heart continued to race, as she thought of those kids and their hostile reception. You couldn't just startle children and expect them to want to play with you. She should have remembered that from her own pool days at the Sheraton. You had to act very, very cool and pretend to be interested in your own Nerf ball and just hope someone might notice you and think to include you.

She continued to tremble halfway to Baltimore–it had been a long time since she'd remembered to eat anything–so she stopped at a crab shanty and ordered half a bushel and a half pitcher of beer and a cup of water for Barry, who rested in the shade beneath her picnic table. When her dinner arrived, she began hammering at it, taking out her frustrations. Crab shrapnel clung to her sweaty T-shirt, and she managed to lacerate her fingertips on her food's armor as she extracted teensy bits of meat. Barry retreated from the noise, but made an effort to be sociable after she rinsed off some morsels of lung for him. The carcasses continued to pile up around her.

The week passed with excruciating slowness. Adriane longed to call Joan but restrained herself, and Joan exercised restraint in turn. When were she and Molly coming back? Wednesday–or was it Thursday? At night, Adriane continued to read *The Godfather*, though it no longer enthralled her quite as much. The violence seemed less principled than before. Michael went on a murderous rampage and was kind of an asshole when all was said and done. Adriane worried that her friends might be avoiding her.

So her relief was great when Joan and Molly showed up for poker on Friday. Adriane tried to read their facial expressions for clues to what was going on. Just a few hands into the game, however, she no longer had to wait, because Monique asked, bluntly, "So, where do things stand with the baby?"

"That's on hold," said Molly, crossing her arms in front of another Hello Kitty tank top, this one dotted with strawberries. "Indefinitely."

No one dared asked why, so final-sounding was Molly's "indefinitely," and Adriane took some small comfort that at least she hadn't asked the nosy question. Molly shuffled the spare deck with mechanical singleness of purpose.

Tamara timidly asked if there was any more asiago. Adriane said, "Deal me out," and took the opportunity to disappear into the kitchen, where she opened the refrigerator, stuck her head in, and took a deep breath of cold air.

Joan said the same and soon appeared beside her. "I'm sorry I've haven't called," she whispered into the fridge. "We've had a bad week. Much turmoil."

"What happened?" Adriane decided it was okay to ask.

As it turned out, the sister, according to Joan, harbored a long simmering antipathy toward Molly's "lifestyle." This came out on the last day of their visit, after Molly had proposed the godmother idea. Joan finger quoted the word "lifestyle" and a few others as well. Being gay was "okay" as long as Molly's "friendships" were "self-contained" and "discreet," but when bringing children into the world entered the equation, Brenda could no longer "abide" and had to make her position clear.

"I knew something was fishy when she'd given us twin beds," Joan whispered, hands finally at rest. "Between you and me, I'm very pissed at Molly."

"At Molly?" Adriane regarded her friend closely.

"This whole idea of having a baby seemed built around Brenda's blessing. Which is totally stupid. It's just pathetic."

Adriane's face grew warm, as though this talk of ulterior, unworthy motives reflected on her somehow. She closed the refrigerator and turned to add some tap water to the potted orchid on her counter.

"I can't believe she didn't warn me something like this might happen." Joan peeked out at the living room and sighed. "I do feel terrible for her though. You won't believe what else her sister said."

She leaned close to Adriane's ear now. "She said she was uncomfortable with Molly staying her kids' godmother."

Adriane winced and muttered, *"Infamita!"* It was her turn to peek at the living room. "Poor Molly," she whispered, surprised by how much she meant it. She watched Molly's stoic profile, and saw her sitting on a stoop in Salisbury, overlooking her sister's large backyard–wearing her Hello Kitty tank and enduring a sweaty arm draped over her shoulder, as her sister swore they were still family and *nothing* could ever change that.

10. sex party

fall 1999–new year's eve

Much as Adriane had loved her father–which was too much, in fact–his golf clubs remained an artifact from a dark and crippling chapter of her past, one she still hoped to overcome some day, ideally by the start of the new millennium, which gave her about six more weeks. So she'd placed an ad. And now, her potential buyer on his way upstairs, she lugged the beige vinyl golf bag out of her hall closet and examined its pockets, where she found a glove, a few tees, and a monogrammed ball: AG–her father's initials, as well as her own. Also a small pewter flask. Empty. And a scorecard dated September 20, 1982. Apparently, he'd golfed a seventy-eight that morning, a great score and the best of his foursome. Though it was hard to surmise the whole story based solely on score. They could have been betting on number of holes won or even hole-by-hole.

She was pretty sure the faintly penciled "thirty" in the upper left corner stood for thirty thousand dollars.

She noticed for the first time a few brown freckles on the side of the bag and began scratching them off with her fingernail. And then, a blip of panic when she realized they must be flecks of dried blood. There were more of them, all up and down the length of the bag, and she tried to scrape off as many as she could, but soon her dog began growling from the couch and a second later the front doorbell rang.

"Coming." She wiped her fingers on her jeans. In the hallway stood a tall young man with sandy hair and studious but chic glasses.

"Stan," he said and shook her hand with vigor while her dog came over to sniff the cuffs of his chinos.

"Here they are," she said, leading him to the bag.

He nodded toward the clubs and said, "How old did you say they were?"

"Brand new in 1981," she said, "and haven't been used since '82."

Not since September 20, in fact, the day her father had checked into the Quality Inn on York Road and blown his brains out. But of course she omitted that background detail. Adriane had not visited her dad's grave in almost a year, not since her fibroid operation. She felt guilty about it, but she'd needed to put some extra distance between herself and death.

Stan was rustling around the barrel of the bag. He withdrew an iron and asked, "Mind if I take a few swings? I'll be careful."

"Feel free," she said nervously, hoping she'd gotten most of the blood off. Her dog was growling softly. "Barry." She called him to her. "Let the man swing."

Stan grasped the club, took up a stance in the center of her living room, rocked his hips back and forth. He seemed to know what he was doing and wielded a fluid golf swing, like someone comfortable in his own body. Adriane stood to the side with her dog and watched. Each time Stan would approach the imaginary ball, he'd glance over at her first, as though this were part of his method. He went on to test most of the irons this way. Unsheathing the three-wood, he asked, "Do you play?"

"When I was little I used to watch my dad and his friends," she said.

Adriane decided to go wash the dishes while Stan continued to make up his mind. But no sooner had she left him alone than he called after her. She ran back in, afraid he'd discovered something appalling in the bag.

"These are beautiful clubs," he said. "But to be honest, I was hoping for something newer. When you said in your ad, *barely used*, I assumed *new*."

"Oh, you're right." She raised a hand to her mouth. "I should have made that clear."

"Hey that's okay! Don't worry about it."

"But that really was misleading," she said. "Would it help if I cut the price?"

"No, no don't do that. I'm happy to get gouged at the pro shop. I just thought I might be able to scoop up a bargain."

"I feel terrible," she said, which was true, especially because the guy was being so nice about it. His lack of disappointment seemed almost surreal. "What if you took the clubs," she proposed, "no money down, and tried them out for a couple weeks? And if you like them, pay me whatever they're worth to you, and if not, just bring them back."

He laughed and said she drove a hard bargain. He would agree to her generous terms on the condition she go to the movies with him.

Adriane had bad luck with impulsive dates, but she did want to disburden herself of the clubs. Plus the movie was a matinee and a documentary–which seemed safer.

Together they squeezed the golf bag into the small hatchback of his car, a brand new hybrid-powered model, the Insight.

"I've never seen anything like this," said Adriane.

"Honda's trying to get my firm jazzed about it, so they loaned us a few," he told her. "Sixty-three miles to the gallon–what do you think?"

"Yes," she said, amazed. "I *think*."

"What do you drive?"

Adriane drove the car she'd inherited from her father. "A '63 Checker Marathon," she said.

Stan smiled at her quizzically, as though unsure whether she was joking, then replied at last, "Old school."

The documentary was about Biosphere 2, a self-sustaining colony in the middle of the Arizona desert, which, though it ran into difficulties–all the bees dying, for instance–impressed Adriane tremendously. The project's scale. The ambition of it. An alternate universe, just about. After the movie, she and Stan went to a Thai restaurant around the corner and sat in a round booth, their knees occasionally touching–which gave Adriane a little brush of adrenaline each time–and talked about alternative energy sources. As an investment banker specializing in the energy and transportation sectors, Stan knew a lot about it. He was also a member of something called the Greater Baltimore Polyamory Society. The first few times he mentioned it, Adriane heard "Pollyanna Society," but basically the GBPS, if she understood right, was some kind of swingers group. The way he described it, though, made it sound more principled and philosophical–even scientific.

Later, outside her lobby, he confidently took her in his arms and, before kissing her good night, blew gently across her forehead. He had just been explaining wind farming, so this odd gesture seemed almost fitting, and she felt a current of energy in herself, spreading from her forehead, down her face, and into her lungs, stomach, and hips. She'd never imagined someone could make renewable fuels sexy.

Adriane drained her pint, then threw a dart that missed the target entirely. "He's environmentally aware!" she shouted over the jukebox in the Fell's Point Stout House. "And a good kisser!" Her friends Joan and Shelley nodded with appreciation.

"And how did we meet this upright smoocher?" Shelley asked crisply.

"He came to buy my father's clubs!" Adriane shouted, then recounted the misunderstanding over *barely used* and *new* and how bad she'd felt about it.

"So he's environmentally aware for a golfer," noted Shelley.

"That's a cute meeting story you could tell your grandkids someday. Do you think he might be the *one*?" asked Joan, while Shelley rolled her eyes and chugged her beer.

Adriane blushed. "Stan's a *poly*," she said, quoting his lingo. "I don't think they're allowed to be the *one*."

"He's a what?" shouted Joan.

"That's the Greek word for *player*," said Shelley. She stood behind the toe line and threw a bull's-eye.

Adriane tried to explain Stan's affiliation with the GBPS, whose members, men and women alike, felt committed to more than one lover and to explore new paradigms in interpersonal relationships. Some members, she now recalled, were "married" to a "primary" partner, but she wasn't entirely sure how that worked. As she relayed this to her friends, she felt a little foolish; everything had sounded more reasonable coming from Stan. Maybe not completely reasonable, but more so; she couldn't convey, for instance, the visionary enthusiasm that animated everything he said. Adriane had never met anyone so forward-looking.

"He's invited me to a New Year's Eve party." She unfolded the invitation, digitally printed on textured paper and featuring a tasteful clip-art photo of a wisteria vine. "Read this."

"What's a Sex Party?" asked Joan, staring at the page.

"What does it sound like, dear?" Shelley quipped.

The three women perused the invitation in the bar's dim light.

Joan finally said, "I thought we were supposed to do something New Year's Eve."

"Oh, I didn't say I was going to this thing," said Adriane, collecting the darts. "But it would be mind-blowing. It's flattering just to be invited, don't you think?" she asked her friends. "Not everyone is up for crossing this kind of frontier."

"That's crazy. You can't go," said Joan. "*He's* crazy."

"Why?" asked Adriane, pacing back and forth in front of the dartboard. "Because he's honest about his sexuality?" Really, when she thought about it, Stan was a man of passion and principle, though in a way that many people, say Adriane's mother–were she alive to comment on it–might fail to appreciate.

"I know you, Adriane," said Joan, in an ominous tone of voice. "You'll hate yourself the next day."

"But what if he's my paradigm shift?" Adriane had been trying to effect a paradigm shift for some time now, had been looking for ways to cultivate *abandon*, which meant behaving in a manner heedless of consequence, indifferent to loss. Or, if not quite *indifferent*, at least somewhat less distressed by it. She had yet to manage this. And frankly, with the new millennium just over a month away, Stan's sex party seemed like a make-or-break opportunity, a crucible in which to reforge herself. If she wasn't even willing to rise to such an obvious challenge when it presented itself . . . ! She winced and glanced down at her thumb, whose skin she'd managed to break with a dart point. Anyway, if she couldn't rise to such an obvious challenge when it presented itself, she might as well chuck the pretenses and admit she was stuck for good in her rut of fear, disappointment, and regret.

"Want me to see if you and Molly can come along, Joanie?" she asked. It would be nice to seed the event with a couple friendly faces.

"I'm not even going to answer that," said Joan.

"Shelley? How about it?"

"Been there, done that," muttered her more libertine friend. "But you should go."

"Do you think?"

"'She who prizes her good reputation is subject to at least as many torments as she who behaves neglectfully of it.'"

"Who's that quote from?" asked Joan.

"The Marquis de Sade," said Shelley, matter of factly.

Joan made a sour face. "What a reasonable source of postfeminist wisdom."

Surprisingly, Joan's objections felt more satisfying; they gave Adriane something to push against in her own mind. The more Joan protested, the more justified Adriane felt to consider going.

Over the next few weeks, Adriane and Stan saw a lot of each other. They viewed an exhibit at the Walters Art Gallery on the progressivist underpinnings of the Arts and Crafts Movement, called "My Fair Chair," and another utopian documentary, this one about the Oneida "Perfectionists," a nineteenth-century commune that prized silversmithing and free love. So the idea of polyamory was starting to seem new only to Adriane. In a way, it was nice that earlier pioneers had presumably worked out some of the kinks.

She and Stan had long conversations about the stock market; he'd been working with a company called Enron that had found amazing new ways to wring efficiencies out of the marketplace. In turn, she taught him a thing or two about betting on pro football. Unlike her father, Adriane was a disciplined sports gambler, not a compulsive one. She was consistently able to generate an income from this, the sole area of her life in which she felt successful. One Sunday, with a hundred dollars riding on the Broncos to beat the Seahawks, Stan shouted jubilantly at her TV set throughout an exhilarating overtime, then raised his fists in triumph.

"It feels like I'm stealing," he crowed.

"One gets over that," she said, smoothing an errant lock of his hair. She opened her wallet and counted out the hundred dollars her bookie would be replenishing the next day. Actually he'd be giving Adriane $600, as she'd placed her own bet on the Broncos. "So, what are you going to do with your winnings?" She held the money halfway between them, as though she would only reward the right answer.

"I'd like to take you to dinner," he said.

"You sure you don't have a date with Polly Amory?" she asked, drawing the wad of bills back toward her slightly.

His brow creased. "Who?"

"All these other women you're seeing, Stan. When are you finding the time for them?" Adriane hadn't meant to ambush him; it just came out. She wished instantly it hadn't. Still, she was pleased when he said:

"I'm not seeing anyone else just now."

"Really?" she said, and took a moment to admire his long lashes.

"I wouldn't withhold something important like that from you. I'd have told you everything. Who she was, or he was. What we did. How I felt."

"He?"

Stan shrugged. "It's possible."

Adriane slid his winnings into his shirt pocket and got up from the sofa. She walked to the French window and stood with her back toward him. Her pleasure from a moment before had evaporated. Not so much because he could entertain lovers of either gender, but because her own need for reassurance struck her as banal and regressive. It made her sick that the millennium was almost upon her and she was no closer to achieving abandon, or even just a workaday nonchalance, than she had been a couple years before. She looked out the windowpanes, past the empty flowerpot and wrought iron balconet, toward the sidewalk five stories below. Five stories really wasn't that far a drop. Or, rather, it wouldn't take long at all to get there–to the ground. Though she knew this was an unhealthy sign, she'd lately allowed herself the occasional morbid fantasy. Not just the usual abstractions about death, but the hard details. As she pictured it now: She would land chin first, her lower teeth piercing the tender pink roof of her mouth, her lips offering the sidewalk a kiss of scorching passion. Then her right shoulder would touch concrete, forming the briefest triangle with her flattened cheekbone before her neck would snap left, and her corpse, her abandoned corpse, might finally settle into repose.

"What if I don't want to know everything?" she said.

Stan joined her by the window and turned her chin upward. She closed her eyes and let him gently blow against her brow, her heart refilling like a sail. She pressed her mouth against his, hungrily tasting the broth of him. Sucked on his tongue and began to fumble with his belt.

Clasping his hand over hers, he said calmly, "I think we should wait."

"For what? Your sex party?"

"It's not my party, but yes, for something like that. Just so we don't go into this thinking it's, um, traditional."

She let go of his belt. "Did I say anything about exclusivity here?"

"No, you didn't, but the subtext. Our first time together," he mused, "should be with other people."

Adriane felt an ache of affection: She could never love someone who wasn't at least a little strange, hard to fathom, and out of reach. And she couldn't really blame him for wanting to sleep with other people. In theory at least. She said, "I'll need more information to even consider going to this thing, this sex thing."

They returned to the couch, where her dog lay his snout across her leg as Stan cheerfully discussed the details, at great length.

"So I wouldn't have to do anything I didn't want to," she made sure.

"Absolutely."

He repeated the rule against drugs or alcohol, then added, "It's a potluck."

"Not even wine with dinner?" She tried to recall what she'd drunk over their past few dates and wondered if he thought she had a problem. "What kind of orgy doesn't have alcohol?" she demanded.

"It's not an orgy," he reminded her. "It's a philosophy. And a way of life." He recommended several books on the subject. "It's not that we don't like a glass of wine with dinner as much as the next person–we just don't want anyone waking up the next morning with regrets."

"You're kidding," said Adriane. "You've actually woken up without regrets?"

Stan smiled and said, "You've got that great sense of humor, Adriane."

She smiled back, but secretly she was imagining a utopia whose citizens awoke every morning without regrets, the thought of which brought a small lump to her throat.

The night of the party, she placed a smoked pig's ear on some newspaper for Barry, though they both knew he wouldn't touch it until she returned. She hated to leave him alone on New Year's Eve–the distant squeal of party favors made him whimper. Also tonight's special agenda only added to her guilt–as though she were hiding something unwholesome from him.

He growled softly when the buzzer rang, and she told the

intercom she'd be right down. Gathering up her cheese platter, she kissed Barry between the eyes and felt deeply hypocritical for urging him to be a good boy. He regarded her without judgment, as she tiptoed toward the front door and closed it softly behind her.

In the car, Stan greeted her with kiss. A deep kiss, even more tender and romantic than his usual. She felt an urge to suggest they skip the party and go back upstairs together, but by then they were already underway. Stan had yet to remove the golf clubs from the back of his car, and they rattled with each stop and turn, as he drove toward the northern suburbs.

At last, he stopped in front of an ivy-covered, Tudor-style mansion, faced her, and said, "You're trembling."

She'd been trembling from the moment she'd gotten in the car, having slept poorly the night before. She'd lain awake obsessing about her utopian society–which she'd named Piafville, after the French chanteuse–where everyone greeted one another with the affirmation: *Je ne regrette rien.*

"I really appreciate your coming tonight," he told her, reaching into the back for his tureen.

How much she wanted him, and how close he now seemed; all she need do was love him in a room full of other people. Maybe it was a huge mistake, but at least it would be her last mistake of the millennium.

"Glad to be here," she said and unbuckled her seat belt.

Carrying her cheese platter up the flagstone path, she asked, "What are the hosts' names again?"

"Guillaume, he's a caterer, from France, and his wife, Sarah."

Adriane comforted herself: At least Guillaume would have heard of Edith Piaf.

An attractive, zaftig woman with Asian features, wearing pleated slacks and a floral silk blouse, answered the door and smiled broadly at Stan. "Happy New Year!"

"Hey, Sarah, this is Adriane Gelki."

"Sarah Hsu," said the hostess, extending her hand. She inhaled deeply in the vicinity of Adriane's cheese platter. "*Formidable!* Guillaume will be thrilled."

Sarah led the way to a brightly lit living room, where seven guests sat in various pieces of what Adriane deemed Daughters-of-the-American-Revolution furniture, which went okay enough with the house, but still surprised her. The group paused in their conversation and each rose to shake hands with the new arrivals. Introductions blurred; a man named Max Pipkin, a Patty or Patsy; it was all Adriane could do to remember the hosts for now. A girl of about twenty introduced herself as Lisette–was she the au pair Stan had mentioned?–and handed Adriane a glass of mineral water with a lemon wedge. Fair and lithe, Lisette radiated a wholesome prettiness. Otherwise, Stan was right: The group seemed ordinary enough, not the menagerie of circus freaks and porno stars Adriane had worried about.

"We've just been discussing *The Ganesha Epiphanies*," said a woman with large green eyes and a long braid. "The author treks through India in search of the Twenty-Three Abundant Truths."

Adriane guffawed appreciatively, as she thought was expected of her, but the braided woman scowled. "Don't mock what you haven't experienced."

"I'm sorry. I was just . . ." said Adriane, glancing around for Stan, who'd wandered off. "So you recommend this book?"

"It changed my life," said the woman.

"I'm up for *that*," Adriane said, reaching for a pen. "What are some of the truths?"

"You really have to read the book."

"Doesn't he explain in there somewhere," said a petite, birdlike woman, wearing a nice set of pearl studs, "that we are in control of our own reincarnation? And we can actually choose the manner and form of our return?"

"Yes," said the braided one. "But not everyone can do it. It takes discipline, an alignment of vision, and a little planning."

In her teens, Adriane had coursed through all manner of religious texts, including some of the Vedas, but she couldn't remember how genuine this particular wrinkle sounded; still, she admired its optimism and nodded eagerly.

The group looked at her. Someone asked, "What have you been reading?"

"Um, right now?" She had in fact been rereading an old textbook called *Tragedy: A View of Life*, but was afraid now of the first impression that might make–snobbish or, worse, glum–so she said, "I'm kind of between books at the moment."

"I always have five or six books going at once," announced the braided one, whose name seemed to be Emma. "I love books. I love everything about them. The way they smell. The way they look on shelves. I arrange them by color, so when I'm in the mood for a green book, I look in my green section."

A slender gray-haired man, wearing a striped apron, swept past them carrying a bowl filled with couscous and lamb.

"*Bonsoir*, newcomer," he called over his shoulder. On his way back to the kitchen, he paused to kiss Adriane on each cheek and drew in a deep breath with his large aquiline nose. "What a charming blazer," he said, taking in the line of her figure. "She is lovely," he added, suddenly in the third person. "Where have you been keeping her?"

She realized Stan had suddenly returned to her side.

"Where were you?" Adriane whispered.

Instead of answering, he introduced Guillaume, who took another greedy sniff before running off toward the kitchen. *"Enchanté, chérie!"* he called over his shoulder.

Stan nodded now toward the birdlike woman with the pearl earrings and said, "Wanda here curated 'My Fair Chair.'"

"Oh, I loved that show!" said Adriane, overstating it, but she wanted, well, she wanted to be *liked*. "I had no idea an armoire could be . . . political!"

A tiny bell rang. "Dinner is served!" announced Sarah Hsu. "Daniel will be here soon. He asked us not to wait."

"He had a better party to go to before this?" asked a preppily dressed young man, whose name was F. Chipper Something.

"No," said Max Pipkin, moving toward the table. "He's coming straight from temple. He's Orthodox," Max added.

"You're kidding," said the preppy.

Adriane felt her bladder tense at the mention of this person. She knew an orthodox Daniel and truly did not want to run into him tonight. She turned toward the man named Max and asked: "Does Daniel look like George Clooney? But with a yarmulke?"

"You should tell him that," said Max. "He'd be flattered."

Adriane took a deep breath, excused herself, and trotted toward the bathroom. Locking the door behind her, she splayed one palm on the marble countertop and cupped mouthfuls of water from the tap with the other. She sat down on the toilet lid and pressed a hand across her breast to feel the reassuring heft of the flask hidden in her jacket pocket. Just before Stan picked her up, she had rinsed the old thing out and filled it with vodka. It wasn't that she was eager to violate the group rules, but just knowing the flask was there slowed her racing heart a little; maybe she wouldn't have to actually drink. She brought it out for a moment and tightened the knob just to feel its ribbed surface across her fingertips, then put it away. This party was the last place she wanted to run into Daniel Minick, manager of Shalom Gardens Cemetery, where her father was buried and where her mother would also be buried, if only Minick had allowed it. Adriane took a last look in the mirror and said, *Je ne regrette rien.*

Back in the dining room, everyone had taken a seat. Stan hadn't saved one for her but instead sat flanked by Lisette on his left and Guillaume at the table head. There were only two open chairs, adjacent to each other, so Adriane took one.

"Guillaume, that turkey is huge!" said Wanda.

"Not just a turkey, *chérie*. It's a *turducken*: a turkey merged with chicken and duck."

The group applauded, and Adriane thought, *Holy cow.* "Is that some kind of genetically modified food of the future?" she asked, and Guillaume smiled indulgently and several of the guests laughed.

"No, they are stuffed, the smaller birds into the larger," he explained, slicing a deep cross section of pinkish fowl.

Adriane blushed pink as well, bit her lip, and repeated affirmatively to herself: *Je ne regrette rien; je ne regrette rien. . . .*

"Guillaume," Stan was saying, a bit testily, "I see you sprinkled minced apples on my butternut squash soup."

"I'm sorry, my dear boy, is that not a good enhancement? Shall I fish them out?"

"No, that's all right. But let's consult together next time," said Stan, and he smiled warmly in the caterer's direction. Guillaume smiled back with easy charm. Kind of an odd exchange, noted

Adriane, who was still preoccupied with her turducken embarrassment.

"Sarah, what's the word on the street?" Max Pipkin called from his end of the table. "Our bathroom remodel's way over budget; we could use another TelePrimus."

"Well," said Sarah, passing a salver of green beans almondine, "I'm very keen on Global Crossing. They've been laying leagues of fiber-optic cable that will grow the sector exponentially. I've used their video conferencing. You wouldn't believe the speed and clarity . . ."

As Sarah went on, Wanda with the pearl earrings leaned toward Adriane and asked, "How did you and Stan meet?"

The question caught Adriane off guard–it seemed so ordinary, so couple-y. She told her golf-clubs anecdote, but softly, as though it were inappropriate.

"That's an unusual way to meet," Wanda enthused. "That's a story you can tell your grandchildren."

Adriane glanced around nervously, hoping Stan couldn't hear any of this "traditional" talk of grandchildren, its old-paradigm, if consoling, notion of legacy. But he seemed lost in conversation with Lisette the au pair.

A half hour into dinner, the doorbell rang.

"That must be Daniel," Sarah announced and went to answer.

Adriane felt her body temperature rise and a sudden dampness under her arms.

Entering the dining room, wearing a black peacoat and carrying a covered Pyrex casserole: Daniel Minick. Adriane recognized him immediately. Almost dashing he looked, and yet, as Adriane remembered him, a complete jerk.

"There he is," said Max Pipkin.

"Shabbat shalom," Daniel answered.

"Happy New Year, Daniel," said Sarah. "My goodness, your face is red. You look frozen."

"I walked," he explained. "It's . . . it's longer than I thought."

"You walked?" several people asked at the same time.

"It's a Sabbath thing," he replied, and that seemed to put an end to it.

Sarah reached for his casserole and asked, "Shall I reheat this?"

"That's okay. It's good cold." He put the casserole down on the table; there was a plate on top, which he set at the open place next to Adriane, then extracted a spatula as well as a knife and fork from his coat pockets. Sarah introduced him to the rest of the guests.

He seemed to know Max and Wanda, and he cocked his head at Adriane a moment before his eyes widened. "How weird! How totally weird is this! I almost didn't recognize you!" he said, as he sat down next to her. "I haven't run into you in ages!" he added, meaning the cemetery.

"Well, I've *been* there," Adriane lied.

Across the table, Stan was holding the platter of carved fowls for Lisette's selection, and he seemed oblivious to any other conversation.

"Are those kosher utensils?" asked someone named Patty Romero, who worked at Sarah and Stan's firm. Daniel acknowledged that they were.

"So, Max," began preppy F. Chipper, "does this mean Dan's more Jewish than you?"

"That depends on how you look at these things," said Max, reaching for a tray of manicotti. "I'm certainly not Orthodox."

"Max is un-Orthodox," said Wanda.

Adriane turned to Daniel. "Why are you here? I mean, are you a regular?"

"Max invited me," he said, pointing his kosher fork in Max's direction.

"Are you even allowed to do this?" she challenged him. "Isn't it a little too . . . New Age?"

Daniel sighed and removed the foil from his casserole dish. He turned to Adriane and said, "Brisket?"

She shook her head.

"The Talmud frowns on the idea," he conceded, lifting some potatoes to his plate. "But the Torah doesn't exactly proscribe it. So, I guess you could say I'm working the gray area. I might just watch."

Although she had taken comfort in the idea that she herself could just watch, it suddenly occurred to her there should be a strict rule against it.

"Don't you have a fiancée?" she demanded. "What's she doing tonight?"

"We're . . . no more," Daniel said in such a strangled way it was clear he'd been recently dumped. Adriane knew she shouldn't feel any pleasure from this, but she couldn't help herself. "Max thought I should come. To get me out of myself," he continued glumly. "And you?" he asked her, "are you here with someone?"

She pointed to Stan and volunteered the anecdote of their meeting. "Aren't you going to say that's a story I could tell my grandchildren?"

"It's not that great a story." He put a forkful of brisket in his mouth and smiled with that infuriating righteousness of his that she always associated with death.

The blood-speckled golf bag, her father's suicide–her anecdote's tarry depths burbled in her throat. Adriane excused herself and trotted down the hallway–past Sears-style family portraits of Guillaume, Sarah, and three angelic Eurasian children, *who were where tonight*? she wondered–then made it to the bathroom just in time. A deep heave, silent except for its splash into the toilet. Luckily the exhaust fan made a loud clatter. Little bits of turducken floated in the bowl, and she flushed them away. After catching her breath, she rinsed her mouth and sat down on the toilet lid. Withdrew the flask from her blazer, unscrewed the cap, and took a long slug of vodka, tinged with rust. She felt disgusted with herself for copping out like this. But if she was going to reforge herself in the crucible of this particular millennial sex party–with Daniel Minick watching, or participating, she couldn't decide which was worse–she needed anesthesia. Stan would just have to forgive her. Perhaps he needn't find out, she hoped, draining the flask. She could hold her liquor well enough, much like her father. Better than. After rinsing her mouth some more, she popped a couple breath mints and returned to the table, where she tried to follow the main conversation, which was still stuck on the whole Judaism thing.

"Wanda, you're not even Jewish at all, are you?" asked the woman with the green eyes and long braid.

"It *is* Wanda *Hayes* Pipkin after all," someone pointed out.

Adriane felt like jumping in. "Just so long as you and Max don't plan to be buried together in an Orthodox cemetery," she blurted.

The table grew quiet, as the incoherence of her remark established itself.

His mouth full of manicotti, Max broke the silence and said, "We'll be buried at Hillside. Why would we want an Orthodox cemetery?"

"I think that remark was directed at me," Daniel Minick said. "Adriane and I share some history."

Guillaume leaned forward and said, "This sounds promising."

Stan looked toward her for the first time since dinner had started.

"It's just a business matter," said Daniel.

"Daniel's my undertaker," Adriane announced, the blood rushing in her head.

"I'm nobody's undertaker," Daniel protested. "I manage Shalom Gardens."

"He wants to bury me next to my father," Adriane added belligerently. "But I'd have to convert first."

"I was just trying to offer you options."

Another silence settled over the table, until Stan declared, "Adriane, this cheese platter is fantastic!"

She beamed, having finally gotten his attention. Those who'd sampled the platter now sang its praises and those who hadn't, insisted it be passed their way. Adriane wondered if she might need to throw up again.

Max moved the conversation along by comparing the varieties of Judaism, but Adriane barely heard him, her pulse still throbbing.

"Listen," Daniel murmured, leaning close, "when your mother died . . . I was brand new. I was trying to follow the rules. Maybe I should have just turned a blind eye and not asked so many questions. I'd handle it differently now, for whatever it's worth."

"Now that you're 'working the gray area'?" Reaching toward his Pyrex casserole, she asked, "So what's this kosher thing taste like?"

"Here." Daniel waved her fork away and used the spatula he'd brought from home. "Let me serve you some."

"Don't you find religious orthodoxy is kind of like the spiritual version of Obsessive-Compulsive Disorder?"

"No, I don't," he said, placing some brisket on her plate.

She felt better for having delivered her nasty remark, and she tasted the brisket now and could admit it was pretty good. "Not I'm-ready-to-convert good, but–"

"That's all right," he said.

After dessert, people began to drift from the dining table to sit in the living room or–in the case of Patty Romero and some guy named Tyler, who played trombone with the Baltimore Symphony Orchestra–disappear from view altogether, possibly into one of the bedrooms. Adriane remembered now that privacy was a theoretical option, though it hadn't seemed like Stan's preference.

Emma was going on about *The Ganesha Epiphanies*, with F. Chipper beside her on the couch, rubbing her shoulders. Wanda Hayes Pipkin sat next to them flipping through an issue of *Gourmet*. Stan and Lisette the au pair were dancing in a far corner of the living room to some kind of bossa nova music, while Daniel pored over the household's CD collection. Max Pipkin ducked into the bathroom. Guillaume and Sarah began clearing the table.

"Let me help you with those," said Adriane, picking up a plate.

"Don't be a goose," said Guillaume. "Enjoy yourself. We'll be out *tout de suite*."

Adriane drifted into the living room and sat in the loveseat, across from Wanda, Emma, and F. Chipper.

"I think every elementary-school child should be forced to read it," concluded Emma. "No, that sounds autocratic. I think every high-school student should be forced to read it."

"As long as somebody is forced," quipped F. Chipper, as he rubbed her shoulders.

"That's right!" Emma laughed. "I'd make a good reading dominatrix. Would you like that, Chippy?"

F. Chipper took this opportunity to whisper something in Emma's ear, after which the two of them stood and quietly headed toward the hallway, passing Max Pipkin on his way back from the bathroom. He was wearing nothing but a pair of blue jockey shorts and argyle socks. He rubbed his hairy stomach and plopped down next to his wife.

"Everything all right, dear?" Wanda asked, still flipping through the magazine.

"That couscous was awfully spicy," he said.

Daniel finally stopped studying the CD collection and meandered toward the couch and sat down next to Max.

"Too much Wagner," he said.

Stan and Lisette began kissing as they danced. Adriane's guts purred sourly, and she averted her eyes and wondered if he was trying to make her jealous, then quickly dismissed the motive as unworthy of him. But when he glanced at her and they locked eyes, there soon passed between them a kind of unspoken question. As though he was testing her to see if she could handle it. Adriane didn't like tests, but still wanted to pass. Tonight, she suspected, she was meant to pay some sort of initiation dues. So she continued to gaze back at Stan, forced herself not to look away, and to her relief and amazement, her initial churning discomfort faded, like haze dissipating in the heat of sunshine. Stan led Lisette by the hand into the living room's center, where they now sat on the carpet at Adriane's feet.

"You look like someone who could appreciate a good foot massage," he said to her, reaching for her ankle. "May we?"

Adriane nodded, apprehensive and a little excited, as Stan

slipped off her right shoe and sock, Lisette the left. They each rolled up the cuff of one pant leg. Lisette produced from the corner table drawer a small vial of aromatic oil; she shook out a few drops onto Stan's cupped palms and her own, then clasped her hands and rubbed vigorously until she was satisfied by their warmth. Stan did likewise, and then they both gazed fondly at Adriane and each grasped a foot and simply held it a moment in their warm oily hands. Lisette smoothed the oil along the arch and bridge, over Adriane's thirsty heel and taut Achilles tendon.

"Close your eyes," Stan suggested, and she did as she was told, letting them drift up into her head. His thumbs urged her arch into the most delicate spasm. She moaned slightly and could perceive on the soft edges of her consciousness Wanda Hayes Pipkin saying, "I want to make this crown roast sometime."

"Oh, look," Sarah Hsu's voice floated softly through the room. "How sweet."

"Dear boy," Guillaume murmured, "allow me to make up to you about those minced apples." As host, perhaps he felt a special concern that none of his guests harbor any regrets. Adriane began to think of him as the unofficial mayor of Piafville.

She heard a zipper and the soft shuffle of denim. Stan continued to massage her foot, though she could tell the angle of his wrists had changed, and the pressure of his fingers became intermittent. Now she heard a moan but was reluctant to view the cause of it. When at last she worked up the courage to open her eyes, she watched as the caterer applied, through the latex membrane of a condom, the most compelling oral persuasion to the object of Adriane's recent fantasies.

Sarah Hsu was sitting by Adriane's side, watching her husband with a look of indulgent affection.

"Doesn't that bother you?" Adriane leaned over and whispered.

"Not really," Sarah whispered back. "Guillaume will always have his impulses. I like being able to keep an eye on him." She tucked a strand of Adriane's hair behind her ear. "Does it bother you?"

"I don't know yet," she whispered. "It's very startling."

Over on the couch, Daniel Minick reached for a pistachio from a bowl on the end table. After popping the nutmeat into his mouth, he glanced around for someplace to dispose of the shell. But not finding anything, he discreetly slipped the remains into his shirt pocket. He coughed. A throat-clearing grumble that seemed to aim its moral undertone at Adriane.

"How did you and Stan meet?" Sarah asked.

But before Adriane could say a word, Stan let out a ululating scream and squeezed the pressure points of her foot with such intensity that she screamed as well, in a seizure of pain.

Wanda Hayes Pipkin looked up from her magazine. A door opened, and Adriane could feel the vibration of people running down the hall.

"Good God," said Emma, emerging topless. "What are we missing?"

Guillaume glanced at Adriane just as he opened his mouth and let go of Stan's penis. Stan himself leaned his head backward and said, with a lilt in his voice, as though he was pleasantly surprised to see her: "Adriane, I want very much to make love to you."

He smiled at her, but upside-down it looked like a grimace. She could feel his trembling fingers intertwined with her toes, and Lisette still grasping the other foot, and Sarah Hsu stroking her hair. The four of them were part of a chain–the five of them, counting Guillaume, who clutched Stan's thighs as though they were a set of parallel bars–some exponentially strong erotic current that promised the kind of liberation, even abandon, she'd envisioned. If she could somehow just push through this awkward moment, she told herself, she might reemerge on the other side transformed–new and unrecognizable to herself. Everyone seemed focused on her, waiting for her reply. She nodded at Stan with a shiver and let Sarah help her out of her blazer.

Stan pulled off his shirt and reached for a fresh condom. His chest glowed palely. A fine tuft of hair sprouted above his navel, and his pubic hair billowed around the base of his penis. Adriane undid the top button of her blouse, but then became aware of Minick again. He appeared preoccupied with retying his shoelaces and seemed to be blushing. He was so painfully uncomfortable it was making Adriane uncomfortable. Her fingers fumbled with her blouse's second button.

She caught Minick's eye. He quickly looked away and reached for another pistachio. Who was he kidding: "Working the gray area"? He could no more work a gray area than she could read Hebrew. He so did not get this, any of it, and she felt sad for him, in a way that angered and confused her. Trying to assuage the loss of his fiancée by sowing some wild oats? The futility of his project seemed obvious and pitiful.

She'd managed to get her second button undone, but was having even more trouble with the third, he'd gotten her so flustered; she looked down at her chest to see what she was doing when she heard a hollow clank–it seemed to come from her left, where Sarah had just draped Adriane's blazer over a chair. And now the winking pewter cap of her flask rolled across the carpet and landed inches from Stan's big toe. He bent forward to pick it up, then looked at Adriane with naked disappointment. Everyone fell quiet, absorbing the fact of the empty flask over there on the floor, and the craven behavior it signified.

They were all so serious–even Guillaume and breezy Sarah had turned stony, as though they'd bitten into something rancid. Where was everyone's sense of proportion? Their sense of humor, for God's sake. *Finally*, some laughter burbled through the room, but Adriane quickly realized it was all coming from her. The harder she laughed, the sterner everyone stared, and the more she had to laugh.

"Doesn't she know the rules?" asked Emma, arms folded across her breasts.

"Dammit, Adriane," said Stan. "What part of 'no alcohol' don't you understand?" He began to get dressed again. Without looking at her, he said, "I should take you home."

"Drunkenness is *not* a turn-on," said Max Pipkin to no one in particular, as he flicked a piece of pistachio shell from his chest hair.

Sarah added, "This is how people get hurt."

"Well," said Guillaume, peeling off a pair of latex gloves Adriane had not before registered, "that was certainly a close call."

Only Daniel Minick regarded her with an expression that looked at all sympathetic, and that's when Adriane stopped laughing and knew she must be in deeper trouble than she'd imagined.

She squirmed against the passenger seat while Stan drove fast. They rode in silence, except for the rattle of golf clubs, and after a while she turned toward him and, for lack of something better, said, "I liked your friends." When he didn't reply, she began to chatter compulsively. "That Guillaume! Maybe he'd teach me some sex tips. I'm sorry I broke the rule about drinking. That guy Minick makes me nervous. He's not just a killjoy; it's like he brings death into the room with him."

"It's okay," said Stan calmly. When he pulled to a stop in front of her apartment building, he left the engine running.

"Come upstairs," she said. "It's not even midnight. We could have great sex right now, you and me."

"That's a nice offer," he said, "but–"

"I was just nervous," she said. "Because I'd never been to one of those things before. Next time I'll know what to expect. Just don't invite–"

"You have a negative energy around you, Adriane," he said, plainly and without any overt meanness. "I'm not sure how else to describe it."

"So? You have a positive energy; we should be magnetically attracted to each other."

"I just don't think you're ready for this approach. Polyamory," he added, diplomatically, "isn't for everyone."

He was right, of course–she couldn't pull it off, couldn't hang with the new paradigm–but she had no philosophy of her own, no way of life, except for her sports handicapping. This tremulous hope of hers, that she might outrun the shadow of loss, was turning out to be a cruel hoax. The night's aborted attempt at abandon had left her more bereft than ever.

"You should take your clubs back," he said.

Defeated, she could only nod. Together they slid the bag out of the trunk.

"Good-bye," he told her. "And good luck to you." She watched the taillights of his Insight diminish, then disappear.

Adriane glanced up at her apartment, marked by the empty

flowerpot on her balconet. She wasn't ready to go up there–afraid to return to her own home.

Car honks signaled people's eagerness for the new millennium, barely an hour away. As she stood before her building, the honking grew more intense and, it seemed to her, tinged with desperation. Hefting her father's clubs at last, Adriane lugged them through the lobby, into the elevator, and finally along her hallway. From behind closed doors, noisemakers squealed in anticipation of the new and the hoped for–the prospects of peace, good health, and fortune. Better sex and more of it. Deeper love. Above all: a clean slate and a fresh start.

Everyone seemed to be counting on it.

11. adriane and the dogs of varanasi

new year's eve (continued)–winter 2000

"It's too late, Miss Gelki. He has expired."

"But, but how?" Adriane stammered. She gazed at Dr. Lal, the young vet manning the graveyard shift at the Greater Baltimore Animal Hospital. "He seemed fine when I left him this evening."

Dr. Lal glanced at the sheltie on his examining table. "Without an autopsy, I couldn't say. He was an old dog. Heart attack maybe."

"I shouldn't have gone to that party," she murmured. "I shouldn't have left him alone on New Year's Eve." She stroked his cold fur. "Barry," she whispered.

"Perhaps," the vet said gently, "you'll cross paths in his next life."

"Reincarnation?" she asked him hopefully. People had been talking about reincarnation earlier at the party, so this seemed like an uncanny coincidence.

"Yes," he said, blinking his long lashes. "I was referring to reincarnation."

Someone paged the doctor's name over the loudspeaker, so he excused himself and left the room.

Adriane hugged her dog, buried her face in his fluffy coat.

Breathed him.

She lifted him to her chest, held him tight, tighter. Fifteen minutes passed and the doctor had yet to return. Adriane didn't know: Was she supposed to take her dog? Was she supposed to leave him? And leave him to what? Unable to put him back down on the harsh metal table, she found herself wandering out of the examination room, still clutching him, determined now to take him with her. As they passed through the waiting area, she cooed into his fur so nothing would appear amiss.

"That didn't hurt so bad," she said in a forced singsong, "did it now?"

"Hell of a way to start the new millennium," said an elderly man holding his wounded schnauzer.

Adriane nodded and kept walking. Soon they were outside. She laid Barry on the passenger seat of her car, draped a blanket over him–something he'd never have tolerated while alive. Somehow, he seemed more vulnerable now.

She started her engine. Eyes slick with tears, she threw the transmission into gear–the wrong gear; she startled when the car lurched backward. Heard the tinkling of broken taillights before she felt the impact. Glancing over her shoulder, she saw the trash Dumpster. Didn't bother to check the damage to her car. Driving now, she kept hearing the doctor's last words and she clung to the promise of reincarnation. She'd often wondered–back in the days when she devoured books about religion–if there was any truth to it. But now her curiosity was real and motivated. She scrambled to remember what all one was supposed to do by way of ritual to grease the wheels. Indeed, there was something about clarified butter. And also the holy Indian city of Varanasi . . .

Her thoughts continued their eastward tide and lapped against the idea of her own karma. And for a moment, the narrower, admittedly childish thought: *What have I done to deserve this?* Adriane was feeling both victimized and blameworthy. Mostly blameworthy. *I shouldn't have left him alone*, she thought again, *not on New Year's Eve. . . .*

She carried Barry into the dingy elevator of her prewar apartment building. His eighteen-pound body stiffening by the moment, she brought him into her kitchen and arranged him on the counter.

Loving Barry had always come so naturally to Adriane. And yes, yes, yes! She *knew* it had been wrong to treat him like a person when he was alive–she had come to understand that at some point. But the shimmering promise of a *next* life–a life in which his noble soul might find refuge in human form–well, entire civilizations had been built around that tender hope. Just because she'd loved Barry so easily didn't mean it would be easy to stop.

Clarified butter, she thought, as she searched her fridge, casting aside old jars of mustard and carryout packets of soy sauce. All she had was a plastic tub of I Can't Believe It's Not Butter.

She heated the spread product in a small pan and skimmed off a few floating bits of impurity. In keeping with her dim understanding of a ritual she'd read about ages ago–or at least thought she'd read about–Adriane would smear a fingerbreadth of the grease across Barry's nine orifices as a seal to keep his soul from dissipating willy-nilly.

Elsewhere in her building, people were partying, the squeal of noisemakers piercing the thick walls of her apartment from various directions; Barry would have whimpered and hid under the piano if he were alive. *I should never have left him alone on New Year's Eve.* She sealed his eyes first, then his ears, then his nostrils. And long pointy mouth; that took a lot of grease. And last, the tip of his penis and crinkly anus. The party noise crescendoed. Adriane glanced at her kitchen clock, which read midnight. The new millennium had begun. Adriane had long pictured the new millennium as an enormous cruise liner pulling out to sea, leaving her on dread's rickety pier, but just now logistical urgencies distracted her from all that.

She retrieved from the linen closet a clothing storage bag and dumped out the wool sweaters onto her mother's piano. Back in the kitchen now, she gently squeezed Barry into the clear plastic, resealed it, and hooked up her vacuum cleaner to a special port and removed all the air, watching the bag shrink around the form of her beloved. Over the vacuum's whir, she thought she heard the phone ring, which she might otherwise ignore except that it must be Stan calling to apologize, so she picked up.

Instead it was Daniel Minick, who said, "I shouldn't be calling you now–"

"That's okay," murmured Adriane.

"No, I mean, I'm *really* not supposed to be using the phone now. But I was worried when you left early like that."

"Not early enough," she mumbled.

"Is this too strange, my calling? Am I interrupting?" he asked. "Is he there now . . . Stan? Not that it's my business."

Adriane didn't say anything, just observed the scene on her kitchen counter: her dog hooked up to her vacuum cleaner.

"I didn't like the way he was treating you," Minick continued, softly, as though concerned Stan might overhear. "You deserve better."

"You don't know that," Adriane mumbled. "You don't know what I deserve."

"I just think you're a good person, Adriane."

The strangeness of that claim hung there in silence; she didn't even know if she'd heard him correctly.

"I was hoping you might like to go out some evening," he said.

"Well, the thing is–" She looked at her counter, trying not to let her voice crack.

"No, forget I said that. Just strike it from the record please."

"Okay."

"Not that I don't want to go out with you, but I didn't want this call to be about that."

"The thing is," she continued, unsure what he meant, "I'm leaving town for a while."

"Oh. Where to?"

"India."

"That is out of town. You didn't mention that. At the party."

"I must have talked about it before you arrived. I've been planning this for a long time," she said, which *felt* true, even if it wasn't. "I'm just not sure how long I'm going to be gone."

"Okay," said Minick and seemed to take a deep breath. "Well, I'll be here when you get back."

She was surprised how vulnerable he had allowed himself to sound; not at all like the Daniel Minick she thought she knew.

"So, happy new millennium then," he said.

"Happy new millennium."

"Actually, I heard somewhere that the new millennium isn't

until next New Year's Eve. That it starts on the year one, not the year zero. Then, of course, there's the Jewish calendar . . ."

He seemed to want to talk about this some more, but it was late, and now was not a good time, so Adriane said good night.

After they hung up, she cleared out her freezer and placed her dog inside. None of this last part–the vacuum, the freezing–had anything to do with Hindu ritual, real or imagined, but she needed to buy herself a little time to figure out how she was going to get them both to India.

Seventy-two hours later–having obtained last-minute visas through an "expeditor"–Adriane and her friend Shelley sat clasping each other's hand through the final flight of their journey, between New Delhi and the holy city of Varanasi.

"Thanks again for not trying to talk me out of this," said Adriane, glassy-eyed with gratitude. "And for coming."

"You need supervision. It's like you're on a bad acid trip," said Shelley crisply. "I'm glad my limbs could cooperate," she added, a blunt reference to her MS, currently in remission. She returned her attention to the *Marie Claire* she'd bought at BWI Airport.

Adriane focused on her copy of *The Ganesha Epiphanies*, which chronicled the author's trek through India in search of the "twenty-three abundant truths." Chief among these, or at least the most central to Adriane's interest, had to do with reincarnation and the ways in which it could be proactively influenced. She wondered idly what she herself might like to return as someday, after she was done with her current bereft guise. Something simple at first, to let her repair her karma slowly–a blade of grass maybe; she did not feel ready for much more responsibility than that.

She read intently through the rest of the flight and was surprised when the rickety plane bounced against the runway. She took a deep breath and closed her eyes, stroked her foot against the green canvas carry-on stored under the seat before her. Yes, she'd missed the extra legroom, but would never trust anything this precious to the overhead bins. Inside lay Barry thawing in his vacuum-sealed body bag, a dozen small animal toys piled on top of him as camouflage, good-will presents intended for a Varanasi orphanage, should any airport inspector happen to ask, which none had; the security guard at BWI hadn't even *looked* at his X-ray screen.

The two women gathered their belongings and descended a metal staircase to the tarmac. Walking to the terminal through humid night air, Adriane at first didn't notice mosquitoes alighting on her bare arms. After she had made it inside, however, she counted more than thirty bites.

"I look like I have hives," she said, and hurriedly withdrew the insect repellent from her purse.

"Spritz me, too, won't you?" Shelley asked and held out her pale arms, also pocked with bites.

They stood in line to prepay for a taxi, and no sooner had they made it outside and into the cab than it began to rain. The taxi's wipers flicked back and forth across the windshield, offering only glimpses of the road into Varanasi. Small bands of men warmed themselves by trash fires under any overhanging shelter. And before long Adriane felt water drip onto her head from a leak in the cab's roof.

"Is the hotel much farther?" Shelley asked their driver.

He shook his head. "Closed. I take you better place."

"I'm sure it's not closed," insisted Shelley.

"Filthy," he said and continued to navigate through the rain. "Better place."

He drove along the narrow streets of the old city and finally pulled before an even narrower alley, through which the taxicab, small as it was, could not pass. Adriane rolled down her window and peered into the dark crevice. The row of four-story buildings on either side looked like dwellings; certainly there was nothing resembling a lobby, nothing even with a front light on.

"Where's the hotel?" she asked, tired and weak from not eating.

The driver nodded toward the alley. "Number five."

"You're not going to escort us?" Shelley demanded.

"Number five." The driver shook his head. "Much better place."

Adriane and Shelley exchanged looks of concern. For a brief moment, Adriane considered returning to the airport, where they would catch the next flight home.

"What should we do?" she asked her friend.

Shelley perked up. "Let's be brave," she said. "I've got mace."

They grabbed their bags and leapt from the cab into the alley, barely wider than an arm span. Blinking back the rain, Adriane looked for number five or, really, any number.

A light glowed from one of the doorways, and the women moved toward it. Closer now, they saw the legs of a man protruding from a portico, and above his sleeping head, the number five.

"This is a hotel?" Shelley wondered aloud.

The prone man's legs twitched. He blinked and regarded the two women. "Welcome," he said, rising now to his sandaled feet. "Hotel is up." A doorman, kind of, he unlocked a metal grille and slid it open, then switched on a long strip of fluorescent lights that seemed to double as a staircase banister.

He reached for Adriane's luggage, and she let him take the suitcase but kept the bag that contained Barry. Shelley quickly handed over her duffel.

"Is it supposed to keep raining?" Adriane asked, as they climbed.

The doorman limped ahead of her, and shrugged. "This will stop soon."

At the top of the stairs, he flicked on another bank of lights, illuminating a small lobby, its floor occupied by the bodies of three sleeping boys. They rubbed their eyes, then trooped behind the front desk and asked their guests to register.

The tallest, who introduced himself as Vinay, produced a long brass key. The two younger boys grabbed at the bags with such speed and conviction they nearly managed to pry Adriane's carry-on from her, but she continued to clutch it fiercely.

Vinay led the way to a tiny elevator, and after all five people crammed inside, he shut its grille, then pulled the control handle a notch clockwise. A toy-piano rendition of "Jingle Bells" accompanied their slow ascent to the fourth floor.

Down a short hallway, Vinay opened the door to a small room with twin beds and private adjoining bath that seemed clean enough but smelled of insecticide–some industrial-strength product long ago banned in the States probably. The boys put down the luggage, and Vinay asked if they could be of any further service.

"Thank you, no," said Adriane and reached into her purse for some coins.

He shook his head. "When you say good-bye, memsahib."

"All right then," she said. "Thank you." She closed the door behind her, and did indeed feel like she'd stumbled into some sort of acid trip. Scratching furiously at her bug bites, she wondered if she was finally starting to lose her mind.

* * *

In the morning, bright sunshine poured through their window, and the alleyway below was so choked with people Adriane didn't recognize it. Sari-clad women carrying bushels of flowers on their shoulders, a man talking on his cell phone as he sidestepped a pair of water buffalo–the crowded alley intimidated her even more than it had empty.

But her body needed food. "And we'd better find some bottled water, too," she decided.

"Couldn't I sleep just a little bit more?" murmured Shelley from under her sheet.

"I can't go out there alone!"

"Just another ten minutes."

"I'll wait for you in the lobby," said Adriane. "Maybe they have some information about the cremation grounds."

"Splendid," said Shelley, who began to snore before Adriane had made it to the door.

"Down, please," she told the middle boy from the night before. He closed the elevator grille after her and immediately the treacle of "Jingle Bells" began. She wondered if it played year round.

"Good sleeping?" the boy asked her hopefully, as the exposed elevator shaft passed before them.

"Oh, yes," said Adriane after she understood his question. "Very good sleeping."

"Good," he said and pulled open the grille for her. "My name is Lalit."

"Thank you, Lalit. I'm Adriane."

"Please remember to say good-bye, Adriane memsahib."

In the lobby, she saw a tall elderly man standing behind the front desk, sorting envelopes. He wore a button-down shirt and paisley necktie.

"Excuse me," she began tentatively, not knowing the extent of the man's English. "Do you have any literature on the . . . um . . . funeral grounds?"

He looked up from his mail and eyed her curiously. "I've a great deal of literature," he said. "Why don't you step into my apartments?" He indicated the open door behind the front desk.

"Oh, I wouldn't want to impose," Adriane said nervously.

"Not at all," said the man, tossing aside a stack of unopened letters. "I'm hardly busy. What brings you to Varanasi?"

"Just a personal interest," said Adriane, "in the funeral, um, areas."

He led her into the first room of the apartment, a library with floor-to-ceiling bookcases covering every inch of wall space. The tile floor was adorned by an ornate, faded rug, and the furnishings consisted of two brass-studded leather club chairs and, off to one side, a large red-topped billiard table. "I have a granddaughter about your age at Stanford. Medical school. I'm Colonel Nanda, retired," he said, adding, "I am the owner."

"What a handsome library," Adriane said.

He peered at one shelf in particular. "I have a number of academic texts that discuss death rites, and also several religious works. Do you read Sanskrit by any chance? What specifically did you have in mind?"

"A brochure," murmured Adriane. "Something with hours of operation and fees."

"I see." Colonel Nanda restored a dusty tome to its place on the shelf. "It is said the pyres at Manikarnika Ghat have burned continuously since before recorded time, so you stand a reasonable chance of finding them open." He grinned in mild, teasing reproach. "Though observers typically gaze from a distance, usually from a hired river boat. Exactly what sort of tourist experience were you hoping for?"

At this point–maybe it was exhaustion or her flagging blood sugar–Adriane sank to her knees and groaned.

"It's my, Barry," she told the carpet. "I brought him here because . . . so his beautiful soul could be reincarnated. Isn't that why people come here? A good reincarnation."

Colonel Nanda offered her a guiding hand toward one of the club chairs. He then left the room and quickly returned carrying a Coca-Cola, which he opened under Adriane's nose, as though the smell might revive her. He handed over the bottle, and she took a long gulp. After she had caught her breath, the colonel asked: "Did you say your beloved is dying?"

"He's already dead," said Adriane.

"I'm very sorry. So you have brought his ashes to scatter on the Ganges?"

"He hasn't been cremated yet."

The colonel paused. "You mean . . . do you mean there's a body in your room?"

Adriane nodded contritely.

"I wonder why Vinay didn't say anything. We'd better have a look." He led the way to the elevator. And after two dozen more bars of "Jingle Bells," they got off at the fourth floor and soon stood before her door.

She withdrew the big brass key from her pocket and, without thinking, opened up.

Shelley stirred in bed, and the top sheet slipped forward, revealing, beyond the gauze of mosquito netting, the pale curve of her breast. Colonel Nanda covered his eyes with both hands and took a step backward into the hallway. "I'll wait here, while you help your friend dress."

Adriane shut the door behind her. "Sorry," she mouthed.

"Who is that?" whispered Shelley, squirming into a clean pair of jeans. Yesterday's clothes hung soddenly over every chairback.

"He's the owner," said Adriane. She went to the closet, withdrew the green canvas carry-on, and began unpacking its layer of animal toys. "He's come to see Barry."

"You *told* him?" hissed Shelley.

"I panicked." Adriane's eyes began to water again.

A knock on the door.

"Come in," Shelley called out.

Colonel Nanda entered and stood over Adriane, who peeled the edges of the green carry-on toward the floor, exposing the plastic bag, blurry with humidity and flecked with dainty blossoms of mold.

The colonel sighed. "Your Barry, then, is a dog."

"Yes."

"You have brought him all this way to enable an auspicious reincarnation."

"Maybe as a man, even . . ."

"Reborn as a man," the colonel mused, adjusting his necktie.

"A good man, preferably in his thirties." She almost added "and single" but stopped; she had already made herself pathetically clear.

"Let us revisit that question," he said gently. "You're welcome to borrow anything from my library on the subject you like. If that will help."

"Have you read this one?" she asked, pointing to her copy of *The Ganesha Epiphanies*.

"I've not heard of that particular title, no," he said, then gazed down at Barry. "The poor creature. Why is there no odor?"

"Vacuum technology," explained Adriane to the colonel, towering above.

"Is it made specifically for this purpose?" he asked, astonished.

"It's for sweaters." Adriane choked back a sob. "You won't confiscate him will you?"

"Surely he represents a health risk," Colonel Nanda pointed out. He stroked his chin and looked down at her with moist eyes of his own. "What would you have me do?"

"Won't you help us, please?" Adriane asked, as earnest as she'd ever been in her life, hating to beg, but it was already clear to her that she and Shelley were never going to pull this off on their own. "Please?"

The colonel glanced back and forth between her and the plastic bag, as though trying to fathom the kind of anarchic life force that could have led to such a moment as this–before, at last, removing his tie and folding it away in his pants pocket.

An hour later, Adriane and Shelley were following Colonel Nanda through the crowded alley, which now smelled of curdled milk, on their way to the cremation grounds at Manikarnika Ghat. Though the ghat lay several kilometers from his hotel, the colonel claimed it would be faster to walk. He took long strides–sidestepping burlap blankets heaped with radishes and spinach for sale–and soon got ahead of them, but luckily Adriane could track the gray curve of his haircut, bobbing above the crowd.

People jostled her as though she were some mere molecule. Out of the corner of her eye, Adriane glimpsed an elderly man washing a small stone shrine carved into a wall. When she tried to get a better look, she almost walked head first into a bamboo pole, part of a scaffold, it turned out, supporting a trio of workmen some thirty feet off the ground.

"Thank God we came during the cool season," shouted Shelley behind her. "My arse is liquefying in these jeans."

They were now separated from Colonel Nanda by more than a dozen yards. The green carry-on bag was slowing Adriane down. She gripped its handles so tightly her palms were beginning to blister.

At an intersection the colonel stood waiting.

"Would you like me to take your bag?" he offered.

"No, thank you. I've got it," Adriane insisted.

The alley disgorged them into a slightly wider street, and the crush eased, but soon there came the added difficulty of cars, auto-rickshaws, and more vendors–selling food, clothing, or beads, as well as stacks of something that looked like dried cow chips. When the two women next caught up to Colonel Nanda, he repeated his offer. "We might be able to make faster progress," he said, extending a hand toward Adriane's carry-on.

She looked into the colonel's kind face, weathered by time, experience, and, she could see, mercy. Slowly, she passed him the bag.

He hoisted it above his head and set off into the stream of traffic. Adriane followed the floating green beacon. She noticed another shrine carved into a wall, a similar stone couple, whose feet appeared to have been recently washed, and she wondered what it meant.

At a new cross street they met a procession of two dozen people chanting *"Ram nam satya hai."* Some of them were carrying a bamboo stretcher, which supported a human figure wrapped in red-and-gold cloth. Leading the funeral party, three men played tarnished horns, a wheezing tune that sounded for a moment like Thelonious Monk's "In Walked Bud."

Colonel Nanda, Adriane, and Shelley made room for the procession, then fell into line behind it, and their progress became much easier. On her right, Adriane could glimpse the brown Ganges, and on the long steps descending to the water's edge stood multitudes waiting their turn for a dip. Adriane imagined the cool water against her skin and felt a flicker of envy at the bathers, even though the thought of joining them butted against her lifelong notions of hygiene and germ theory.

Still following the mourning party, Adriane began to hear the sound of an ax and its echo, like the ticking of a large unseen clock. Soon, she saw the fruits of all that chopping: a woodpile three times taller than the colonel. Beyond it lay a concrete patio smaller than a basketball court: the cremation grounds of Manikarnika Ghat.

Colonel Nanda set down the green bag, crossed his arms, and waited while representatives from the mourning procession approached a man holding a clipboard in the center of the patio.

In the farthest corner, several men stood around a bonfire in full flame, while across from them another small group waited for the new pile of logs to catch beneath the white-shrouded figure of their own loved one. Just beyond the ghat, children played a game, and the roiling sounds of street traffic nearly drowned out the crackling of firewood. Wisps of smoke and cinder drifted through the air, blackening the turrets of a nearby temple. Adriane wished for a handkerchief to cover her face, but there was nothing to do but inhale the airborne traces of the dead.

The ghat's manager, in the slightly regal manner of a maitre d', pointed the newly arrived party to a corner of the platform where there smoldered the final remnants of a spent bonfire. Its mourners had already left. Two charnel attendants shuttled the smoking embers, as well as a largely unburned leg, to the river's edge and set all of it adrift in a cloud of steam.

A scrawny, matted dog trotted near, carrying in its mouth a curved stick, the end of which broke off by Shelley's feet. The piece looked vaguely vertebral.

"Sweet Christ," she whispered, as the dog continued on its way, "is that a spine?"

The funeral workers quickly assembled a new pyre for the red-and-gold corpse, whose kinsmen now laid their bier on top.

By this time, the manager had walked over to a chair in the shade, and this must have seemed to Colonel Nanda like a good moment.

"You will need to wait here on the periphery," he instructed Adriane. Only then did she notice the other funeral parties were all men. "It might be best for me to speak with the manager first alone."

Adriane nodded, overwhelmed. Colonel Nanda picked up the green canvas bag and set out.

The raging pyre in the farthest corner had settled into a regular rhythm, and a young man wearing a white tunic and carrying a wooden staff moved toward one end of the bier. Chanting a few words, he then brought down the blunt end of his staff onto the charred head of the deceased, smashing it open.

Adriane gasped: "Oh my God."

"I imagine it's part of the standard package," whispered Shelley.

The mourners seemed to be taking it in stride, but Adriane's stomach continued to knot. "Promise you won't do that at my funeral."

"Don't be silly," scolded Shelley. "I shan't live to see your funeral."

On a landing above the cremation grounds, one of the attendants was shouting at a German tourist, demanding the film from his camera. The tourist, a sinewy man wearing jogging shorts and a muscle shirt, refused, until a nearby policeman brandished his club.

The incident's shame seemed to attach itself to Adriane; she felt suddenly embarrassed by her whiteness, and she imagined the Varanasi locals working and mourning nearby now glanced at her with apprehension. They understood that, like the German, she too was guilty of insolence: Spoiled American, she could travel halfway around the world on behalf of a pet. To appropriate and pervert another culture's traditions as it suited her. Adriane cringed at her own naïveté and gall. Yet all of this shame, heavy as it pressed on her, did nothing to displace her grief. And so, when she saw Colonel Nanda opening the green canvas bag to show the manager its contents, she felt as though a surgeon were prying apart her ribs.

The manager put on a pair of glasses, which had been suspended around his neck, and peered into the canvas bag–at her exposed and broken heart–then spoke at length with Colonel Nanda, who finally pointed to Adriane. The two men looked over at her, and she waved awkwardly, and soon the colonel was back at her side.

"They refuse to take it on," he said, his own voice neutral, without judgment. "They will not allow a dog to be cremated here."

"Oh," said Adriane. She could feel Shelley's hand clasping her own.

"There is one other place we should try," he announced, then led them up the stairs to the street, where they hailed an autorickshaw and piled in tightly, the colonel sandwiched between the two women, the green canvas bag on his lap. "Harishchandra

Ghat," he instructed. The auto-rickshaw sputtered into the sea of traffic and pedestrians.

Adriane had no idea how she'd have negotiated any of this without the colonel's help. She wanted to thank him, but he seemed all business at the moment, so she kept quiet.

The sky was hazing over as they debarked at Harishchandra Ghat. In addition to several wood pyres, there stood a large gray building, taller than it was wide, plumes of smoke floating from its chimney. An electric crematorium, explained Colonel Nanda–the marriage of tradition with modern efficiency.

"We may find the management here more open-minded," he said.

He left Adriane and Shelley on the sidelines and disappeared into the building. A cluster of waiting mourners turned their bleary attention toward the two foreign women. Shelley wandered off toward the water, but Adriane stood frozen in the grip of anticipation and self-consciousness.

Five minutes later, Colonel Nanda returned, shaking his head, and Adriane murmured: "They won't cremate a dog, either?"

"The gentleman I spoke with claims he would have cremated an Indian dog, but not a foreign dog. The vacuum bag, alas, tipped him off. Where's your friend?"

They found Shelley and then another auto-rickshaw. Adriane climbed in feeling completely undone. The sky filled with bruise-colored clouds.

"Now Barry will never be reborn as a man," said Adriane.

The colonel cleared his throat. "Yes, I've been meaning to discuss that idea with you. To start, you are describing not so much a *rebirth* of the soul as some sort of *merging* of souls, which I've never heard of."

"But can't it happen like that, *too*?"

He regarded Adriane in a lingering way that seemed intent on measuring her delusion. "The ideal of dying in Varanasi is to achieve something called *moksha*. To *avoid* rebirth, you see."

Adriane looked at the patient but tired colonel. Then at her friend Shelley, who appeared jaundiced with exhaustion, the reprieve of her disease pushed to its limits. In the street, a tea vendor rinsed his cups in a puddle of rainwater, gripping them between his elbows. She thought of the boys having to sleep on the hotel lobby floor, better off though than the men gathered each night around sidewalk trash fires. Over her shoulder now, she took a last glance at the clusters of mourners. The everyday misery of the world.

"Yes, of course," she said.

"Don't despair," said the colonel, wiping a silent tear from Adriane's cheek with his handkerchief.

"I'm sorry to be so much trouble," she murmured. "And all for a dog. You must think I'm insane."

"To love a soul is to love," the colonel said gently. "Meet me in the library this evening around nine. And we shall reassess our options."

Later that afternoon it began to drizzle.

While Shelley lay in bed, perusing the same worn copy of *Marie Claire* and munching from a bag of pistachios she'd bought at Harishchandra Ghat, Adriane read from one of the textbooks Colonel Nanda had lent her. The small shrines they had passed earlier in the day, she learned, were "sati stones," marking the spot were a wife had died on her husband's funeral pyre. A supreme gesture of devotion, supposedly, but there seemed to be other reasons as well: The prospects of impoverished widowhood, a marauding army at the gates. Loneliness. The misery of the world. Were most satis, she wondered, simply suicidal anyway? Maybe they had the suicide gene she herself had grown increasingly worried about.

She thought of her mother, whose note declared the intention to "rejoin my husband." He'd already been dead ten years, but still, maybe there was something sati-like about her mother's death that Adriane had failed to appreciate. In the West, suicide was such a taboo, but here the sati at least seemed to be considered a special case. Did they achieve *moksha*, or did they have to come back? If Adriane were to go through something like that, she would definitely not want to come back.

She walked to the window, looked down on the muddy alley below, and scratched at her raw arms, brooding now over the mechanics of the whole thing. She pictured one of the carefully built pyres at Manikarnika Ghat and imagined herself lying down next to the beloved deceased and closing her eyes, trying to lull herself into a state of calm before the tinder was lit. Was that how one did it? Or did you wait for the fire to rage, then throw yourself on it, so that you would burn more quickly and everywhere at once?

"Penny for your thoughts," said Shelley.

Adriane looked at her. "You've been a good friend coming all this way."

"I always wanted to see India," Shelley replied, returning to her magazine.

They napped until shortly before their nine P.M. appointment, then gathered up the green canvas bag and entered the elevator, Shelley bringing her magazine along in case they had to wait.

"Checking out?" asked the smallest bellboy.

"Jingle Bells" tinkled in the background as they began to sink.

"Not checking out yet," said Shelley.

"Please remember to say good-bye," he said.

"Of course," said Shelley, and the boy smiled brightly at her.

Colonel Nanda was waiting for them in the library, seated in one of the brass-studded club chairs, as was another man, of young middle age, wearing a flowing white tunic and billowing pants and no shoes.

"Ladies," said the colonel, "this is my friend, Panditji. He is a priest."

"Good evening," said Adriane, bending slightly at the knees and waist in some combination of a bow and curtsey.

The priest rose and shook hands with both women. "Nandaji has told me about your dilemma."

"Yes, my foolish dilemma. You were right, Colonel Nanda," she said, returning his book to him. "I garbled everything."

"Existence is easy to garble," the priest said, generously.

"Panditji," asked Adriane, "since Barry didn't die here in Varanasi but he's here now . . . what *will* become of his soul?"

"Many things are possible," said the priest. "He could yet achieve *moksha*–escape from the cycle of death, rebirth, and worldly suffering–or he could enjoy an auspicious rebirth, possibly as a human being, even."

"But not," mumbled Adriane, "as a man of my own age." Though she understood how wrong she'd been, she could not stop lashing herself with her own stupidity.

"Ah yes, the soul-merger, or takeover Colonel Nanda was describing to me: That is not the common opinion here, and, frankly, it strikes me as too whimsical. What I find worth mentioning is the matter of perspective. There is the point of view of the deceased–that is to say, what would be most auspicious for him? Then, to be sure, there is your own point of view: your attachment to his soul. These two points of view, one might ask, are they congenial? Are they harmonious?" His gaze seemed to Adriane at once benevolent yet demanding. "Our most pressing concern, however," the priest added, "is to facilitate his last rites. Since the cremation managers have refused, we must take matters into our own hands."

The priest slipped a clear plastic poncho over his white tunic while the colonel handed Adriane and Shelley each a poncho, then donned one himself.

"How can I ever repay you for this?" Adriane asked the priest.

"It is traditional to gift a cow," he said. "Do you have a cow?"

Adriane shook her head.

The priest turned his attention to Shelley. "Then perhaps you are finished with that magazine? I like to keep up with the West."

Shelley immediately handed over her *Marie Claire*, which he tucked under his poncho. He then turned to the colonel. "The boys have prepared an *arthi*?"

"They're waiting by the shed." Colonel Nanda led everyone to a back staircase, then to a small veranda behind the building. Vinay and Lalit sat there, smoking cigarettes and watching the rain. Propped against a storage shed stood a bier, similar to the one used in the procession to Manikarnika Ghat, only shorter, more like a stepladder.

The priest asked Adriane to set down her green canvas bag, after which he spoke to the boys in Hindi. Vinay tied a handkerchief around his mouth and each boy pulled on a pair of long rubber gloves. The older one removed the plastic bag from its canvas outer bag and prepared to open the vacuum seal.

"Good lord," said Shelley, beginning to cough. Adriane, too, had a hard time choking back her nausea. The boys lifted the sodden corpse onto a length of white cotton and began to swaddle Barry as tightly as possible, after which they tossed the empty vacuum bag, and the green canvas bag for good measure, into a metal barrel, doused both with kerosene and lit them on fire. Colonel Nanda wafted the smoke outward toward the alley, and soon the stench of decay was masked by the acrid odor of burning plastic.

Panditji sprinkled a handful of marigold petals over her dog's shrouded form. He then lit a small bouquet of incense, cupped a hand over top, and said, "Let's make time."

The boys hoisted either end of the bier. Colonel Nanda held a large black umbrella over Barry. And with the priest leading the way, everyone set out into the drizzle, Adriane and Shelley in the rear, carrying the large kerosene bucket between them. The boys' shirts quickly became transparent, and Adriane felt guilty there hadn't been enough ponchos to go around.

Panditji softly chanted *"Ram nam satya hai"* as they trekked from one alley to another, passing no one except for the occasional pair of legs–or single leg–poking out from an alcove. The perfumes of incense mingled with whatever whiffs of putrefaction escaped the cotton shroud. It was chilly enough for Adriane to see her breath. She kept a lookout for sati shrines but didn't see any. As kerosene sloshed onto her sneakers, she thought once again about her own possible suicide gene. If ever it was going to declare itself, she thought, now would be the time.

"You've been a good friend," she whispered again.

Shelley gave her a sour look, and Panditji chanted louder, which Adriane took as a subtle rebuke not to talk.

As the little procession passed another recessed doorway,

Adriane glimpsed a glowing pair of eyes, low to the ground, tracking the bier's progress. And soon the eyes emerged from the shadows and began to follow.

The group continued their march toward the river, pellets of rain dropping from the rim of the colonel's umbrella and from the small opening around Adriane's face. The poncho fit snugly and made her claustrophobic, and she couldn't scratch her mosquito bites. She wanted to remove it, then, ideally, shed her own skin. She tried to focus on Panditji's chant: *"Ram nam satya hai."*

The next time she glanced over her shoulder there were two pairs of eyes keeping pace, and after the procession rounded another bend, there emerged a third pair: three animals following silently.

Adriane motioned for her friend to look back. But Shelley continued to watch the ground, her whole body hunched from the strain of carrying her half of the bucket.

Soon their group stood at the edge of a promontory over the river. The stairs at this particular ghat were jagged and haphazard. "Be careful not to trip," the colonel advised as they stepped from rock to rock. Adriane glanced behind her and saw five dogs, it turned out, quietly trailing. Her foot slipped–a wave of kerosene sloshing against her leg–and she felt her heart race in the moment it took to regain her balance.

"Careful," hissed Shelley.

Vinay looked back and shouted something at the dogs. Adriane kept her eyes on the ground in front of her. The funeral party approached the riverbank and soon they were at the very edge of the Ganges, more or less cornered, by the river of eternal life.

Just shy of the water, the boys laid their bier across two large stones, suspending it a foot off the ground, while Colonel Nanda continued to shelter Barry with the umbrella.

Panditji began to ladle kerosene over the shroud, and Adriane felt her knees weaken. The dogs maintained their distance now, watching from a ledge of rock. Panting heavily, the one on the far left limped to a puddle of rainwater, took a drink, then lay back down with the others.

Under Colonel Nanda's umbrella, Panditji lit a torch. "It is time to say good-bye," he declared. "Have you any parting thoughts to tell your beloved?"

Don't leave, Adriane thought, *come back to me, I miss you*–a great store of parting thoughts along those lines, amassed, it seemed, over a lifetime but none she could say out loud, none that would help him, or make sense to the people who were offering their kindest service, or even make herself feel better. She shook her head ruefully. Shelley took her hand and led her a few steps farther from the bier.

Adriane couldn't bring herself to look. She closed her eyes and tried not to faint. Behind her, she heard the swooping wing of fire, and she buried her face in her friend's shoulder and cried out, a gasping cry that got no traction, just whistled through her throat like a canyon wind. She pictured herself joining the pyre, throwing herself on it, the way she had from the safety of her hotel room, but now that she could actually feel its heat on her back, she leaned closer to Shelley and held on tight. Adriane was no sati. Maybe someday she would come to see this as cause for gratitude–that at such a moment of truth she would cling to her own absurd life–but right now her inability to kill herself, the loss of suicide as an option, seemed one more thing to mourn. She began to howl, a raw howl that drew its breath and sound and bile from the deepest corners of her gut. A second fire burned inside her. She clamped her mouth around a hank of her friend's long hair trying to mute the sound, but it was no use, because when she needed to breathe, the howl exploded once again. Shelley hugged her close, but this only made Adriane howl louder, at the prospect of her dear friend's own funeral–only a matter of time and which Adriane would very certainly now live to see.

During each gasp for breath, she heard an echo, the dogs howling from the bluff above, urging her on. Louder and longer. She wept now with abandon, the complete abandon she'd often imagined, except never like this, never toward her pain, always away from it, and yet this was abandon, too. The howling grew, fed on itself, as the fires, both the one inside her and the other, continued to rage for what seemed like a very long time. Only when they'd begun to burn themselves out did the heat against her back and insides gradually start to ebb. At last, she heard a great sigh of steam, and she turned to face the river in time to see a small raft–what little was left of the bier and body–floating downstream. A glowing ember bobbed on the water, and as Adriane watched it grow smaller and dimmer, she tried to deem what might in fact be most auspicious from the point of view of the deceased, what would a good person wish for him, were she a good person, or at least were she mindful of becoming that good person in the new millennium, another year away apparently, giving her more time to work on some things, but in the meanwhile, she watched the bobbing ember and mouthed the word *moksha*.

Vinay kept his eyes toward the ground, scuffing his sneakers against the dirt. Then he idly picked up a leftover piece of the bier and, without anything better to do, tossed it into the river, making a small *plunk*.

Next thing Adriane heard: the sudden scrabbling of claws over stone, as the dogs raced down the bank then lunged past the funeral party–brushing against people's legs and nearly knocking Shelley over–on their way to the water. They dove in and paddled furiously toward the stick. The largest got to it first. Then they all swam back to shore. The stick bearer dropped it at Vinay's feet, before each dog shook out his coat, sending forth a spray of river water.

The big dog pawed the ground, stared at Vinay, and barked. The boy glanced back at Colonel Nanda and asked something in a trembling voice.

"Move gently, Vinay," said the colonel. "And throw it again, I suppose."

Vinay gingerly reached for the stick and threw it back into the river, sending the largest dog and two others in pursuit. But the remaining dogs seemed to be waiting for sticks of their own, so Panditji found another and tossed it and then Lalit did as well.

Soon the sticks were coming back in shifts, and Vinay, Lalit, and Panditji kept throwing them into the water, trying to tire the dogs, whose play, for all one knew, could turn fierce at any moment. The dog with the lame paw emerged now from the river and after limping over to Adriane, shook off a coatful of Ganges water and dropped his stick in front of her.

She looked at him, and he barked, asserting his desire. Answering some persistent instinct of her own, Adriane plucked the stick from the mud and waved it under his snout. Then threw it into the ever-moving river.